From the Case Files of Charlie Madison, P.I.

The Unusual Clients

3 Novellas

Milo James Fowler

Copyright © 2023 by Milo James Fowler

All rights reserved

DOPPELGÄNGER'S CURSE © 2015 Milo James Fowler
Originally appeared in *Future City Blues*

UP IN SMOKE © 2018 Milo James Fowler
Originally published by the Society of Misfit Stories

DEATH DUEL © 2016 Milo James Fowler

This eBook or any portion of it may not be reproduced or used in any manner whatsoever without the express written permission of the author—except for brief quotations in glowing, 4.5-star reviews. (Your reward will be waiting for you in Heaven.) The stories contained within this eBook are works of fiction. All material is either the product of the author's overactive imagination or is used in a fictitious manner. Any resemblance to actual persons (living or dead) or to actual events is entirely coincidental—and worthy of further investigation.

For Sara

The Case Files of
Charlie Madison, P.I.

Now accepting...Unusual clients:

DOPPELGÄNGER'S CURSE

UP IN SMOKE

DEATH DUEL

GIRL OF GREAT PRICE

IMMATERIAL EVIDENCE

YAKUZA TERRITORY

CHIMERA EFFECT

THE GIFTED ONES

DOPPELGÄNGER'S CURSE

I

They called it the City of Angels, once upon a time. But that was before the fallen variety started roaming our congested streets and dark alleys, seeking whom they might devour. Figuratively speaking. The only demons I'd ever seen were flesh and blood—human beings who'd lost track of their humanity. Too many to count.

For the past quarter century or so, the city was officially designated as Sector 51.7634 by the United World government. Had a nice ring to it, but probably wouldn't look too good on one of those *I Heart* T-shirts. Not that tourists visited our town much anymore. There were other places to go and things to see—like that big green lady with the torch on the east coast. What was left of her reminded folks of the good old days, back when immigrants by the thousands flocked to our shores seeking freedom and a better life.

Now they came seeking refuge from the Eastern Conglomerate's warmongering.

The woman seated in my office was no immigrant, neither Russian nor Japanese. But she shimmered like a heavenly creature, and if I hadn't known any better, I might have confused her with the real deal. Gorgeous copper hair flowed over the shoulders of her raincoat, every centimeter charged with a protective layer of static. One of the best ways to keep the acid rains assaulting our fair city from ruining one's fairer complexion, or from burning holes through what could have easily been a thousand-credit coat.

"I need your help, Mr. Madison," she said, leaning toward me. She sat with her legs crossed, her form-fitting skirt ending at the knee. Her electrostatic overlay ran down to the soles of her flashy scarlet pumps, ensuring that not a viscous drop of rain touched her flawless skin. The girl glowed, but I had a feeling she would have been just as gorgeous without the protective layer. Her emerald eyes stared at me from a curtain of long lashes that had yet to blink. "My life is in danger, you see."

Such was often the case when folks came to see yours truly: Charlie Madison, detective.

"Have you gone to the cops?" A perfunctory question. I already knew the answer: your average citizen tended to avoid local law enforcement. Even the police who weren't tied to the mob had their own ideas about looking out for the common good, and justice seldom entered the equation.

"They wouldn't believe me." She clutched a black-sequined handbag on her lap. "It's too bizarre."

I leaned back in my faux-leather desk chair until it squeaked. Fizzing raindrops drummed against the windowpane behind me like impatient fingers. Amber light from the streetlamp eight stories below filtered through venetian blinds, painting the woman before me in dim, diagonal stripes.

"Maybe you'd better tell me all about it," I said.

"Then you'll take my case?"

I held up a hand to slow her down. "Haven't agreed on anything yet."

"Money is no object, I assure you." She paused, cocking her head to one side. "You have no idea who I am." Her tone wasn't conceited. She sounded curious, like I was a lone oddity in her privileged life.

"You have the bearing of a woman with means. Other than that, I'm sorry, no." Her face didn't ring a bell.

"Does the name *Forsythe* mean anything to you? As in Alexander Forsythe?"

"Sure." The man had made a fortune on our city's mass transit system, back in the day. The hyperail was still in working order, last time I checked. But call me old-fashioned; I preferred taking a cab or hoofing it rather than trusting my life to a bullet train. "You're too young to be his daughter."

"Granddaughter." She smiled slightly, lips curving at the corners into small dimples. "Amanda Forsythe."

I nodded. "And you're saying the cops wouldn't be any help to a Forsythe?"

"I may have..." She cleared her throat, eyebrows contorting. "They don't take me seriously, Mr. Madison. Over the years, I have unfortunately...cried *wolf* far too often, if you catch my meaning."

"I see."

"But those days are far behind me now. I'm a mature woman, not a silly girl looking for attention."

She still looked girlish. Couldn't have been more than twenty-five.

"Regardless, you've garnered some unwanted attention. Is that it?"

"Why, yes." She went back to unblinking mode. "Someone wants to kill me. I've received threats—"

"That's nothing new though, is it, Miss Forsythe? There's always going to be some nut job out there wanting a piece of your pie. Or maybe this is something different. Someone suffering from unrequited love?"

"No, it's nothing like that. It's—" She dropped her gaze, fingers tensely massaging her purse. "You're going to think I'm crazy too."

"Try me."

"All right." She sat up straight, chin held high. Probably learned that posture in finishing school. "There is a woman who looks exactly like me. She's stalking me, Mr. Madison. She's sending me threatening messages, and I'm not afraid to admit I'm just about at my wit's end."

"How long has this been going on?"

"Every day for the past two weeks. She will leave a note—handwritten, not a ping on the Link—on the windshield of my car, beneath the wiper. Or under the mat by my front door. Or delivered by a waiter in a restaurant or coffee shop." She popped open her handbag and pulled out a sheaf of half-sheets creased down the middle. "Here. I've kept them all. I don't know why. Maybe to prove this is really happening to me, that I'm not losing my mind. Not yet."

I leaned forward, reaching across the desk to take them. Each note had been written in the same penmanship—all caps—on the same sort of stiff recycled paper. Nothing sent over the Link, which would have been possible to trace.

"There's no room in this world for the both of us," I read one of the notes aloud. The same message appeared on every piece of paper in one form or another.

"Then I received this one less than an hour ago." She handed me another note. "My driver found it slipped into the doorframe of my car as he opened the door for me."

SAY GOODBYE TO THIS WORLD

I glanced up from the paper. "How do you know she left it?"

"Because she's always there—fifty, a hundred meters away—when I receive one of these. She watches to make sure I've gotten it, then she vanishes into the crowd."

"Couldn't it be a hologram? Somebody projecting an image of you to get your goat?"

"No, nothing like that. Our neighborhood does not allow the use of obnoxious holo-advertisements and the like. There's no way it could be one of those holograms."

Of course not. The high society end of town would have field dampeners installed to prevent such garish displays of free enterprise.

"No offense," I said, "but how can I be sure I'm not looking at a hologram right now?"

She blinked, bewildered. Then she noticed my gaze briefly trace the outline of her static cling.

"Oh, forgive me. I forget to deactivate it sometimes." She pressed a small node behind her ear, and the energy shield dissipated, revealing the gorgeous girl minus the glow. "I get so used to wearing it when I'm out in weather like this."

"Of course." Only the fanciest of toys for the rich and famous. For the rest of us, we had that trusty protective polymer we sprayed on our coats. Extended their lifetimes by a year or two, if we were lucky. "Miss Forsythe—"

"Amanda."

"I'm not sure how I can help you. If a threat has been made on your life, then you have to go to the police."

"I told you. They won't help me. But I don't need them anyway."

"You need a bodyguard."

"I have one." She nodded toward the front office beyond my closed door where Wanda Wood, my personal assistant, was busy babysitting the big guy in the tailored suit. "What I need is *you*, Mr. Madison. I need you to find out who this woman is and what she wants from me."

"I'd say it's fairly clear." I gestured toward the notes strewn across my desk. "What about this?" I sorted through the papers and held up one in particular that had stood out from the rest.

NO ONE CAN HELP YOU

Her slender shoulders shifted up and down. "What about it?"

"If she doesn't want you going for help, she won't be too happy about you coming to see me." If she existed at all. "Couldn't this be some sort of harmless prank? Maybe a long-lost twin you never knew about?"

"I'm an only child, Mr. Madison. And I don't have any cousins, if that's what you're going to ask me next." She leaned forward without a hint of levity in her cool-eyed gaze. "I'll pay double your rates for the evening. I'll wine you, dine you. If she shows up, you'll follow her and find out who she is. If she doesn't, you can forget you ever saw me." She paused. "Because I'll probably be dead by this time tomorrow."

Overly dramatic? Maybe. But with the possibility of four hundred credits staring me in the face, I wasn't going to argue.

I stood, buttoning my suit jacket. "How am I dressed?"

She almost smiled. "You'll do nicely."

2

Grabbing my trench coat off the rack across from Wanda's desk, I nodded to Amanda's hired muscle and noted the metallic sheen of his left hand. Most likely a fellow veteran; but unlike me, not all of his limbs had come back from the war intact. Wish I could say I'd returned home unwounded. But not every injury inflicted by the Eastern Conglomerate could be seen by the naked eye.

"You can go on home," I told Wanda. "See you in the morning."

I didn't need to remind her to lock up. Between the two of us, she was never the one to forget.

"You goin' out?" She rose to her feet at her desk, leaving her Underwood to sit untended. The thing had been rigged to work with her Slate, antique keystrokes working in conjunction with a touchscreen. The girl was quirky all right, and I wouldn't have had her any other way.

"Miss Forsythe is treating me to dinner."

Wanda looked Amanda over with the mistrust born of class distinctions. Don't get me wrong, Wanda was as classy as they came; she just wasn't born with a single silver spoon in any of her mother's kitchen drawers.

"We're glad to have you as a client, Miss Forsythe," Wanda said in a clipped tone. "Payment for Mr. Madison's time—"

"Has already been wired to his account." Amanda didn't

bother to grace Wanda with a glance. Activating her rain shield, she took the arm of her imposing bodyguard who'd yet to show a single facial expression, and the two of them exited into the main hallway outside. "Coming, Mr. Madison?"

I leaned over and gave Wanda a peck on the cheek. The girl smelled like lavender soap, and she was a real looker with those bottomless blue sapphire eyes, blonde curls that bounced across her shoulders, and legs that wouldn't quit. Smart too, blessed with what they called a perfect memory. Nothing ever slipped past her unnoticed.

"You don't usually date your clients, Charlie," she said quietly, turning her back to the door and leaning against her desk.

"They don't usually pay me double." I gave her a nudge. "You jealous?"

"Of her? Yeah, right. Spoiled brat's got a stalker, right?"

"You guessed it." Unless she'd been eavesdropping. Wouldn't put it past her.

"Dangerous?" She gazed up at me.

"We'll see." I patted the slight bulge under my left arm where I kept my .38 Smith & Wesson snapped in a shoulder holster. "Don't you worry."

"Not you I'm worried about." She nodded toward the hallway where Amanda and her escort waited patiently. "It's Little Miss Sparkle Toes."

"We get a few more cases that pay this good, you might be able to buy your own fancy rain shield."

"That'll be the day, Charlie."

Probably right. But at least I'd be able to pay the rent on this place as well as my apartment. As of late, it tended to be a financial juggling act when the bills came due. The last thing I wanted was to live out of my office; but if push came to shove, I'd sooner lose my flat than my place of business.

At least the office made money—every now and then.

3

Our first stop was Leonardo's, an Italian bistro on Broadway where Amanda's driver remained parked at the curb under the pouring rain in a slick black sedan. Her bodyguard sat at the bar, keeping his eyes on us in the mirror behind the rows of wine bottles. Amanda and I took a table for two by the front window where we both had a decent view of the deluge and vacant sidewalks outside. Not to say it wasn't crowded out there. Hovering right outside the rain-spattered glass like small UFOs were half a dozen weather-beaten paparazzi-cams vying for the best shot of Miss Forsythe and her mystery date. She didn't seem to take notice of them at all.

"Popular spot." I glanced across the heads of our fellow patrons, numbering close to a hundred and packing the place, wall to wall. Not a single flowing copper lock among them to be seen.

"Safety in numbers, right?" She deactivated her electrostatic shield and surveyed the menu, swiping her index finger across the display in the glass tabletop. "What looks good to you? The lasagna's a little heavy from what I recall, but the sauce is to die for."

Being stalked by her own doppelgänger—not to mention those cameras—hadn't affected her appetite, by all appearances. "Your call."

She glanced up. "You're easy."

"Just along for the ride."

She studied me for a moment. "Have you always been a detective, Mr. Madison?"

"Depends on what you mean by always."

"Fine." She tapped the menu, ordering two plates of lasagna and a bottle of the house merlot. I didn't usually drink on the job, but I wouldn't mind filling up on rich Italian fare tonight. "How long, then?"

"A few years."

"And before that?"

"The war. Same as your bodyguard, if I'm not mistaken."

She nodded. "Brock was a surgeon. Lost his right arm and both legs overseas."

The arm I'd noticed, not the legs. Prosthetics were getting better all the time at mimicking natural human movement.

"I don't think he likes me." I glanced at his reflection in the mirror. He eyed me coolly.

"He's just overprotective, that's all. It's been hard on him, these past couple weeks. He wants to keep me safe." She tried to laugh it off, changing the subject. "What about you, Mr. Madison? Did you lose anything in battle?" Her gaze drifted down my torso.

"Nothing that shows." Seeing my gunner squad mowed down by a platoon of E.C. mandroids with meter-long bayonets, slicing through them like sickles through bloody wheat—that sort of thing sticks with you. Changes you on the inside where nobody can see. But while it's one thing to be a haunted man, it's something else entirely to let it interfere with your work.

"You ever feel like we're waiting for the other shoe to

drop?"

"How's that?" I focused on her.

"This supposed *cold war*—it's like a pregnant pause, really. We're just waiting to see who will make the first move. Us or them."

"Let's hope they take a nice long while deciding." The Eastern Conglomerate would never join the United World; China and her allies had made that clear enough from the start. But the current global stalemate was the closest thing to peace our weary old planet had experienced in decades. I didn't mind it one bit.

She smiled faintly. "So you came back a war hero, and you—"

"Never said that."

She shrugged. "You made it back alive. I figure that qualifies you as a hero. So you get back to the city, and then what—you decide to become a detective? Just like that?"

"I liked the idea of being my own boss." After years of taking orders from pig-headed UW commanders, I knew I'd never be able to work for the government again. Or anybody else, for that matter. "Thought I could make a difference."

"Here?" She scoffed. "This town is the pits, in case you haven't noticed. Between the mob and the politicians, it's a wonder we haven't been quarantined. Why stay? You're not tied down here, are you? Do you have a family or something?"

Nothing like that. I had friends. I could count them on one hand, but they were all the family I needed.

"Some might say this city's a lost cause, but I don't see it that way. Sure, Ivan's mob runs things, and most of the cops are on his payroll. But there are still people in this town who want to see it cleaned up. I figure if I can help out some of those people, I'm doing what I can to make this city a better place."

"People like me." She smiled, revealing perfect white teeth; they hadn't come cheap. "Honestly, Mr. Madison, I wasn't sure you'd still be in business. I found you listed on the Link, but nowadays you don't hear much about private investigators anymore, you know?"

"We're a dying breed." The Link now made it possible for just about anybody to play detective—as long as what you were after was in range of the nearest vid-cam. But for dark business that often took place off the grid, your local gumshoe came in real handy. "Not that I mind the lack of competition."

The waiter arrived with our steaming lasagna, bread sticks, and wine. I kept an eye on Amanda's bodyguard as we ate. His gaze hadn't wavered from our table; his face remained an expressionless mask.

"Has he seen your double?" I nodded toward the bar as I dug into my meal.

"Brock? Yes. Every time. Jerry too—my driver."

"How many times would that be now?"

"More than a dozen."

"With the notes increasingly threatening?"

She nodded. Then she stared, open-mouthed. Not real ladylike, showing off that half-chewed mouthful of mush. But as I turned to follow her gaze outside, I saw what had attracted her attention.

She stared for good reason.

There stood her doppelgänger in the pouring rain, sheltered under a flimsy umbrella and wearing a slick black raincoat. Same gorgeous copper locks flowing over her shoulders, but no sparkling electrostatic protection.

Keeping the umbrella between her and the paparazzi-cams, she pointed a revolver straight at Amanda.

4

"Get down!"

I knocked our table over and grabbed Amanda by the wrist, pulling her behind it just as a shot took out the front window. Glass exploded in razor-like shards, skittering across the tile. Gusts of cold wind swept the invading rain inside Leonardo's.

"This way, Miss Forsythe," said Brock the bodyguard, standing between Amanda and what remained of the shattered window. Somehow, he'd managed to launch himself more than twenty meters from the bar in the blink of an eye. Now he stood brooding over her like a hen protecting one of its chicks.

"Where is she?" Amanda demanded, furious but weak in the knees.

"Gone." I stepped outside, crunching glass under my shoes. I squinted into the rain as I put on my hat. Not as fancy as an electrostatic shield, but it did its job. "You get all that?" I shouted up at the floating cameras.

Lenses flared and retracted, whirring in midair. Remote-controlled by some nameless, faceless voyeur who got paid to sit on his ass all day. Laziest job in the world, if you ask me. But good work if you could get it.

Remembering what Amanda had said about her double always leaving a note, I headed down the street toward her car.

Jerry the driver stepped out, shielding himself uselessly against the rain with one hand. The hybrid sedan sat with its engine off.

"Is Miss Forsythe all right?" Jerry said in a shaky voice.

I nodded. "You see which way the shooter went?"

He pointed back the way I'd come.

"Same woman?"

"What?"

"Miss Forsythe's stalker."

"I believe so."

"You saw the whole thing?"

He nodded.

"Didn't think to tap the horn or anything? Scare the woman off?"

Jerry cursed. "I had no idea she was armed!"

"She ever tried taking a shot before?"

He shook his head. "Should I call the police?"

"Yeah. I really think you should."

I backtracked past Leonardo's, heading up the sidewalk, looking for any sign of the woman. Zilch. No idea who she was or what she wanted, but one thing I knew for sure: this was a police matter now. Attempted murder was nothing to sneeze at. Whether or not the cops believed Amanda's story was beside the point. She had witnesses—including footage soon to be all over the Link—of that woman pulling the trigger. It was no ghost of her attention-seeking, overactive imagination. It was the real deal that could, apparently, disappear into the night without leaving a trace.

Too bad those hover-cams hadn't been tasked with following the shooter. The paparazzi were too busy selling their footage to the highest bidder.

By the time I hoofed it back to the restaurant, the owner had already activated an electrostatic barrier in place of the missing window to keep the rain out, and the patrons had settled down somewhat. Brock stood in the street where Amanda's car was now double-parked, engine silently idling. He held the rear door open as she slipped inside.

"Hold on," I said as I approached. "The cops will want to question—"

Brock slammed the door shut before I could make eye contact with the girl. He turned to face me, his mechanical hand landing squarely on my chest.

"Miss Forsythe's safety is my only concern, Mr. Madison," the bodyguard said in a low tone. I noticed the bullet hole in his right shoulder, torn straight through his suit jacket. Good thing there was only a metal prosthesis underneath, or he would have been bleeding out. But in order to intercept that round as it plowed through the front window, he must have seen the shooter before Amanda or I even laid eyes on her. "The police will be directed to Forsythe Manor. They will question her there. Her dealings with you are over. Permanently."

Not exactly the case. She'd paid me for two days' work, minus expenses, and so far I'd worked less than an hour. I planned on finding out who that doppelgänger was, and why she wanted Amanda dead—whether or not Brock the cyborg let me anywhere near her.

I wasn't a dog with a bone. I was just a man who liked to see things through.

5

When I got back to my office, I expected the place to be empty. But Wanda hadn't followed my instructions too good.

"Had a feeling you'd be back," she said as I let myself in. "Once I saw this."

She detached her Slate from its Underwood dock and handed it to me. Displayed across the glass touchscreen were multiple Link facets, each playing the same scene on a loop: the umbrella-carrying shooter out front of Leonardo's; the massive bodyguard lunging in the way of a speeding bullet; yours truly on the floor with Amanda Forsythe behind an overturned table, covered in shattered glass. Had to hand it to those paparazzi-cams; they'd gotten some decent footage.

Oddly enough though, none of the scrolling headlines had anything to do with the attempted murder. Instead, they focused on—

"See right there? *New love interest,*" Wanda pointed, reading over my shoulder. "*What could socialite Amanda Forsythe possibly see in one of the last private eye's to hang a shingle in this town?*"

"Shingle?" Who used that term anymore?

"*Has she grown desperate in her old age—*" Wanda continued to read.

"The girl's not even thirty, for crying out loud!"

"—*or just slumming it for kicks?*"

"Next time I see a paparazzi-bot, I'm considering it open season." I patted my holstered .38 and handed the Slate back to her. "They don't care that somebody took a shot at her. All they're concerned about is her love life."

"Is there any?" Wanda raised an eyebrow, folding her arms.

"We barely got into dinner. And I have a feeling dessert wasn't on the menu." I rubbed my face with both hands and blew out a sigh. "Listen, since you're here—"

"Actually, I'm on my way out. My boss told me to go home early, but you know, I had a few things to finish up. Now that's done, so..." She placed her Slate back into its typewriter housing and reached for her coat. "I'll see you tomorrow, Charlie."

"Would it make any difference if I needed your help?"

She paused. "Would it pay overtime?"

"Time and a half."

"Double."

The kid drove a hard bargain. "Deal." I pointed at her Slate. "I need you to dig up whatever you can on Amanda's bodyguard, Brock. Her driver, too: name's Jerry."

"Last names?" She slipped her phone over one ear.

"No clue." I gave her a wink. "But that shouldn't be much trouble for you, Tech Wiz."

"Caveman," she muttered with the makings of a smile, her gaze already transfixed on whatever invisible facets she'd opened in her mind's eye.

That's how the Link worked; it took everything you'd normally finger-swipe through on a touchscreen and projected it into your field of vision—but only yours.

Nobody else could see what you were looking at. Phones hijacked your visual cortex or something, transmitting audio along with the visual stimuli. Real fancy, but I'd sooner be caught dead than wear one of those things. Machines and me hadn't gotten along real well since the war; I had no desire to rely on technology in any of its forms. Besides, all it would take was another EMP airstrike from the Eastern Conglomerate, and the Link would go the way of its much more impressive predecessor, something they used to call the *Internet*.

"What do you want to know?" Wanda said, smacking that signature wad of gum.

"How long they've been working for the Forsythe clan. What their backgrounds are. Brock's a veteran, half-machine." From the moment I met him, I got the feeling he didn't approve of Amanda seeking out my help. Why? Didn't he want to know who that stalker was?

"And this Jerry guy?"

"He saw the whole thing—that woman with the umbrella opening fire on the restaurant. Said he hadn't noticed a gun in her hand. Guy with eyesight that bad shouldn't be driving for anybody."

She nodded, looking like she was staring at the office door; but I knew those gorgeous unblinking blues were taking in all manner of data on Amanda Forsythe's hired help.

"You've got a call coming in from the 37th precinct," she murmured, multitasking. "Sergeant Douglass would like to speak with you about the incident at the restaurant."

That was fast. But then again, the *incident* did involve a photogenic city socialite.

"Route it through my intercom," I said, opening the door to my office.

"Already done," Wanda replied. Tech Wiz at work.

Navigating my way through the dark office, I managed to make it to my desk without banging my shins into anything. Lights out kept the electric bills low, regardless of the bruises. Collapsing into my faux-leather desk chair, I flipped the switch on the intercom.

"Charlie?" Douglass's brogue came through louder than necessary.

"Who else?"

"Right." He chuckled. Nothing in the world could dampen his spirits. One of the last honest cops in town, a man I was lucky to call my friend. "Listen, I just need to verify you were at Leonardo's this evening—when the shootin' took place."

"You know I was." Otherwise, he wouldn't have called.

"Yeah, sure," he hemmed and hawed. Then he came out with it: "I hate to do this to you. I know time's are tough and all, and I'm sure Miss Forsythe is a real big fish."

"Paid me double."

"You don't say? Well, that makes this twice as hard then." He paused. "You've gotta step off the case, lad. This is a police matter now, and we've got the girl in protective custody. You know how that goes. No interference from the private sector." Subtext: I'd be arrested on sight if I didn't follow his advice, and there was nothing he could do about it.

"Have your detectives questioned her yet?"

"Heading over there now. Stankic and Bellincioni—"

"Stinkin' and Blinkin'," I muttered with a curse. Dirty

cops, both of them. Detective Stankic was a slob with an affinity for garlic and onions and sauces that stained every tie he knotted around his mottled throat. Detective Bellincioni had a nervous tick that caused her to blink one long-lashed eye more often than was necessary. Hence my nicknames for them—which sounded more than a little like their actual surnames. They didn't like it, but that was all right. We had what you might call a working antagonistic relationship.

"Hey, I don't like 'em any more than you do, Charlie. But the captain assigned 'em this case. I'm just holdin' down the fort tonight. If Miss Forsythe doesn't agree to come over and ID the shooter, they'll keep her home under watch until the perp is apprehended."

"You see that footage on the Link?"

He scoffed. "Damned hover-bots. Damned paparazzi! Didn't even think to swoop lower and get a good look at the shooter's face, now did they?"

"I saw her face."

Douglass paused. "Did you now?"

Didn't matter. I was off the case. "You wouldn't believe me if I told you."

I signed off and returned to Wanda's front office. She held up a finger to keep me from breaking her concentration. Then she pointed that finger at her Slate. Spilling across the screen were rapid-fire mental notes she was making as she concluded her Link search.

"Well, Charlie, that will either put you to sleep tonight or put your mind at ease." She rubbed at her eyes as she removed the phone from her ear and slipped it into her purse. "Either way, it's late, and I'm goin' home."

I retrieved her Slate from the Underwood. "Everything

here?"

"Everything I could find." She pulled on her coat and stifled a yawn. "Both upstanding gentlemen, by all accounts. Been workin' for the Forsythe clan for years. Came highly recommended, the usual."

"Easily accessible information?" I raised an eyebrow.

She graced me with a sly smile. "Sure. If you know where to look. See you tomorrow, Charlie." She opened the door to the hallway and gave me a wink. "Don't stay up too late. You need your beauty sleep same as anybody else."

With that, she was gone. And I was left to scroll through virtual pages of notes on Brock Moynihan and Jerry Gunderson, two men who'd been in the employ of the Forsythe estate for decades. Amanda's father had hired them both around the same time, back when she'd started high school. Had he been worried about the boys at her school? Jerry had been her driver from the start, and Brock her bodyguard, escorting her to and from classes. That had to be fun for the poor girl. Not much room for a social life.

But things had changed when she went away to college, out of state. Neither fellow went with her. Both men started working for her father instead. Brock lost a leg in a car accident, protecting Mr. Forsythe from an oncoming vehicle—so not all of his prosthetics were thanks to the war. Amanda had been wrong about that. Jerry's eyesight was never brought into question. Both men appeared to be above reproach.

When Amanda's father became ill, she returned home from college and never finished out her senior year, choosing instead to sit at her father's bedside. Her mother had passed away a year or two before, but that hadn't interfered with

Amanda's studies. Daddy's girl? Oh yeah. When her old man finally kicked the bucket, the entire Forsythe estate became hers. Who needs an education when you're set for life?

Brock and Jerry stayed on, reprising their roles as her personal bodyguard and driver. Life went on—until just a couple weeks ago, when this doppelgänger showed up out of the blue.

A knock sounded against the frosted glass of the office door. Outside, I could make out the shadowy form of someone standing in the hallway. Wanda? Had she forgotten her keys? Unlikely. The girl was like an elephant in the memory department.

With her Slate in one hand, I unlocked the door—of course she'd battened down the hatches on her way out—and pulled it open. Smiling at her, I said, "Forget something?"

My smile faltered. I didn't say anything more. I thought about going for my gun instead.

"Mr. Madison?" said Amanda Forsythe, dripping wet in a slick black raincoat. She held a collapsed umbrella down at her side. "You're Charlie Madison, right? The detective?"

6

I nodded toward my name on the door.

"Right." She blinked up at me. Her hair wasn't as immaculate as Amanda's and her facial art—mascara, lip rouge, the rest—wasn't as pristinely maintained, but this girl shared the same face. Uncanny. Her voice, however, was lower by an octave. She'd spared no expense to look like the socialite, but tampering with the voice box was tricky. Maybe she hadn't wanted to take her obsession that far. "You were at the restaurant—"

"So were you. Target practice?"

"I'm sorry about that. I didn't—" She nodded with determination. "I've been afraid something like that might happen."

"That you'd try to kill her?"

"That I'd lose it. You can only press someone so far, Mr. Madison, before they...break."

She appeared to be speaking from personal experience. "The cops are looking for you," I said. "Attempted murder on a local socialite? Not something you'll be able to put behind you anytime soon."

"I wasn't trying to..." She squeezed her forehead, swooning all of a sudden as she stared at the hallway's tile floor. "I didn't want to kill her. Not really. I just...wanted to scare her—in a big way."

"Her bodyguard took the bullet."

"Brock's half-machine. He'll be fine." She raised one hand and leaned against the wall. Her emerald eyes glanced past me at my dark office. "I could really use somebody to talk to."

"Are you armed?"

"Search me." She opened her raincoat. No electrostatic filter for her. This doppelgänger was a commoner like the rest of us. "Or take my word for it. No, I'm not. I tossed that gun as soon as I could. Can't believe I fired the thing."

I studied her umbrella for a moment. Lethal in the right hands, sure; but those hands of hers didn't look like the type. Deciding to give her the benefit of the doubt—whoever she really was—I stepped aside and gestured for her to come on in. Pointing at the futon couch next to Wanda's potted lily, I waited for her to take the hint and sit herself down. Then I closed the door to the hallway, but not before making sure it was empty outside. She hadn't been followed by cops or hover-bots—or any accomplices, from what I could tell.

"So, you like to write." I set Wanda's Slate into its Underwood moorings and leaned back against the desk.

"Write?"

"Threatening notes, mostly. By hand. Old school, but I can respect that. I'm something of a Luddite myself." I folded my arms. "What I can't understand is what you hope to get out of it. Having yourself surgically altered to look like her. Stalking her. Scaring her. What's your endgame?"

"You should ask her the same thing. It's been going on for weeks now. I can't figure it out. Believe me, I've tried. Do they want me to lose it and kill myself? Is that what they're after? With me gone, do they think they'll get everything? Live off my inheritance and die of old age together?"

"They?"

"The imposter and her cronies—Brock and Jerry. They've been plotting against me!"

Crazy talk.

"You mentioned Brock before. War veteran, upstanding guy from what I can tell. Lost his second leg protecting Amanda's father."

"No, he didn't." She cursed mildly under her breath, her fingers kneading the hem of her raincoat. "*My* father told that to the press to cover up what really happened. He didn't want them to know about Brock's weird little hobbies."

"Your father?" I almost smiled. Before I had a chance to weigh the potential consequences of challenging a sociopath's delusion, I said, "I see. You actually think you're Amanda Forsythe."

"Of course I am," she said wearily, shaking her head. "Who else would I be?"

A delusional doppelgänger—the spitting image of Amanda Forsythe with some sort of malicious intent I couldn't for the life of me figure out.

"How do you think Brock lost his leg?" I said.

"Playing with explosives. It's his thing. He's something of a mad scientist, really. He makes these gas-bombs and uses them as practical jokes. Believe me, growing up with that guy around all the time? It got old real fast."

"So you're saying the woman I had dinner with, the woman wanting me to track you down—" I paused, looking her over. "You're saying *she's* the imposter."

"That's right." She raised her chin regally.

"And her hired help are working with her—assisting in the charade?"

She nodded. "I need you to help me reclaim my life, Mr. Madison. I can't go to the police, they'll never believe me." She bit her lip for a moment. "I used to be quite the spoiled brat, you see. When dear old Mommy and Daddy wouldn't bestow enough of their kindly attention on me, I would call the cops, tell them I was being abused. Neglected, perhaps, but never to the extent I fabricated for local law enforcement. I'm a laughingstock to them now. They probably read about me stalking her and think she deserves it. Because they think she's me!"

Short of administering a DNA test, how was I to know if she was who she said she was? "Amanda—the other Amanda—paid me double to take her case. What can you offer?"

The fire went out of her eyes. "I barely have enough to live on. They've left me with that much, you see. I rent a flat off Market Street, and I can buy food. But that's it. They cancelled two of my credit lines, and the one I have left is closely monitored. The balance is never more than what I need for the day." She paused. "They're keeping me alive so I'll lose my mind. So I'll off myself, and they'll be rid of me without getting their hands dirty."

Either she had an incredibly inventive imagination, laced with all manner of paranoia, or she was telling me the truth. In which case the first Amanda had played me for a fool, hoping to include me in her staged play. But to what end? She said she wanted me to find out who her stalker was, follow her and find out what she wanted. All right. The stalker had come to me instead, and I'd found out more than I bargained for—assuming any of it was on the level.

According to this woman, she was the real Amanda

Forsythe, and all she wanted was her life back. Simple as that.

My job was done. Now what? Contact my client and tell her what I'd discovered? That would go over well.

"I can't pay you now, but when this is over—" she went on.

"She's in protective custody. It won't be easy to get to her." Detectives Stinkin' and Blinkin' would see to that, not to mention Brock the bodyguard. A gas-bomb hobby? Weird. "That's what you want, right? To confront her?"

She blinked. Her eyes were glassy. "I don't know. But I can't let her steal my life from me. This has to stop."

"If you show up at her place—your place—you'll be arrested." I paused. "But that could be for the best. Get everything aired out, once and for all. They could run a DNA test on the both of you—"

"I want you to prove she isn't who she says she is." She got to her feet, gripping the umbrella down at her side. "That's all. Can you do that?" She pulled open the hallway door and stepped outside. "Mr. Madison, please." She was struggling to maintain her composure now. "Will you—even though I can't pay for your services?"

"If what you say is true, then you've already paid me." Via her imposter. "And if it isn't, well...She paid me double, like I said." So I had another day to see how the case panned out. "I'll do what I can."

"Thank you." She nodded vigorously, causing either tears or viscous raindrops to ooze down her cheeks. "I'm sorry I got your couch wet. I have to go. Good night." She shut the door, and her heels clopped quickly down the hallway outside.

7

I briefly considered following her back to wherever she lived, to corroborate that part of her story, but that's when a ping came through on Wanda's Slate. Incoming message—video file. Addressed to me.

Curious, I tapped it open and watched as a scene from earlier that evening replayed before my eyes. The vantage point was different this time. Instead of looking at Amanda from behind my desk as she sparkled there in her electrostatic shield, I now hovered near the ceiling. Strange. I didn't recall there being any sort of recording device in my office at the time. I wouldn't have allowed it.

Maybe this was standard operating procedure for the rich and famous; they did seem to enjoy being on camera at all hours of the day and night. And a personal micro-sized hover-bot could have been concealed under an invisibility cloak or some other illegal tech. But that's not what bothered me most about the footage.

The audio had been doctored.

"I need you to take care of her," Amanda was saying. "Permanently."

"I'm no hitman," I replied. My voice, but I'd never said that.

"Detective, hitman—you'll be whatever I need you to be. I've wired payment for your services, double your rates. I expect that girl to be dead by morning. You've killed before. You were in the war. This should not be a problem for you."

"Maybe if I knew who she was...Why she has to die."

"She's a dangerous psychotic. She's surgically transformed herself to look identical to me. And she's threatening my life. I'm scared, Mr. Madison. Won't you help me?"

I watched as the on-screen version of me stood and buttoned his suit jacket. "How do I look?"

Amanda smiled. "Like a killer."

The video ended there. No message attached. No clue who'd sent it. Wanda would have been able to find out where it originated, but I'd have to wait until morning for her help. In the meantime, all I could do was play the video back a couple times and marvel at the seamless audio overlay. Our lips moved completely in sync with a bizarre script we'd never written.

"What the hell is going on here?" I muttered.

Was someone setting me up for an impending murder? Implicating Amanda (or her imposter) in the death of her stalker (or the real Amanda Forsythe)? Why drag me into this mess?

No chance I'd be going home now. Sleep had retreated far beyond my grasp. I clenched and unclenched my fists, staring at the frozen image on the screen. Me standing there looking like a doofus, ready to do my mistress's bidding. Any tech wiz worth their byte would be able to tell the video had been tampered with. Right? No way anybody would take it seriously.

Then why was my pulse racing?

There were two police detectives already on this case who wouldn't think twice about locking me up: Stankic and

Bellincioni, providing protective custody for Amanda—the first Amanda who'd come to see me. If whoever had sent me this video sent them the same thing—

My intercom bleeped. Wanda had it set up in her absence to receive and send calls without her Link interface. No way to screen the caller with my low-tech device, but that didn't matter. Right then, I needed a diversion.

Dropping into my desk chair, I flipped the switch and answered, "Madison."

Silence answered, punctuated only by the rain drumming and sloshing against the windowpane behind me.

"Hello?" I checked the intercom, making sure the thing was still plugged in.

"Drop the case," came a man's muffled voice. Unrecognizable.

"Did you send that video?"

"Forget about Amanda Forsythe."

"Can't do that." She came to see me twice, after all.

"He wants her dead."

"Who does?"

"With the police hanging around, he'll force you to do it. He wants her out of the picture. He can't do it himself. He's...not right."

"Who? Give me a name."

"I've already said too much, Mr. Madison."

He ended the call.

I flipped off the intercom and cursed, rocking back in my chair. Who was that? Brock the bodyguard? Jerry the driver? The second Amanda had said they were working with the imposter. Had one of them gotten cold feet, decided to cut me loose? Too late for that. One of them had sent the video, had rigged a silent, invisible camera to record the whole thing when the first Amanda sought my help. Which one was more likely to possess the requisite audio-tampering skills? A cyborg who liked playing with explosives? Or a chauffeur with poor eyesight?

Better question: which one was more likely to lose his nerve?

8

I had to get out of there. Figuring some fresh air would do me good, I shut down Wanda's Slate and tucked it into a bottom desk drawer. Paranoid? Maybe. I could have deleted the video, but I needed her to check it out first, find out who'd sent it. Verify the audio was fabricated.

Forgoing the elevator in favor of a little exercise, I took the stairs down the eight flights to the ground floor. I pulled my fedora down low and popped my coat collar, going for as much protection as possible as I stepped out into the acid rain. My destination: the news stand on the corner of the block.

Sure, it was late—or early, depending on your sleeping habits. But I had a feeling old Mr. Newspaper would be at his post. He always liked the wee hours before dawn, said they set him at ease. He wasn't one of those people who needed noise to distract him from his sorrows. He was comfortable in the quiet. Lucky devil.

I may have saved his frozen ass once in the war, back when we were stationed in St. Petersburg during the dead of winter. He was my commanding officer in those days, a time we'd both worked hard to put far behind us. For the most part, I'd say we succeeded.

I found him arranging stacks of periodicals bound in twine beneath his stand's rain-battered awning. All that paper—it was hard to believe eReaders had been so hot on everybody's New Year's Eve list when I was a kid. Some tech fads just had a way of dying out, helped along by the Eastern Conglomerate's EMP bombardment of major United World cities.

"How's it hangin', Charlie?" He glanced up at me with a grin around his chipped pipe.

"A little uptight," I admitted. "Nothing a little poisoned rain can't cure."

He chuckled. "I think we're immune."

He'd once told me the chemicals we were exposed to in the war had already done all the damage anybody could take, and he was now impervious to whatever else this crumbling world had to throw at him. Maybe I subscribed to the same theory.

"Popular girl." I gestured toward a pile of tabloids he'd dropped onto a stack of newspapers that would go out in the morning. Amanda Forsythe's face was all over the covers.

"Our city's little darling." He raised a bushy eyebrow at me. "How was the dinner conversation?"

"Cut short." I glanced at the text splashed across one of the cover photos. There it was, in black and white—the same thing Wanda had shown me on the Link. The gorgeous socialite was slumming it with a washed-up detective. Not those words exactly, but that was the gist. "I might be in over my head on this one."

"You two run in different circles. What were you expecting?" He was ribbing me, of course. I could see the look in his eye. "But you're not here about your love life."

"No problems there."

"Because it's nonexistent."

"Less trouble that way."

He snorted and grinned. "You find out who the stalker is?"

"Found out who she thinks she is."

"And that's thrown you."

"A bit." I tugged one of the tabloids free and stared into Amanda's beautiful eyes. Only two-dimensional, but more than reminiscent of the real deal. "The men who work for her—they might've hatched some harebrained scheme. Maybe it's about money, I don't know. But it's taken a dark turn, and they've roped me into the middle of it."

"They expect you to play a part in their game?"

"They're gearing up to force me to."

"Well then. You know what to do about that." He stared back at me. "Do what you always do—what they least expect!"

"Right." Easier said than done.

Part of me wanted to head over to Market Street and start ringing doorbells until I found the second Amanda. But that would be playing right into their hands—whoever had sent that video. If I found her dead, it wouldn't look good at all. I'd be the prime suspect. Another part of me wanted to go straight to the first Amanda's mansion where Stinkin' and Blinkin' had her under watch. Tell her about the video and her double. See how things panned out.

Which was the more unexpected course of action? If only I could've cloned myself and headed both directions at once. That sure as hell would have surprised all parties concerned.

"I'll go home and get some shut-eye. Nobody will see that coming."

He shrugged. "Sure. Sleep on it. An answer may reveal

itself to you in dreamland."

I would've laughed if that had never happened before.

"How much?" I nodded at the rag in my hand and reached for my ident card.

"You know your money's no good, Charlie. If it helps with your case, consider it gratis." He paused then, eyebrows contorted as he stared into the night for a moment. "You know, now that I think about it, I remember something in one of the gossip columns about her bodyguard. The big guy with the prosthetics. Back when she went off to college and left him behind, he got hurt. Lost his other leg."

"I've heard the stories. It either involved a berserk vehicle or an explosion."

"Add this to your list of culprits: rumor had it he did it on purpose. For attention. Maybe he felt neglected and abandoned."

"He thought she'd come back. But she didn't."

"Not even for her own mother's funeral. He didn't stand a chance."

"You're saying he was sweet on her." More than that. Obsessive.

Mr. Newspaper tapped his wrinkled earlobe. "I hear things is all. Sometimes the voices make sense, you know?" He gave me a wink and went back to sorting through his stacks.

I'd made up my mind. I wouldn't be paying a visit to either of the Amandas, and I was too amped to head home with any thought of sleep. Instead, I decided to head over to Brock's domicile.

9

Very few perks came along with being a veteran of the United World Armed Forces. If you came home in one piece, you counted yourself lucky. I'd learned long ago not to expect anything in return for my years of service. The United World government was too busy licking its wounds, grateful for the current cold war respite to regroup while the Eastern Conglomerate did the same. But as a detective, I found my ever-helpful VA rep. to be a virtual fount of information.

"What's that name again? I've got the files open here." Carol was on the east coast, three hours ahead. Still early, but not so bad that she'd let my call go straight to the mailbox.

"Brock Moynihan. Ran into him just yesterday. It's been years, you know?" I kept my back to the half dozen patrons in Howard's Tavern, each one silently drinking alone. Before me in the cramped phone booth, a dingy wallscreen the size of a file folder glowed with my rep's image on it. She hadn't gotten ready for the day yet, and she didn't seem to mind me seeing her in slinky pajamas. Adjusting her glasses, she parked stray strands of her graying brunette hair over one ear and peered at the Slate in her hands.

"Were you stationed together?" Her eyebrows knitted as she finger-swiped the tablet's screen.

"No, but we might have gotten a little drunk before we shipped out."

"Might have?" She glanced up at me.

"I'm a little fuzzy on the particulars. It was a crazy night."

"I'll bet." She went back to tapping on her Slate.

"I should've asked when I saw him yesterday, but it all happened so fast. We each had places to go, people to be."

"How's the private eye gig working out for you, Charlie?"

"It pays the bills." Sometimes.

"Well, this is interesting." She glanced at me again. "Says here you both have someone in common: a Miss Amanda Forsythe. Does that name mean anything to you?"

"She's a client."

"Apparently, Mr. Moynihan works for her as a bodyguard." She paused, chewing her lip. "What's this really about, Charlie? Did you even know Brock Moynihan existed until yesterday?"

Should've known better. She was almost as sharp as Wanda. Almost—because nobody on the planet was, as far as I could tell. Wanda's perfect memory had a way of setting her apart.

"A woman's life is in jeopardy. I think Brock Moynihan can help."

She blinked at me. "Well, that's all you had to say." She rattled off his address, and I filed it away, pretty sure I'd remember even without Wanda's total recall. "Is there anything else I can do for you, Charlie?" She dropped the Slate beside her and slipped off the glasses. The vid-cam's perspective shifted upward, and I saw that Carol was sitting in a large bed with rumpled sheets. She smiled at me and toyed with the top button of her purple silk pajamas.

"Never enough time in the day." I gave her a wink and tapped the screen, ending the call.

10

Brock Moynihan didn't live on the bad side of town. But he wasn't in the same zip code as his employer, either. Plenty of holograms glowed into the night, up and down his street, advertising everything from cold medicine to birth control. I had a feeling he'd still be with Amanda and the cops at Forsythe Manor, and I hoped to have free run of his place. I couldn't help but wonder what kind of mad scientist's laboratory I might stumble upon as I picked the lock and let myself in.

I found nothing of the sort. Not right away, anyhow. The place was bare, Spartan. A torn, overstuffed couch faced an old cabinet-style TV. I shut the front door on the dark, fourth-floor hallway outside and went room to room, keeping an eye out for what might turn up. The guy didn't spend much time there; that much was obvious. A couple bottles of beer in the otherwise empty fridge, a bag of low sodium potato chips in one of the cupboards. If he was obsessed with Amanda, it made sense he would spend all of his time around her. And if she was an imposter, then it also made sense he'd be close by to make sure she kept up appearances.

No computer. No file cabinet. No paperwork of any kind stored anywhere. The place had the feel of a well-worn safe house to it. The bed was made, military fashion; the closet contained one change of clothes. Looked exactly like the suit he'd worn earlier.

I don't know what made me check the back wall of the closet. Detective's intuition, maybe. The storage space was far too small, considering the size of the sliding door. There had to be some kind of partition covering additional storage.

There was another sliding door in the rear of the closet, padlocked shut. Interesting—just enough to get me to draw my revolver and break the lock. The door jerked aside, half-sliding with stubborn resistance as I shoved it open. Impenetrable darkness met my eyes along with the sharp odor of cleansers and other chemicals. Odd place to keep such things—right next to your bedroom.

I felt along the wall inside that secret room, but there was no light switch. I drew my lighter and flipped the cap. The flame leapt upward, splashing its flickering glow across the prison cell walls. That's what the space looked like, without the niceties. Instead of a steel toilet, there was a dentist's chair bolted to the floor. Instead of mostly naked ladies, only one woman's picture graced the walls in dozens of photographs. Each one had been taken of the girl lying in that surgical chair, undergoing various procedures. Plastic surgery, by the looks of things. Each before-or-after photo was labeled in black marker with a date. Seven years ago—that's when they'd all been taken over the course of six months. That's when this red-haired girl had undergone her transformation. In this cramped, sterile room, Amanda Forsythe's double had been created.

But the process wasn't complete. Recent images lined the edge of one wall: photos of Amanda's neck and throat alongside anatomical diagrams of the larynx. Handwritten notes had been made, a date set for the following week. Dr. Brock Moynihan was preparing to take Amanda's double under the knife one more time.

Would he ever be satisfied with her? Or was that her curse—to exist in the shadow of the real Amanda?

The front door creaked on its hinges, echoing in the front room. No footfalls. I must have neglected to shut it all the way. Old buildings tended to have warped doorframes, either too tight or too loose. Closing and pocketing my lighter, I kept my revolver out just in case I'd be dealing with unwanted company. For the time being, I left Brock's secret surgical lair and passed through the short hallway toward the couch and TV.

A large man in a gas mask faced my direction, shutting the door quietly behind him. The insectoid eye sockets and elephantine proboscis of the mask gave him a decidedly non-human look as he squared his shoulders and stared at me. Streaks of dim light from the streetlight outside cut through slats in the window blinds by the couch. Otherwise, the place was draped in silent shadows.

"How did you get this address?" Brock's muffled voice came through the thick rubber.

"Pays to have connections." I raised my .38 toward his shoulder of flesh—the left one. "Why the mask?"

"Because of this." He held up what looked like a gas grenade. No wonder he didn't keep much around the place, if this was what he liked to do in his free time.

"Planning on stinking up the joint?"

"Put down your gun, Mr. Madison. I would hate for you to wake my neighbors. They are elderly citizens, most of them. They need what little sleep they can get."

"Very considerate of you." I cocked the hammer. "Listen, since I've got you here, I've been hearing some conflicting stories about that leg of yours. The one you didn't lose in the war. First it was a vehicle you intercepted on its way toward Amanda's father. Then it was an explosion in your gas-lab. Less than an hour ago, I heard you may have done it to yourself. Blew off your own freakin' leg, just to get a girl's attention."

He lobbed the grenade at my feet. As soon as the canister hit the floor and rolled toward me, gas billowed from it in every direction. I pulled my coat over my head and dashed straight for the window, running full-tilt into it and expecting to crash through the glass onto the fire escape outside. Instead, I bounced off the reinforced plasticon and landed awkwardly sprawled across the couch.

"You were supposed to go after her, once you received the video. To make sure she was all right. But thanks to my little wasps, I saw that you had come here instead." He gestured vaguely at the air in the room. "You can't see them, of course. Micro-cams the size of insects. My own ingenious design." Brock loomed over me like something from a nightmare, swaying as the room spun behind him. He held the canister over me as the gas spewed forth. "Breathe deep now, Mr. Madison."

I shot him in the face—or tried to. My arm wouldn't cooperate. It moved in slow motion. And my trigger finger wouldn't curl. The room was getting darker. Soon I'd be out cold, and there was nothing I could do about it.

"You will kill her, Mr. Madison," the monster said, slapping the gun out of my hand with his steel arm. The revolver clattered across the floor. I heard every bounce it made across the wooden planks. "You will kill her, or you will lose a limb. Perhaps I will start with your shooting arm. Every day that you procrastinate, one of your limbs will be taken from you in your sleep. To prove this can be done, you will go to sleep now. And when you awake...there will be a nasty surprise waiting for you."

He didn't laugh like a maniacal fiend. He just stood there, watching me, as impenetrable darkness swallowed my senses.

II

A crushing blow to the jaw woke me. I sat up with a start, finding myself on the couch in Brock's apartment. The glow of the streetlight outside had been traded for morning daylight, overcast and gray. Enough to see by.

Brock held the gas mask in his steel hand. He'd used the other one, made out of flesh and bone, to welcome me to the day. Thank God for small favors.

I quickly patted my arms and legs, checking if they were still there. "You didn't do it."

Brock ran a hand through his mussed-up hair and stared at the floor as he paced. "No. I couldn't go through with it." He'd tucked my revolver into the waist of his trousers. For now, he left it there. "Not saying I won't. Just saying I may have lost my nerve a bit. It's been years since I've operated on a man. The plastic surgery, that's different. Superficial. But to amputate..." He shook his head. "I wasn't sure I could risk it."

"Because you're not a killer. Not anymore." I watched him. "What the war made us do, that's not who we are."

"What do you know about it?" He glared at me.

"Lost my entire gunner squad to a platoon of mandroids. Spent some time afterward avenging their deaths—trying to. Did plenty I'm not proud of."

"Eastern front?"

I nodded. "You?"

"Nagasaki."

It's a wonder any piece of him had survived that hell zone. We lost most of the Japanese islands to E.C. firestorms at the height of the war.

"We've seen enough death to last us multiple lifetimes." I paused, watching him. He was staring at his prosthetic hand like it belonged to someone else. "How could you want to harm another human life?"

"Have you ever been in love, Mr. Madison?"

"Sure. Once or twice."

"Was that love returned to you? Or was it unrequited?"

I had a feeling I knew where this was going. "If you love her, how can you even think of killing her?"

"I can't." He shook his head. "I can't face her. She has power over me, you see. I can't explain it. Her very presence overwhelms my soul."

"She's just a kid—"

"She's a *goddess*!" His eyes flashed wildly.

"I assume we're talking about the stalker, right? The real Amanda Forsythe?"

"Of course. When the media attention became too much for her, back when she was in high school—perfection incarnate, immortal beauty walking the earth—I convinced her parents it would be in their best interest to hire a body double, one we could use to distract the paparazzi while Amanda went about her daily life. I had it all figured out, you see, and when we found the right girl, Mr. Forsythe allowed me to be responsible for her makeover. Every detail had to be perfect, and I knew what had to be done. Amanda was a priceless painting I'd studied for years, a flawless angel.

I knew every centimeter of her body, and I knew how to mold that girl into her image."

My skin was crawling, but I tried not to let it show. "You did a standup job. If it wasn't for the voice—"

He cursed foully, pounding his fist into the steel palm of his prosthetic. "I could never get that right—not without surgery on her larynx. I tried to convince Mr. Forsythe that it would be worth the effort, but he was satisfied with the girl's appearance. Besides, he wanted her to keep her mouth shut, you see, to avoid suspicion. I disagreed, and my views were duly noted. But that was all. And because of it, she will never be *perfect*—not until I make that much-needed adjustment."

He was staring again. Had he lost his train of thought?

I cleared my throat. "Listen, I can see you care for the girl—"

"I thought we would have more time together. With her double leading the media on diversionary paths throughout the city, Amanda and I would be able to truly connect. No distractions. Just the two of us."

"But she wasn't interested."

"Such a flippant way to describe my pain." He stared at me, and I had to wonder if he was getting his nerve back. Which would be the first to go—my shooting arm? I seemed to remember him mentioning that before, while I was in a gas-induced stupor. "But of course you're right. That's all it was to her, a matter of interest. She didn't find me *interesting*. She tolerated my presence. While I worshipped the ground she walked on, while my heart raced anytime she shared the same roomful of air, she never saw me as anything more than a servant. An older man. A *cyborg*," he spat. "I had to think of a way to earn her affection—"

"But that didn't work out so well either—injuring yourself. So you've finally decided to kill her. If you can't have her, nobody will. Something deranged like that, right?"

He ground his teeth. "You are a man without fear."

"I'm not afraid of you, if that's what you're getting at."

"You really should be."

I shrugged. "You can't kill the girl. You can't cut my arm off. Seems like all you can do is run your mouth." I got to my feet. Too quickly—the room swayed a bit. I still wasn't over the effects of the gas, the smell of which lingered in the room like an ashen ghost. "So how about we part company, and we both go back to doing what we do best. I'll solve my clients' cases. You can take bullets for well-crafted doppelgängers. Deal?"

He drew my revolver and aimed it at me. Not a good feeling to stare down the barrel of your own weapon. I felt more than a little betrayed.

"You will kill her for me, Mr. Madison. Or I will give that video to the police, and you will be finished in this town. I happen to know that the two detectives at Forsythe Manor are not fans of yours. Not at all. They will be more than happy to put you in your place!"

That's when a shot rang out. But it hadn't come from the muzzle of my .38 Smith & Wesson. It came from the front door—a door that was now open, framing Amanda in a black raincoat with a smoking gun in her hand.

12

"No..." Brock staggered forward a step as blood ran into his eyes from the exit wound, a hole the size of a golf ball in the middle of his forehead.

Amanda met my gaze. "Thank you," she said. "From both of us."

Brock squeezed the trigger on my revolver, and I hit the floor as one round after another plowed into his couch, right where I'd been sitting a few moments before.

"Amanda—wait!" I shouted as her heels dashed down the hallway outside and descended the stairs.

Doors flew open along the hall as neighbors cried out, "Did you hear a shot?" and "Call the police!"

"Amanda..." Brock groaned, collapsing to his artificial knees. He emptied my gun into the defenseless couch and kept pulling the trigger with his steel finger, clicking on each vacant chamber.

It's a wonder he didn't die immediately. Must have had something to do with his mechanical parts, wired to his brain. As long as they were functioning, they required cerebral impulses. But he would die eventually; of that there was no doubt. Nobody takes a round to the head like that and lives to tell about it.

Amanda hadn't dumped that gun of hers, after all. Made me wonder who she'd been aiming at when she shot up

Leonardo's. Had that been her first attempt on Brock's life?

I was out in the hallway before my feet knew what to do with themselves. Nearly tackling an elderly lady in a flowery kimono, I steadied myself against the wall and made sure she was all right.

"The police are coming, mister," she said, the skin around her eyes crumpled like old parchment. She clung to my arms. "You won't get far."

"Wasn't me." I shook her off and stumbled down the hallway, navigating my way around the other scowling neighbors. "Which way did she go?"

But of course none of them knew who I was talking about. By the time they'd filtered out of their units, Amanda had been well out of sight.

"You think you can come in here and shoot up the place, mister?" Mrs. Kimono called after me, earning a low murmur of discontent from the other locals.

"He killed Brock!" hollered a hoarse voice from Moynihan's open doorway.

Fighting waves of vertigo, I managed to make it down the three flights of stairs to the ground floor just as the foyer doors swung open and two dark silhouettes faced me. One looked like an unshaven whale stuffed into a rumpled suit. The other looked more like a scarecrow with poor posture.

"Madison!" Detective Stankic bellowed. "I had a feeling you'd be mixed up in this."

"Stay right where you are," said Detective Bellincioni, whipping out her cuffs and heading straight for me. "You have the right to remain silent—"

"Did you catch her? Amanda Forsythe? She must have passed right by you!" I gritted my teeth as Bellincioni slapped on the cuffs and cinched them tight.

"—anything can and will be used against *you*—" she rattled off my Mirandas.

"Forsythe was here?" Stankic belched. "She gave us the slip back at her place. The chauffeur said this Brock guy might be in trouble. Crazy love triangle or something?"

"Something like that," I muttered.

"How the hell do you fit in, Madison?"

"I'm the hit man. Don't you know?"

"Yeah, I saw that video. Looking to make a little extra money on the side, eh?"

"Can't really picture this one as a hired gun," Bellincioni said. "His aim's never been too good."

"It does the job." I jerked my arm free of Bellincioni's claws. Being cuffed was bad enough; I didn't need her paws on me. "But your Amanda didn't shoot Brock the bodyguard. That was her stalker." Who happened to be the actual Amanda Forsythe. Had she known Brock was planning to kill her?

Stankic took a long draw on his soggy cigar stub before blowing the rank smoke into my face. "You'll have plenty of time down at the station to get your story straight."

13

Once Stinkin' and Blinkin' escorted me inside the bustling chaos of Precinct 37 at dawn, Sergeant Douglass saw to it that I didn't end up downstairs in a crowded holding cell full of drunken degenerates. Instead, he took me straight to his makeshift office—otherwise known as the staff lounge—and booked me there.

"Can I trust you not to make a run for it?" he said, unlocking my cuffs.

"I wouldn't get too far." I glanced out the door into the noisy bullpen. "Thanks for getting me out of their clutches."

"Stankic and Bellincioni? They didn't have squat on you. The video, sure, but our tech crew is workin' on that as we speak. They'll guarantee it's a fake." He heaved his broad shoulders, equal parts fat and muscle, and blew out a sigh. The man had the build of a pro rugby player whose glory days were a couple decades past. "But what about Amanda? Any clue where she's gone off to?"

"Which one?" Talk about a femme fatale—times two. "From what I've gathered, Amanda Forsythe and her double could have been in cahoots from the start. Getting rid of the bodyguard was a common goal. He had plans to kill the real Amanda and take the look-alike under the knife, do some work on her voice box. Make her sound like the genuine article. Real creepy-ass stuff."

"So she reaches out to the real Amanda, and they hatch out a plan to do him in—before he can harm either one of them. That about the shape of things, lad?"

I nodded. "But why they included me? No idea."

"Diversionary tactic, maybe. The bodyguard had his own endgame in mind: killin' off the real Amanda and livin' off her fortune with the imposter. Only he didn't figure the two of them would want anything to do with each other."

"And now they've both gone off the grid?"

"For now. But we'll find 'em eventually. If it's a priority, that is. The commissioner may want us to leave well enough alone. Could be argued Amanda Forsythe acted in self-defense."

"At my expense." I wouldn't soon forget Brock pointing my gun at me while she ended him. If he'd pulled that trigger a split-second sooner... "I'll be wanting my revolver back, by the way."

"Soon as it's out of evidence, I'll make sure you get it. Forensics was busy prying it out of Moynihan's mechanical hand, last I checked."

"The guy had it bad." I rubbed my wrists where Bellincioni had over-cinched the cuffs. "Old enough to be that girl's father. Obsession in the extreme."

"Not to mention the gas mask. What the hell was that all about?"

I shrugged. "Guy was a freak."

Even so, he'd needed serious help. Not everybody had returned from the war with their heads on straight. I'd wager a guess that most of us hadn't. Brock Moynihan had jumped into his work as a bodyguard with both feet, but that didn't mean he'd been ready for it. He had a few screws loose, but not in his prosthetics. They'd been the only parts of him not prone to malfunction.

"Am I free to go, Sarge?"

Douglass nodded. "You do good work in this town, Charlie. I don't care what the likes of Stankic and Bellincioni have to say about it."

They tended to see me as a chronic interferer in police investigations. They even went so far as to call me a soulless mercenary, while they, in contrast, rode a pair of high horses. They were paid by the city to look out for its best interests, after all. Problem was, those interests were usually tied straight to the mob.

"Thanks, Sarge. If either one of those Amandas makes contact, I'll be sure to let you know." Technically, the first one was still my client until sundown.

He chuckled. "Let's hope they leave you be. I have a feelin' you won't be signing on for any more doppelgänger cases in the near future!"

"You got that right."

14

By the time I made it back to my office, Wanda was already at her desk, fresh and ready for the start of a new day.

"I may have left a facet open on your Slate," I said, hanging up my coat and hat.

She nodded. "I might have played it twice. Some video."

"What did you think?"

"Whoever switched out the audio did a pretty good job. It would have been believable—if I hadn't heard the actual conversation between you and Miss Forsythe. Or her double, rather."

"You make a habit of eavesdropping?"

"Sometimes." She smiled up at me. "But what we really should be discussing is countermeasures. You know, maybe some sort of defense system to keep invisible cameras from floating in unannounced. The privacy of your paying clients demands it, don't you think?"

I gave her a wink. "Good idea."

She glanced at my vacant holster. "Where's your gun?"

"In evidence. Amanda's bodyguard emptied all six rounds at me right before he died."

"Yikes." She neglected to blink. "You all right, Charlie?"

"Will be, once we get ourselves another case. The rent doesn't pay for itself, sweetheart."

"You know what? There might be a girl in my building

who could really use your services."

"Oh yeah?"

"Only..." She wrinkled her nose. "Maybe it's not a good fit. You see, she's got this evil twin, and—"

"I'll be in my office."

It was later that night when a courier from the precinct showed up at my office door. I'd already sent Wanda home for the day, and the place was dark and quiet. Just the way I liked it after an unpredictable twenty-four hours. Perfect for dozing.

"Yeah?" I said as I opened the hallway door.

"Sign here, please." The young woman thrust a Slate at me. Her cap was pulled low, the bill keeping her features out of sight.

I took the Slate and saw the image of my .38 revolver—which the courier proceeded to retrieve from her messenger bag in a transparent snapcase. I signed off on it, and we traded. As she slipped the tablet into her bag, I popped open the case and flipped out the cylinder on my revolver.

"Cops couldn't spring for any ammo?" The chambers were as empty as Moynihan had left them.

"You'll have to take it up with them." She turned on her heel, and as she did so, I noticed the copper sheen of her hair, pulled up tight and tucked under the hat. No shimmering static shield tonight, but her natural glow was just as angelic as it had been the night before.

"Where will you go?"

She was halfway down the hallway before she stopped. Turned. Smiled back at me. Amanda's double, judging by the tone of her voice. I had a feeling that somewhere downstairs, the actual police courier was sleeping off a knock to the noggin in her skivvies. Wouldn't be fun waking up from that.

"We're thinking Mexico."

"Nice down there this time of year." I stepped out into the hall and leaned against the doorframe as I holstered my revolver. "Good plastic surgeons."

"That's what we hear." She hesitated. Unconsciously, she stroked her neck. Her voice was her own. Would she try to get her face back? "Thanks, Mr. Madison—for your help."

"Not sure I did much of anything. She pulled the trigger."

"Brock...was dangerous. He had me fooled, though. He made me think he loved me, that we had a life together. That Amanda deserved to have everything taken away. She was always such a bitch to me..." She shook her head. "When I saw what he was planning—with my voice—"

"You saw? How?"

"I tasked one of Brock's wasps to follow you. I saw everything in that secret room. Heard everything he said to you." She hesitated. "He would have killed her, and I never would have been good enough for him. We had to get rid of him. There was no other way."

Not sure I agreed with that, but I wasn't one to pontificate on particulars. "What about Jerry? Is he next on your hit list?"

She smirked. "Jerry's an idiot. Harmless, really. If he's smart, he'll get out of town and stay the hell out of our way."

I could see it in her eyes: she was a force to be reckoned with now. Not a victim under the knife in those surgery photos. Not an imposter naively believing the promises of a dangerous man. She was becoming her own woman, even as she wore the face of another.

"You two try to stay out of trouble."

"We'll give it a shot." She smiled and gave me a little wave. Then she trotted off.

I shut the door and locked it behind me, taking a moment to imagine the two Amandas on a beach along the Mexican Riviera, tossing back margaritas under a high intensity SPF shield. That fair skin of theirs would broil, otherwise. Would they enjoy the good life together? Or would they team up as cold-blooded assassins for hire? No way to know. But I had a feeling they'd be remaining off-grid for a while.

Would I call Douglass about her visit? Sure, after I gave the girls a healthy head start south. Amanda was no longer my client, but I figured I could give her that much. She had paid me double, after all.

As for Charlie Madison, private investigator, he was headed home to sleep in his own bed. The night may have been young, but if it knew what was good for it, then it would keep quiet and let him catch up on some much-needed winks.

This case was closed.

UP IN SMOKE

I

"Somebody wants me dead, Mr. Madison."

The guy looked scared out of his mind. I'd seen that look plenty, back in the war. But this fellow wasn't a grunt in a gunner squad with no place to hide on the frozen tundra from a platoon of red-eyed mandroids.

He was well-dressed, and if only his suit had done the talking, it would have said he came from money, that he'd never worked a day in his life, that despite the postwar economic downturn infecting the rest of the city, his family had done all right. Maybe he had to sell his muscle-enhanced horse; no more polo matches for the poor kid. But then again, everybody had sacrifices to make.

I wasn't immune. I'd either have to give up my flat and start living out of my office like a glorified hobo, or I'd have to let my assistant go. And there was no chance of that happening. I'd be lost without Wanda. Some sacrifices were sure as hell worth it.

But I digress.

The guy's thousand-credit suit was still talking, telling me he had a dozen others like it, but his closet used to carry twice as many. That's the thing about the rich and wish-they-were-famous: floating so high above the rest of us when the market collapsed, falling for them was merely a change in altitude. Sure, their standard of living had downgraded a bit, but they were nowhere near bottoming out.

"I need your help," he said.

I gestured to the armchair across from my desk and settled into my faux-leather desk chair—the most expensive thing I owned, and a wise investment if I ended up living here. The thing was all sorts of comfortable, and I may have fallen asleep in it on one or two occasions.

"I don't know what to do." He squinted into the light of the setting sun, stripes of orange and rust peeking through open slats on the blinds behind me. Sunshine was a rare commodity in this town; I took full advantage of it whenever I had the chance. Helped keep the electric bills low without any lamps on.

"Have you received death threats?" I said.

"No, nothing like that." He wrung his hands like an amateur stage actor.

"Gone to the police?" Had to ask.

He shook his head and cursed under his breath. "They're no better than the Russians in this town. Father says they're more than likely on Ivan's payroll."

"Your father sounds like a wise man. So why seek me out?"

He shifted his shoulders uncomfortably, like his tailored suit wasn't quite so well-tailored all of a sudden. "Your reputation, Mr. Madison. You're known to...help people? It's not just about the money for you—"

"I've got a living to make, same as anybody else."

"Of course, and I intend to cover your rates and expenses," he said, retrieving a monogramed nubuck wallet—genuine leather, not that synthetic crap—from inside his suit jacket, "whatever they may be."

I held up a hand to slow him down. "I haven't agreed to take your case. Not yet. How about you start at the beginning?"

He blinked, taking a moment to realize his mistake. "Of course. Forgive me." He left the wallet alone for now. Beads of perspiration stood out on his brow. "It's a bit warm in here, isn't it?"

Not at all. But I humored him. "I'll open the window." I always humored paying clients.

"Thank you."

I slid the window up and locked it in place. A cool gust of air wafted inside through the open blinds, carrying the dull tang of pollution along with dissonant chords from the urban cacophony eight flights below.

"Better?"

He nodded, dabbing at his forehead with a fancy silk hanky. Only the best for Little Boy Blue.

"My name is Edgar Talbot." He paused as if that name should've meant something to me. Unfortunately, it did not. I was surprised he didn't divulge his middle name in the process. Pretentious types usually did. "My father is the founder of Talbot Enterprises, you see."

I nodded to show he had my attention, but the company name wasn't filed away in my mental cabinet. Sure, I was born in this city, but I didn't know everybody. For one thing, we boasted a population just shy of five million. Kind of tough to keep that many names straight. For another, the war had taken me far away for a lot of years. Corporations had come and gone in the interim, some seeming to spring up overnight.

Imagine my surprise when I returned to the Unified States to find my entire hometown under the thumb of a *bratva* kingpin named Ivan the Terrible. No kidding. Those of us not affiliated with Ivan's fan club referred to him as the Russian Devil. For all I knew, the Talbot clan was so well off because of their mutually beneficial business dealings with the local mob.

"We are in the import-export business," Edgar said, wiping his brow. Sweating like a nervous wreck now. "Textiles, mostly. We supply all of the tailors in the city."

That explained his fine threads.

"So you're being targeted." Not uncommon these days. The *have-nots* always wanted the *haves* to share their bounty in times like these. Spread the wealth around a bit, fill in the gaps. "Someone's blackmailing you?"

"No, nothing like that," he repeated in the same tone as before. Irritated, like he assumed that by going to see a private eye, the detective would immediately understand his situation. "It's more of a feeling I'm getting." He leaned forward in his seat, sweat standing out like crystal drops, glistening across his face. "I can't shake it. I just know somebody is trying to kill me!"

I was getting a feeling of my own: the guy had a serious perspiration disorder. He didn't look sick, otherwise. Poison maybe?

"Who might want you out of the picture, Mr. Talbot?"

"Call me Edgar, please. Mr. Talbot is my father, and we don't...get along all that well." He paused a moment, then threw up his hands, the hanky fluttering in his grasp. "That's just it! I don't have any enemies, no one who would benefit from my death. No one has threatened me. I have no idea what's going on. It's all so very *frustrating*!"

"How old are you, Edgar?"

He blinked, apparently stumped by the question. "I-uh just turned thirty. Why?"

"It hits us when we least expect it." For me, it had been on that frozen tundra, out on the Eastern front. "How mortal we are."

He shook his head, his face flushed now. He struggled to unbutton his collar and eventually managed, loosening his tie. Forget what I said about him not looking ill. Now he was positively feverish, his wide eyes sporting a manic gleam.

"I'm burning up," he said hoarsely.

"Maybe we should call a doctor—" I reached for my intercom.

"No doctors." He had his wallet out again. "Not this time. I have to know." He shoved his ID at me, no doubt loaded with all manner of credits. "Will you take my case, Mr. Madison?"

I took the ID card and fingered it idly. "Has this happened to you before?" Whatever this was. Sudden onset pyrexia? Hot flash?

"No. This is new." Rivulets of sweat trickled down his ruddy face. "Last time, it was asphyxiation. I was smothered. Before that, strangulation."

"Get a good look at your attacker?"

"No attacker. Nobody there." He stood up suddenly like his britches were on fire. "Just like now. Somebody's trying to kill me, but nobody believes it!"

I had to talk him down, get him to relax, take a breath or few. But before I had a chance to lure him back from the rooftop's edge of insanity, Edgar Talbot burst into flame.

A head-to-toe blazing inferno.

2

"Spontaneous combustion? That's your story, Madison?"

Police detective Stankic surveyed the charred corpse on the floor of my office and chewed the soggy end of an unlit cigar. He probably figured there was already enough smoke to air out of the place without adding his own rank variety. He carried a foul odor as it was. A real slob, he had an affinity for garlic and onions and sauces that stained every tie he knotted around his mottled throat.

"That's my story." I'd never seen anything like it, not even during the war. There had been plenty of horrors, don't get me wrong. Just nothing like this. A guy bursts into flames, right before my eyes? Tough to explain.

Wanda had charged in to the rescue with the fire extinguisher—smashed open the glass case in the hallway outside and everything. Girl was always quick on her feet. But the retardant had no effect. It was like Talbot had turned into a raging conflagration with so much fuel for his fire, the flames wouldn't go out until their entire supply was exhausted.

Wanda didn't give up easy. She emptied the whole canister. Then I beat the poor guy with my coat, thinking maybe there was a sliver of a chance he'd live through the ordeal.

No such luck.

"So...he was one of your clients?" Stankic nudged the remains with the toe of his shoe. Ash formerly in the shape of Talbot's right shoulder crumbled to the scorched carpet and scattered. Stankic shook his head and cursed, always one to contaminate a crime scene.

"You want access to my records, you'll need a warrant."

"Easy, Madison." He graced me with a gruesome smile. "We're just having us a conversation here. Biding the time, see, until the crime scene geeks show up."

"I told you—"

"Combustion. Right." He picked at his nose and shrugged. "Hell, maybe you didn't like the kid. Maybe he owed you money. Maybe he looked at you funny."

"So I torched him—in my own office?"

"How should I know? I didn't see it go down. And I'm glad of it." He cursed under his breath, head waggling with incredulity as his little piggy eyes remained fixed on the victim. "You get a name before this impromptu bonfire?"

"Edgar Talbot."

Detective Stankic stared at me. His jowls sagged as his mouth flopped open. In an impressive display of coordination, he caught the cigar as it fell from his face.

"Welcome to the big show, Madison." He pointed at the remains. "The tabloids will be all over this. They can't get enough of that kid!"

"Didn't realize he was a local celebrity."

"You should Link up more often. That's why you're still playing amateur hour while the real detectives are getting the job done in this town."

"Too bad you're not one of them."

For a split second, I thought he'd go for his gun. Not to

shoot me, of course. He wouldn't want to deal with the paperwork that would entail. But he was never above doling out a hearty pistol-whipping whenever the situation called for it.

As Detective Bellincioni strolled into my office with a well-manicured air of indifference, Stankic opted to favor me with a wicked scowl instead. I didn't mind. Not much he could do to make his face look any uglier.

"Got all I could from the secretary," Bellincioni said, hands on her slim hips as she surveyed the scene. Might've seemed aloof, but I knew from experience that she had a keen eye for detail. Two equally keen eyes, and both of them afflicted with a chronic twitch, one a tad worse than the other. "Emptied the entire extinguisher, she says. Didn't do squat."

"Can't fault her for trying," I offered.

Stankic and Bellincioni—or Stinkin' and Blinkin', as I usually referred to them in my interior monologues—looked at me like I was something they needed to scrape off the bottom of their collective shoe.

The feeling was mutual. I was just a little better at playing nice.

"You'll never guess who that was," Stankic said to his partner. He nodded toward the corpse.

"Don't have to." She whipped out a handheld scanner and swept it slowly across the charred remains without touching anything. Whistling through her teeth, Blinkin' shook her brunette bob as she read the DNA results on the screen. "The one and only Edgar Harrison Talbot. Damn... You sure stepped in it this time, Madison."

"That's what I told 'im." Stinkin' chuckled. Sounded like a

clogged toilet. Or something even more disgusting. "Just wait till the tabloids—"

"Not yet," she said.

Of course not. The cops couldn't allow the public to know about Talbot's death. The tabloids would get the story once Stinkin' and Blinkin' were sure its broadcast wouldn't scare off the killer. Assuming there was one. As a rule, people didn't catch fire without a little help.

"What kind of trouble was he in, Madison?" Blinkin' turned her steely gaze on me.

"I'd say it was obvious."

"Don't be cute. You'll strain yourself," Stinkin' growled. "Shoot straight with us, and we won't haul you down to headquarters as Suspect Numero Uno."

"You've got nothing on me, and you know it."

"Hasn't stopped us before." Stinkin' shrugged his bulky shoulders. "You really want to sit in a filthy cell for twenty-four hours? Fine. But I have a feeling your pretty little secretary might wilt behind bars."

"Assistant," I muttered, glancing at the burnt carpet.

"Yeah." He licked his teeth, his gaze creeping toward Wanda's front office. "I might need to *assist* with her interrogation. The strip search, anyhow." He snickered lewdly. Blinkin' rolled her eyes.

They wouldn't be locking up Wanda—or me. Fingering Talbot's ID card in my pocket, I nodded slowly.

"All right," I said. "Seeing how you seem to know more about my client than I do, how about a fair exchange of information?"

"No promises." Stinkin' and Blinkin' folded their arms in unison. Did they practice that in the break room? "Talk."

"Hey, Wanda?" I called, keeping an eye on the two so-called detectives.

"Yeah, Charlie?" She peeked her head into the room, her loose blonde curls swaying. Her blue eyes sparkled in the soft light of my desk lamp.

"You can go on home. I've got things covered here." I looked from Stinkin' to Blinkin', daring them to contradict me. That was the deal: I'd tell them what I knew, but they'd have to let Wanda go.

They conferred silently, meeting each other's gaze with the most negligible of shrugs. Okay by them. The assistant could leave.

"You sure, Charlie?" There was a distrustful look in her gorgeous eyes as she glanced at the two cops. "I don't mind sticking around—"

"See you in the morning, Miss Wood." I gave her a direct look. Using her surname got my point across, or so I hoped.

She didn't like it, but she didn't have to. The farther away from these crooked detectives she was, the better. Not because I was worried their creeping crud would affect her any; Wanda was a straight arrow, immune to their diseases. I just didn't want them thinking they could use her to get to me.

"All right, Mr. Madison. Good night." She left without another word. Gathering her little handbag, her Slate, and her raincoat, she stepped out into the hallway and shut the door to our front vestibule behind her.

Watching her go, Stankic made an obscene noise at the back of his throat. "You tapped that yet, Madison? Because I'm thinking I should be first in line."

That's when I slugged him, knocking him to the floor

with a right hook. It hurt; the guy had a granite jaw. But it felt so good at the same time.

Well worth the ensuing trip to police headquarters in the back of Blinkin's car with her cuffs digging into my wrists.

"Had to get me alone?" I winked at her in the rearview. "If it was any other woman, I might be flattered."

She braked hard at a red light, throwing me against the steel grate separating us. If my hands hadn't been cuffed behind my back, I might have stood a fighting chance. As it was, the right side of my face broke my fall, and I groaned on impact. Sure to leave a fetching waffle-shaped bruise.

"We'll see how charming you are, crammed in a cell with a dozen other low-life scum," she said.

"They all sucker-punched your partner?"

She growled a curse, jamming her foot onto the accelerator and throwing me back into my seat.

3

News traveled fast around a precinct like the 37th, and the place had its share of private-eye haters. More than its quota, you might say, seeing how so many of these fine, upstanding civil servants served two masters.

Sergeant Archibald Douglass wasn't one of them. No sir. The deep pockets of the Russian mob couldn't tempt him to stray from the straight and narrow path. He refused to turn a blind eye to their sordid atrocities in the city. Ivan the Terrible might have owned everybody from the mayor to the street sweeper, but he couldn't lay claim to a single hair on Douglass's fuzzy head.

"What's goin' on here, Detective?" A small giant of a man with the build of a Scottish rugby player past his prime, Douglass barred the way through the bullpen with a deep scowl set in his ruddy face.

"Oh no, not this time, Sergeant." Bellincioni got right up in his personal space, dragging me behind her. "You're not getting him outta this."

A crowd started to gather. Uniformed eyes dulled by overwork and bloodshot by undersleep brightened at the sight of a certain local gumshoe in cuffs. That's right. I had the opposite of fans.

"Hey, Madison—nice bracelets!" called out one of the beat cops with a big smile, enjoying the show.

"You and Bellincioni goin' steady?" heckled another.

Catcalls ensued. It wasn't pretty. But I smiled back and scratched at my nose nonchalantly with my middle finger.

"What have you gotten yourself into this time, lad?" Douglass said, his brogue thicker than usual. A stress-induced dialect.

"I might've KO'd her partner in crime," I said.

He guffawed. Probably imagining my eighty-odd kilos going up against Stankic's hundred fifty or more. Conservative estimate.

"Besides assaulting a police officer..." Blinkin' squeezed my bicep, her talons digging through my shirt sleeve. Unpleasant. "He's wanted for questioning."

"Regardin' what, exactly?" Douglass folded his brawny arms and stared her down.

"A murder," she snapped, glancing away. Seeking moral support from the crowd?

Douglass raised an eyebrow at me. "You know anything about this?"

"Saw it happen, Sarge," I said. "But it was no murder. Not like any I've ever seen. This guy just...burst into flames."

"Spontaneous combustion," Blinkin' sneered. "Right. Now if you'll excuse us, Sergeant, I've gotta get Mr. Madison booked—"

"C'mon Sarge, help me out here." I turned sideways and shook my cuffed hands behind my back. "There's no need for this."

"Nothing doing," said Blinkin'. Her grip on me tightened. "Outta my way, Douglass."

He didn't budge. "The way I see it, knockin' out that partner of yours was a service to the community." He narrowed his gaze at her. "Uncuff 'im, Detective."

"Like hell I will." She stood close enough to count his gray nose hairs. "I don't care if this private dick is your pet project. He's in *my* custody—"

"Not anymore." Douglass reached past her and grabbed hold of my other arm. "Because you're releasin' him into mine."

She cursed and tugged. He cursed and tugged.

"Make a wish," I muttered.

"Throw your weight around all you want. See what good it does," Blinkin' said to Douglass. "You don't outrank me."

He had his keys out, and a split-second later my shackles slipped free. "You don't like it, take it up with the captain." He handed her the cuffs.

She still had a hold on my arm as I massaged my wrists, flexing my bicep against her claws.

"You can let go of me now, Detective," I said.

She met my smirk with dark, smoldering eyes. Her fingernails dug in, close to drawing blood. Her last stand.

"Don't try leaving the station. I'll shoot you myself." Giving me a shove, she released my arm and cussed to herself. Her heels jackhammered the tile floor as she stormed off, presumably to find the captain.

"You really slugged Stankic?" Douglass almost grinned as he ushered me toward his cluttered desk in the middle of the bullpen.

"Guy went down like a tree." Or what I imagined a felled tree would look like as it hit the ground, back when there were such natural wonders around.

"Back to work," Douglass advised our audience.

They dispersed reluctantly, murmuring among

themselves. A few lingered at the periphery, pretending to be working, probably hoping Blinkin' would return with the captain and a whole new batch of fireworks would start up, ending with me cuffed again and probably stuck in a stuffy interrogation room. Or a holding cell. Whatever they had available at the moment.

No love lost between the cops and yours truly, I'm afraid. I knew most of them were dirty, no matter how upstanding they pretended to be. The only member of the 37th precinct who had my respect was sitting right across from me. And I was lucky to call him my friend.

"So let me get this straight. A fella dies in your office, and you see fit to knock out the police detective on the scene." Douglass clucked his tongue quietly. "What were you thinkin', Charlie?"

"He had it coming."

"No doubt. He's been diggin' his way under your skin for a while now. I get that. But what sent you over the edge this time? You're usually better at keepin' your cool, lad."

I shrugged. Maybe it had something to do with Stankic's remark about Wanda. Maybe it was because I didn't like the cops' attitudes. Or maybe I saw my office as my territory, and they had no business invading it, making lewd comments and insinuating that I had something to do with Talbot's death. I'd mistakenly believed I could do whatever the hell I wanted on home soil, and that including busting up a cop.

Reckless. I hadn't been thinking at all.

Wartime was over. Things had cooled down between the United World and Eastern Conglomerate. I needed to do the same.

"Sorry, Sarge. Won't happen again." I got to my feet and

stuffed my hands into my pockets. My fingers slipped across Talbot's ID card. "Please tell me I'm free to go."

Douglass leaned away from his desk and blew out a sigh. "Promise me you won't leave town."

"I don't make a habit of it."

"Give me your word, lad."

"Or you'll shoot me yourself?"

"No, but the captain would have my head. She might anyway. Mount it on her office wall with all the others." He heaved himself to his feet. "I'll walk you out. You're in my custody, after all." As we navigated our way out of the bullpen and past the front desk where a pencil-necked deskman played solitaire on his computer, Douglass lowered his voice and leaned toward me. "Got any leads?"

I fingered the card in my pocket. "I just might."

But I'd need Wanda's help to hack into Talbot's account without being traced. Glancing at my wristwatch—a cheap timepiece that did its job but was no status symbol—I noted it would be eight hours before she reported for duty at the office.

I didn't want to go back there until the cops cleaned up the mess and vacated the premises. It would take some doing to get the smell of roasted flesh out of the carpet, and I was pretty sure they'd leave that part to me.

"Best if you lie low for a while." Douglass turned as we reached the wall of bulletproof glass doors at the front of the precinct. The night outside was both pitch-black and unlively. "Stankic and Bellincioni will be gunnin' for you."

Not literally, I hoped. "Why does she stick with him? Stankic gives sexist pigs a bad name."

"Tough to say. She might have a screw or two loose."

"Guess that explains it." And the eyeball ticks, to boot.
"Stay sharp, lad." He nodded goodnight.
I saluted him. Old habits died hard. "Thanks, Sarge."
He lumbered back to his desk as the door closest to me sensed my presence, sliding open with a rush of cool, humid night air. More rain on the way, by all indications. The city that never dried out, thanks to the acid wash wearing down our crumbling buildings a piece at a time and sweeping the detritus out to the polluted sea.

Sure, she was ugly. But I had a thing for this town.

"Douglass!" the irate voice of Detective Bellincioni shrilled from the bullpen as the door slid shut behind me.

I took my cue and dashed down the front steps, sprinting across the street and into the first dark alley I came to. If Blinkin' wanted me that bad, she'd have to work for it.

4

I needed to do some research, and I knew just the place. Open all night. Sure, I could've gone on the Link, but that would've required using a phone or a computer. Neither of which I had on my person, because neither of which I owned.

Gadgets and me? We didn't get along so well; not since the war, anyway. Seeing those inhuman EC mandroids butcher my gunner squad right in front of me was enough to make anybody leery of anything too dangerous and too smart for its own good. The Link also fell into that category.

Back in my grandmother's day, they had something called the Internet. Oh, what a tangled web that thing was. Information by the ton, images and video, most of it unresearched and invalid. People's opinions mattered as much as the facts in those days, often more so, and global narcissism knew no bounds.

When the Eastern Conglomerate decided to drop their EMP's over major cities of the United World, the Internet died. Just like that, it lost its hold on citizens—the hold they'd allowed it to have. People didn't know what to do with themselves. Sure, they could still stare at their screens if they wanted to, but those black mirrors only showed them what they'd become: sallow social misfits.

Then about a decade later, the Link came online. In some

ways, it could never hope to be as robust as the Internet; the global impact was no longer there, thanks to the EC's warmongering. But according to the majority of the UW populace, the Link's interface couldn't be beat. Virtual reality sans those goofy goggles they had when I was a kid. While it was still possible to Link up using a phone or Slate, most users opted for the wearable tech—over-the-ear models, in particular. Instead of staring at a screen, they saw everything right behind their own eyes, thanks to some kind of connection with their optical implants. Wouldn't be long before the wearable tech was replaced by a subdermal plug. Just tap and go into your own little world.

No thanks.

I used Wanda's phone to Link up from time to time, but usually I let her take care of that sort of thing. She was the resident tech guru at the Charlie Madison Detective Agency. I preferred the old black, white, and read all over: tabloids printed on slick recycled paper sporting the smiling mugs of the rich and infamous. Members of the yakuza and the bratva shining like stars right alongside our lesser suns—politicians and Link actors.

My source for such research? Mr. Newspaper. Open as late or as early as his insomnia allowed.

"Charlie, how's it hanging?" the old man shouted his customary greeting with a toothy grin. He reclined on a tied stack of newspapers beneath the green awning of his corner newsstand and puffed away on his signature pipe like he didn't have a care in the world. Didn't seem to bother him at all that I was his only customer.

Unofficially, he was my prime informant. If the cops or the Russians ever found out about it, there'd be hell to pay;

but Mr. Newspaper seemed to think helping me was worth the risk. He also seemed to think he owed me.

I might have saved his frozen ass once in the war, back when we were stationed outside St. Petersburg during the dead of winter. He was my commanding officer in those days, a time we'd both worked hard to put far behind us. We'd grown out our crew cuts as fast as we could once we returned stateside, and we never reminisced about the glory days.

War was hell. When you're drafted to fight, you do your job and you do it good. But the only reliving you do is in the middle of the night, when the ear-splitting explosions won't let you sleep. That's more than enough, trust me.

"How are things in the world?" I stuffed both hands into the pockets of my slacks. Truth be told, I felt almost naked without my coat and hat. Blinkin' hadn't seen the necessity of stopping for them on our way out of the office earlier. I probably should've thanked her. She'd gotten me out of there before Stinkin' came to.

"The usual. Wars and rumors of wars." He nodded toward the magazine racks. "And plenty of shiny people to take our minds off it all."

"No news then." I caught sight of Edgar Talbot right away. Tough not to. The guy graced half a dozen of these rags. And he wasn't alone. Beside him in every photo, most likely taken by paparazzi hoverbots as he proceeded about his daily business, was a mystery woman. No face. Just a superimposed white oval with a big, black question mark front and center.

"You got that right." He cleared his throat conversationally. "You workin' late on a case, Charlie?"

"Something like that." Only my erstwhile client was no more. And these tabloids seemed to have no idea he was gone.

I picked up one issue at random and inspected the cover image. Good work, but I knew a fake when I saw it. The lighting was never perfect. Talbot had been alone when the photo was taken. The image of the faceless woman had been added later.

"Flavor of the week," Mr. Newspaper said with a chuckle.

"How's that?" I looked up, meeting his wrinkled gaze.

He pointed at my magazine with the end of his pipe. "That Talbot fella. Rich playboy type. Most eligible bachelor in town, according to these folks."

"Somebody spots him with a girl they don't recognize..."

"And there you have it. This week's special: the *mystery woman*." He chuckled drily. "Gotta say I'm impressed, though. It's been days now, and nobody's snapped a photo of her. I hear the bounty's up to five thousand credits for first blood."

My eyebrows arched involuntarily. "I'm in the wrong line of work."

He shrugged. "A good hoverbot costs twice that. And the insurance on one of those gizmos..." He whistled through his teeth. "Through the roof."

"They do make tempting targets."

"Right." He grinned. "Skeet shooting with prizes!"

As long as your bullet didn't damage the camera or its memory stick, they'd be prize enough.

"So what's the big deal?" I replaced the magazine on the rack. "These guys date a different girl every other night, don't they?"

"Sure they do. But the paparazzi recognize 'em. Young socialites, Link actresses, daughters of local politicians and mobsters, usually. But that girl." Again with the pipe-pointing. "No clue who she is. And no clue how she's been able to keep the hovercams off her."

"Localized EMP?"

"That's the stuff." He nodded, liking the idea. "Would take some tech-savvy know-how. And underworld connections, EMP's being illegal and whatnot."

"Does that ever stop the rich and infamous?"

"No sir, it does not."

I glanced up the street toward my office building, not ready to survey the damage yet. Would there be police tape across the door? Talbot's remains on the floor?

"You're looking a little peaked, Charlie. Why don't you head on home for some shuteye. This bunch'll be here in the morning." He gestured at the glossy covers.

"Maybe you're right." I still had my own flat; might as well make use of the place while I could afford the rent. The bed, in particular. "Let me know if they find out who she is. This mystery woman."

"Always one for a good puzzle, aren't you."

I gave him a wink. "Vocational hazard."

5

The office still smelled god-awful, but at least the crispy remains of Edgar Talbot were no longer taking up valuable floor space.

"I never should've left," Wanda said unhappily.

She stood beside me as we surveyed the scorched carpet. A cool breeze swept in through the open window behind my desk. The ambient light from a gray, overcast morning filled the room.

"If you hadn't, they would've dragged you in too."

"What for? I didn't slug anybody."

"You might have, given time." Then it would've been Wanda with the assault charge hanging over her head instead of me. "You locked the door?"

She nodded, glancing back at our client receiving area that doubled as her office. The door leading out into the main hallway sported CHARLIE MADISON, DETECTIVE on the frosted glass in bold lettering. Backwards from our point of view.

"Not good for business, Charlie."

"Don't need any right now." And I didn't need Stinkin' or Blinkin' waltzing in unannounced. I had a feeling they'd show up soon enough. Stankic had a score to settle, after all. "We've already got a client."

"Who?"

I whipped out the ID card. "Edgar Talbot, deceased."

She stared, her wide eyes a beautiful shade of blue the sky over our fair city hadn't seen in weeks. Her gaze darted from the card to me and back again.

"You can't be serious..."

"About hacking into his account?" I raised an eyebrow at her. "Serious as a stroke."

She smacked her signature wad of chewing gum, but the sound could have easily been a cluck of disapproval. "Robbing a dead man? Not like you, Charlie."

"All I want is his address—for now." I handed over the ID card, and she took it with some reservation. "And the last half-dozen places he made any purchases. Before he...showed up here."

"Blew up, more like." She winced at the memory and headed toward her desk in the front vestibule. "You really need to do something about that smell."

I doubted anything short of new carpet would do the trick. And there was no chance we'd be able to afford something like that anytime soon.

"Spray some of your perfume around. I'm sure it'll work wonders." She always smelled good, like fresh lilac blossoms.

She paused at her desk and glanced back at me like I'd said something funny.

"I don't wear perfume, Charlie."

"Oh." I didn't know what else to say, so I changed the subject. "This Talbot guy, I hear he was something of a playboy. All over the tabloids."

Her narrow shoulders shifted up and down as she scanned Talbot's ID through the reader on her Slate. She had the tablet connected to an old Underwood typewriter, augmented so each keystroke tapped the keyboard interface like a stylus. Quirky? Oh yeah. That was Wanda all over, and I wouldn't have had her any other way.

"I don't pay much attention to that stuff. I'm more into the next-gen tech rags." She winked back at me and mouthed *computer crap*.

I graced her with a dramatic shudder. Meeting those killer robots on the open battlefield had hardened my heart against machines in general and smart ones in particular. So I was more than lucky to have Wanda as my resident tech wiz.

"Holy cow..." She let out an appreciative whistle. "This guy was loaded!"

I was tempted to have her withdraw my retainer then and there, before the cops thought to freeze his assets. But I restrained myself.

"For now, let's focus on his place of residence."

"Right." She nodded, buckling down. Her fingertips danced across the keys on her Underwood, and the Slate's screen responded. "Looks like he was living at his family estate in the Hills. No other address on record."

She rattled off the street and number, and I looked for a pen and scrap of paper, figuring I'd take a cab over to that side of town where the rich, the famous, and the infamous lived together in perfect harmony, far away from our mean city streets.

"Can you backtrack the path he took to get here?"

Another nod. "Yeah, a cab picked him up out front of his gate. Mansions have gates, don't they?"

"Most do." I shrugged.

"Rode it straight into town, where he stopped off at a tailor shop. From there, he must've hoofed it over here."

"How close is that shop?"

"Five, six blocks away."

"Did he make any purchases?" He hadn't been carrying anything with him when we met.

She shook her head. "He was there for only five minutes or so—judging from the time the cabbie let him off and the time he arrived at our door. Factoring in the sunset stroll that brought him here...that would leave about five minutes for the tailor."

"No other scans in the past twenty-four hours?"

She wrinkled her eyebrows a little, her gaze riveted to the screen. "Looking at these charges, the guy hasn't been getting out and about much, Charlie. Not lately, anyway. The previous charge, before the cab, was from three days earlier. Scanned at that same tailor shop."

I had a feeling I'd be visiting a certain tailor in the near future. But first there was the matter of a fleshy fist pounding on the door and an ogre-shaped shadow of a man in the hallway outside.

"Open up, Madison," Detective Stankic bellowed, sounding just shy of murderous. "I know you're in there!"

"Time to clear out." I took Wanda by the elbow and escorted her away from her desk. Not toward the door. "Get your coat."

She got mine off the rack too while she was at it.

"You don't want me to stay and fend him off?"

Nothing I wouldn't say or do to keep her out of Stankic's oily clutches. Of course she could take care of herself, and she'd proven it many times before. But today—

"Best if we stick together this time." I pulled on my coat and nodded for her to follow me into my office—straight toward the open window and the overcast skies outside.

And the fire escape.

"You sure about this, Charlie?" She had that familiar little crease across her brow as I ducked out through the window and stepped onto the iron landing with a clang from my hard-soled shoes. "If the cops are after you, then shouldn't—?"

A bullet ricocheted off the ladder rungs above me. I dropped to one knee and drew the snub-nosed .38 from my shoulder holster.

"Next one hits meat, Madison!" Detective Bellincioni stood in the alley below, eight floors down. Glock in both hands.

Stinkin' ready to bust the door down. Blinkin' squeezing off pot shots. Just the two of them. Out for payback, with or without the blessing of their superiors. Wouldn't have mattered anyway. They had their own idea of what it meant to protect and serve, and justice seldom entered the equation.

I kept my hands where she could see them as I leaned carefully over the railing. "Nobody has to get shot today, Detective."

"You're right about that," she called up to me, her gun aimed straight at yours truly. "Drop your piece, Madison."

The doorframe came apart in the front office as Stinkin' plowed inside like a raging bull. In a couple seconds, he'd be on top of us.

"C'mon." I tugged at Wanda's arm and headed down the fire escape as fast as I could move, my revolver clanking against the ladder as I descended hand over hand. Wanda's heels followed me down.

"I said *drop it!*" Blinkin' hollered.

I was banking on two things at the moment: that she wouldn't really shoot me or Wanda, and that Stinkin' would have a hell of a time hauling his girth down the fire escape after us. Maybe by the time we reached the last rung and dropped to the pavement below, he might have squeezed himself out the window. No chance he'd be able to catch us. He'd have to be content with hurling foul epithets and impotent threats instead.

But that's not how things played out.

Instead of following us onto the fire escape, Detective Stankic proceeded to draw his own Glock and commence with some poorly executed target practice. The guy's aim was all right on a good day, but right now with his heart pounding overtime? Not so much. Good news for Wanda and me as we cringed, making it down to the alley in record time. Bad news for Detective Bellincioni. She caught a ricochet from her partner in the shoulder and went down hard, cussing me instead of the idiotic culprit.

"Watch your language. There's a lady present." I kept my revolver on Blinkin' as Wanda and I backed out of range. Blinkin' kept her semiautomatic trained on my forehead and glared bloody murder. But she didn't pull the trigger as I offered a piece of advice: "Stay out of my way, Detective, and I just might solve this case for you."

She ground her teeth and spat something obscene, advising me to eat excrement. I declined the invitation.

Once we were out on the main boulevard, we slowed from a sprint to a casual stroll. Wanda nudged me with her elbow and leaned in like she was my accomplice or something.

"Where to now, Charlie?"

I tugged at the lapels of my coat as thunder grumbled across the charcoal sky. "Gotta see somebody about a suit."

6

He was a mid-twentieth century cliché, complete with the measuring tape draped over his neck like a scarf that would never measure up.

"Welcome, welcome!" He greeted us brightly as I let the shop's front door close on my heel with a soft jingle of sleigh bells. Not the real deal. A motion-sensored sound effect played through ceiling speakers.

No actual bells. No actual tailor, either.

He glowed in the center of the cramped shop like a ghost from Christmas past, hands extended in a gesture that promised anything we could possibly need at a fair price.

"New suit? Coat? Perhaps something nice for the lady?" He grimaced as he glanced past us at the wet street outside. "Miserable weather, isn't it? We've just received a fresh supply of poly-sealant. With a protective layer like that, no acid rain will eat through your coat or hat!"

"Sure, how about the works?" I flapped my lapels. I needed to get the stink of Talbot's smoke off me. But I knew better than to think I had enough credit to cover a new wardrobe. "How much will that set me back?"

The hologram tailor smiled pleasantly. "Yes, of course. We have everything you need right here. An assistant will arrive shortly to take your measurements."

"Only so much an interface like this can do," I muttered to

Wanda.

"I'm surprised you spoke to it at all, Charlie."

I looked the holo-tailor over. The original owner, maybe? "Gives me the creeps, every time I see these things."

"Next it'll be robots, right? Put us all outta jobs."

"Nobody could replace you, kid." I gave her a wink.

"Will the lady be needing anything today?" said the hologram.

Wanda had left the office without her purse or her Slate, so she wouldn't be making any purchases either. But she sure looked good in that lavender dress. Her coat was open in the front now that we were inside, out of the weather, and she stood with her hands in the pockets.

"Can't really think of anything," she said, looking over the suits on display—other holograms that rotated on invisible bodies, alternating as they turned to show every available variation in color, fabric, and style. "Guess I go more for dresses and skirts, y'know?"

"Just how interactive are you, anyway?" I narrowed my gaze at him.

"Beg pardon?" Holo-Tailor leaned toward me as though he were hard of hearing. Nice touch.

"Do you keep a record of your customers?"

"No. But I do," said the young woman who stepped though the hologram from the back of the shop. The old tailor evaporated without another word, disappearing like the high-tech ghost he was. "A strange question for someone interested in buying some new threads."

"Interested. Right." I nodded. Then I shook my head. "Can't afford any."

The woman was in her early twenties, close to Talbot's

age. And Wanda's. The younger generation, born into war. No memories of what life was like before the United World and Eastern Conglomerate decided to stake their claims all across the planet and duke it out.

"You cops?"

Wanda stifled a chuckle.

"Better." I allowed half a grin to make an appearance. "We actually help people." Usually when they weren't already burnt to a crisp. "Name's Madison. I'm a private investigator, and this is my assistant, Wanda Wood. That hologram—is he the owner?"

She smirked. "A hundred years ago, yeah. My great-grandfather. My sister designed the hologram as a tribute to him. The shop is mine now."

"Get a lot of business?"

"We do all right."

"Just you and holo-Gramps?"

"My sister. We run the place." She retreated a step.

A door in back led to where all the magic happened, I presumed: the alterations, the stitching, the mending. For all I knew, she had a small army of robots that did her bidding. An unsettling prospect.

No tape measure over her shoulders. Instead, she held a stylus-like device, which she twirled from finger to finger. Some kind of laser? No chance I'd be letting that thing anywhere near my inseam.

"And since you're not a cop with a warrant, Mr. Madison, I don't have to tell you anything about my customers."

"Fair enough. Your clientele—locals, mostly?"

She gave me the steely eyes. Her great-grandfather had been much friendlier. Or her sister had programmed him to be.

"Any high-rollers?" I ventured.

She narrowed her gaze. "Why do you want to know?"

"My client, Edgar Talbot. He may have done some business here recently."

Her lips parted. Her fingers stopped twirling. "Edgar Talbot is your client?" she asked in wonder.

How did everybody seem to know about this guy? How famous was he?

"Why would he need a private eye? Can't his own people do his dirty work for him?" she said.

I might have wondered the same thing if I hadn't known he'd been afraid for his life, unsure whom to trust.

"I may not be squeaky clean, Miss, but I do my best to make an honest living. No dirty work going on here, trust me." I hadn't used Talbot's credit yet, after all. Tempting as it was. "I'm just following up on a couple leads."

"And they led you here."

"That's right. You see, according to Edgar Talbot's recent expenditures, this was the only place of business he visited recently—besides my office." I paused. "All very routine. Part of my job involves backtracking, finding out where my clients are coming from. I'm sure you can understand."

Her eyes looked glassy now. The steel was gone. "Is he dead?"

That threw me. But I did my best not to let it show. "What makes you say that?"

"Answer the question," she snapped. She was holding herself together, but not by much. Some kind of super fan? Or did she know Talbot on a first-name basis? His personal tailor who wished she could be more?

"Mr. Talbot passed away yesterday evening," I almost said.

Only I couldn't. According to Wanda, Talbot's death hadn't hit the Link yet, which meant the cops were still keeping a lid on it.

"He thinks somebody wants him dead," I divulged. Better than the whole truth.

"Yeah." Her eyes widened briefly as she stared at the carpet and covered her mouth with one hand. Then she shook her head and dropped her hand to her side. The stylus started twirling through her fingers again, a nervous tic. "I thought he was just being paranoid at first..." She snapped to attention and took a step toward me. "He hired you to help him?"

"That's what I do."

"Have you been to his house yet?"

"Talbot Manor?" I smirked.

"Our next stop," Wanda said.

The tailor nodded. "Talk to that wicked bitch of a stepmother. I'd bet you this entire shop that she's out for blood."

"All right." Time for me to narrow my gaze at her. "And you know this how, exactly?"

"Edgar and I..." She swallowed. "We're close."

"Creepy fan-girl close, or—"

"I'm Rachel." She pointed at her chest, her expression hard. She glanced at Wanda, then back at me. Like the name should ring some kind of bell. "Hasn't Ed mentioned me?"

Maybe he would have, eventually. If our conversation hadn't been cut so short.

"Let me guess: you're head of the Edgar Talbot Adoration Society?"

She cursed my ignorance. "I'm his damn girlfriend!"

7

Thanks to Wanda's nearly superhuman memory, we had no problem telling the cab driver where to take us: straight across town to where the better half lived.

"So." Wanda nodded back toward the tailor shop as the cab left the curb with a splash of acid rainwater and accelerated to rejoin the busy traffic. "Was Talbot slumming it, or is the girl just delusional?"

"Remains to be seen." I shook my head. "Two-person outfit? Don't know how that shop stays open."

"Don't forget the hologram, Charlie."

"No chance of that."

"I know what you mean, though. Don't most guys buy their suits on the Link?"

"Not this guy." I tugged at my lapels. And wrinkled my nose a little. I seriously needed to get this coat deep-cleaned. Talbot's smoke was in its pores. "But I guess I'm not most guys."

"No sir, you are not." She nudged me with her shoulder. "But I wouldn't have you any other way."

"Right back at you, Sweetheart."

She was quiet for a moment or two as our driver dodged and weaved around other vehicles on the slick streets, leaving part of my stomach behind in the process.

"Are we gonna talk about it?" Wanda said at length.

"Might help if you were a smidge more specific." I gave her a wink.

She wasn't smiling. The twinkle had left her eyes. "Those cops. Stankic and Bellincioni. The reason why you're dragging me along on this case."

"Hey, if you don't like my company—"

"You hardly ever let me tag along, Charlie."

I shrugged. "You've always got work to do, back at the office. Keeping us organized." Had to rephrase that: "Keeping *me* organized."

"You're protecting me from something." She gave me a hard stare. "Spill it. Why are we on the run?"

I glanced up at the rearview. So far, the driver was keeping his eyes on the road where they belonged, and we were still headed in the right direction. No reason yet to think he might be working for the cops.

"Stinkin' and Blinkin' have been looking for an opportunity to get me into serious trouble. They think I might've had something to do with Talbot's death."

"And that wasn't enough? You had to go and slug one of 'em—and get the other one shot?"

"Hey, it's not my fault her partner is a moron."

"They're gonna keep comin' after us, aren't they?"

"Sure they will. But once we find out who wanted Talbot dead, the cops won't have any reason to pin this on me. And they won't be able to use you to get to me."

"What's that supposed to mean?" She narrowed her gaze. "You don't think I can handle myself? C'mon, we can take 'em."

"You shouldn't have to. This is my mess, and I'll do whatever I have to..." I shook my head. "To keep you away from those dirty cops."

The twinkle came back into her eyes. "My hero." She gave me a playful nudge. "And they say chivalry's dead. But wait a minute. You're assuming I'm the one they'd catch. What if they get *you* first?"

"Douglass might be able to help me out." Again? Unlikely. "But I doubt it. Withholding evidence. Interfering with a police investigation. Oh yeah, and cleaning Stankic's clock. Three strikes, I'm out."

She nodded resolutely. "So we've really gotta find out who killed Talbot. And fast."

"We do that, I can show my face around the 37th again—as a free man. Stinkin' and Blinkin' won't be able to make anything stick. The end justifies the means in this town, even for a lowly gumshoe."

She was quiet again. "So you think somebody murdered him?"

"I don't think he set himself on fire. Do you?"

"I don't know what to think, Charlie." She shook her head. "You think you know how the world works, and then you see something like that. Guy goes up in smoke, right there in front of you. Nothin' you can do about it."

"Quick thinking with the fire extinguisher. You kept a level head. I just stood there like a dope. Couldn't believe my eyes."

"Fat lot of good it did. Guy's still dead." She paused. "I don't think anything would've put out those flames, Charlie. It was like...some kind of chemical reaction, you know? That fire was unstoppable."

"Try to get it out of your head, or you won't sleep."

"Didn't sleep much last night." She looked up at me, her

sapphire eyes searching for something. "You saw some pretty awful stuff in the war, didn't you?"

I nodded. Not much to say about it.

"How do you keep it from gettin' to you, Charlie?"

"Tough not to, sometimes." I cleared my throat. "You know how I am with computers."

"Machines in general, is more like it. Except for the intercom on your desk. That doesn't seem to bother you."

"I can understand that thing. But smart machines? The Link—jacking a computer into your vision? No thanks."

"Because of the war?"

"I can't forget what we went through over there. I shouldn't forget. But when I remember, I want it to be on my own terms. Good people died. Happens here, too, off the battlefield. Wish it didn't, but people do bad things. It's up to the rest of us to stop them." Half a grin tugged at the side of my face.

"Something funny about that?"

"Something my grandmother used to say. That just because we're living in a fallen world doesn't mean we have to wallow in it. She'd say God gave us the responsibility of lending a hand, helping folks up out of the gutters."

"She was religious?"

I nodded. "Even dragged me to church on Sundays, if you can believe."

She smiled, and it was the most beautiful thing I'd seen all day. "Charlie Madison, choir boy?"

"Not even close."

The cab slowed as it approached a massive gate. Not the single mansion variety of wrought iron. This filigreed monstrosity kept the rabble at bay from poisoning an entire neighborhood. That and the ten-foot wall of stuccoed concrete that surrounded the wealthy, imprisoning them with their own kind.

A pair of armed, well-built men in rent-a-cop uniforms stood at the guard station. Neither one looked impressed by the sight of a dingy city cab idling at their threshold.

"This is as far as I can go, folks," said our driver. He tapped the scanner on the rear-facing screen in front of us. "Your charges. Assuming they let you two in—or out. You want me to wait?"

"No, thanks." I paused, fingering Talbot's ID card. Then I swiped it.

Why not give Stinkin' and Blinkin' a little help? Locating me should have been the least of their worries. There was a pyromaniac murderer on the loose, after all. Might as well play sportsmanlike. Otherwise, where was the fun in an easy victory?

And besides, Wanda was right. We could take care of ourselves.

"You okay with the cops tracing that?" Wanda said quietly as we exited the cab.

"Counting on it."

8

It took some doing to get the guards to open the gate for us. I insisted I was there on behalf of Edgar Talbot, that he was my client, and that I had something to give his mother. Stepmother. A real witch, according to Rachel the tailor.

The two armed beefcakes insisted on patting us down. The one who assigned himself to Wanda took his sweet damn time—tried to, anyway. She nonchalantly stepped back onto his toe with her heel and proceeded to apologize profusely as he lurched away from her with a yowl.

"Can't go inside with that." The other guard gestured at the holstered Smith & Wesson under my arm. "Gotta leave it here with us."

"How will I protect myself from the rich and wanna-be famous?" I slipped off my coat and unbuckled my holster.

"Leave that to her." He grinned at Wanda with appreciation.

His partner with the bruised toe kept his eyes to himself.

"Point us in the right direction?" I handed him my snub-nosed revolver with the shoulder rig wrapped around it.

"The Talbots are at the end of the street. Can't miss it." He raised an eyebrow at his partner. "Good to go?"

He nodded and hobbled into the guard station without a word. A moment later, the gate creaked open, parting in the middle and swinging out to the sides.

"Welcome to the Hills."

I nodded politely, not liking the idea of walking into unfamiliar surroundings unarmed. Wanda took my elbow, and we entered the hallowed grounds of the west coast's old money, set apart from the Russian mob that controlled most of the city under Ivan the Terrible's hairy fist. The folks who lived behind these walls could trace their lineage all the way back to Hollywood, the NBA, and the NFL. Long before the Link made it possible to experience any virtual fantasy under the sun, the ancestors of the Hill's exclusive residents were busting their butts entertaining the masses: big name actors and producers, directors, athletes, singers and performers of every distinction. Trained monkeys along with their trainers.

"Think we'll see anybody famous?" Wanda's head was on a swivel as we strolled along the sidewalk.

Manicured lawns protected by electrostatic shielding on one side; pristine, litter-free streets on the other. Judging by the way the mid-morning drizzle failed to fizz and bubble across my coat and hat, it was safe to assume the Hills had some sort of protection in place over the entire neighborhood. Oh, the things money could buy.

Testing my theory, I took off my hat for a moment and tilted my head back, opening my mouth to let the raindrops tickle my tongue—something I hadn't been able to do since I was a kid.

"Charlie, are you crazy?"

"Most likely." I shrugged. "Go on, try it."

"No way. You want to burn your tongue off, be my guest. I like being able to taste my food."

The rain tasted clean, fresh. Filtered and purified.

"Suit yourself." I wiped my forehead dry and replaced my

hat. "Oh, you've got to be kidding me." I pointed at the pretentious placard out front of the house at the end of the street. "When I referred to it as Talbot Manor, I had no idea."

That was the official name of the place, according to the signage. And as fancy as the rest of these domiciles looked, they paled in comparison to the Talbot's mansion. By all appearances, it had been modeled after the White House from Washington, DC, back during the days of the Republic—before the place was burned to the ground.

"Wow..." Wanda said. "You really think they're gonna let us inside?"

I fished Edgar's ID card out of my pocket. "This might help."

We made our way up the winding pathway, not pausing to admire the lush, well-groomed greenery, as much as we would have liked to. Passing between a pair of Corinthian arches as alabaster-white as a swooning goddess's brow, I approached one of the two massive doors. Faux-ironwood or the real deal? No idea.

"What are you doing?" Wanda whispered as I swiped Edgar's card past the doorside sensor.

"Getting us inside."

The twin doors parted much like the gates down the street, but they did so without even a hint of a squeak.

"I don't know about this, Charlie..." Wanda slid behind me.

So much for her being my protector.

"Welcome home, Master Talbot," greeted the short, boxy automaton, rolling toward us on rubber treads across the spacious entryway's pink marble. "May I take your coat?"

I stared at the thing. It stared back—without eyes or even

an anthropomorphic face. This was no mandroid; it was barely a meter tall with no weapons in sight. But its presence inspired a cold dread to finger my intestines, regardless.

"Pardon me," it said, halting abruptly with both spindly arms hovering in midair. Its tinny voice had been programmed to sound something like a posh British butler. "I may be in error. Are you Edgar Talbot or Charles Madison, private investigator?"

"Madison. Edgar hired me."

"Why, may I ask, are you in possession of Master Talbot's ID card?"

The bot must not have had a facial recognition program. It had scanned both of the ID cards on my person—mine as well as Talbot's.

"He left it with me. For safe keeping."

"I see." The robot swiveled in place indecisively. "Is Master Talbot in some sort of trouble, Mr. Madison?"

"Not anymore." I stepped past the machine toward the main hallway. "Is Mrs. Talbot home? I'd like to speak with her for a moment."

The robot wheeled around to face me. "Mrs. Talbot is not receiving visitors at this time—"

"She'll want to receive me." I shrugged out of my soggy, sooty coat and tossed it over the robot. "Take care of that, won't you?"

I nodded for Wanda to join me, but instead she took my coat off the jerking bot and bent over at the waist as if she were talking to a child.

"You'll have to forgive Mr. Madison," she said to the machine. "When he's on a case, sometimes he forgets about the proper pleasantries and stuff." She shook her head at me as I turned away and headed into the biggest, most luxurious living room I'd ever seen. "His manners aren't always so good," she added, her voice echoing after me.

I would've glanced back, maybe even offered a wry quip, if I hadn't been otherwise distracted. I was too busy staring at the young woman who sat alone on the spacious sofa sectional in the center of the room. She had the looks of a femme fatale not living up to her potential. Writhing in silent, slow-motion ecstasy, she was garbed in a rose-colored silk robe that twisted around her, sheer and lacy. Her eyes were closed, her mouth open, gasping. Over one ear perched a Link interface, blinking with virtual activity. I had a pretty good idea what kind.

Clearing my throat, I stepped toward her, doing my best to keep my eyes directed toward the grand piano across the room.

"Miss, my name is Charlie Madison..." I trailed off.

No response. I tried again—both the throat-clearing and the formal introduction. She gave no indication that she recognized my existence. Some rich people were like that. But I had a feeling this had more to do with her Link activities.

How long had she been online? Was she already a brain-fried zombie?

"As I told you, Mr. Madison," said the robot as it rolled beside me. "The lady of the house is currently indisposed, and she is not receiving visitors. You may leave Master Talbot's ID card with me. I will make sure that he gets it."

Unlikely.

9

"What is the meaning of this?" blustered a bathrobed fellow on the other side of middle-aged, entering the living room with an amber drink sloshing around the tumbler in his hand. "Who are you people? What are you doing in my home?"

"Mr. Talbot, this is Charles Madison, a private investigator," said the robot, pivoting to face its owner. "And this is his assistant, Wanda Wood."

"How the hell did they get in here, Jeeves?" Before the automaton could respond, Mr. Talbot caught sight of the woman on the sofa, moaning and convulsing with pleasure. "Dear heavens, woman, have you no shame?" He grimaced and turned away, tossing back his drink. Nothing like a morning whiskey to get the blood pumping. "Mr. Madison and Miss Wood, whoever you are... Welcome to my home. I am George Edward Talbot, of course, though I need no introduction. I see you've already met Jeeves." He glanced back at the sofa and cringed. "And as for my—"

"Daughter?" I ventured, following his gaze.

"My wife." Mr. Talbot belched, turning his back on her and gesturing for us to follow him out of the room. "Young people and their gadgets. Am I right?"

"Oh, *Edgar*!" the woman screamed suddenly. Enraptured, oblivious to everything beyond her virtual world.

I turned back to find her sitting bolt upright, clutching onto the side of the sofa, her head thrown back. Quite the dramatic pose.

"Are-uh...she and your son close?" I said.

"What is your business here?" George Talbot demanded. He faced me now, close enough to smell the sour alcohol on his breath.

"Your son hired me." I handed him Edgar's ID card. "Said somebody was trying to kill him."

Talbot snatched the card away and peered at it. Squinting at arm's length. "Where's Edgar now? He should have been here hours ago. No. Don't tell me." His upper lip, sweaty and unshaven, curled back in disgust. "He's slumming it again with that little seamstress!"

"Rachel?"

"She has a name? Probably. Most whores do. But how the hell should I know? Don't ask me what he's thinking, running around with that simpering gold digger. Can you believe he had the gall to bring her to dinner? Here, in *my* house?"

"I'm sure that didn't thrill his mother either. Stepmother," I corrected. "Close in age, aren't they?"

He narrowed his gaze at me. "What are you implying, sir?"

I shrugged. "Just wondering if Mrs. Talbot married the right Mr. Talbot."

"Show them out, Jeeves!" he bellowed, his entire face and neck blossoming as crimson as a ripe tomato.

The robot rolled quickly to obey.

Talbot jabbed me in the chest with a hairy sausage of a finger. "If you see that son of mine in the near future, Mr. Madison, whoever you are, you tell him to stay away from that beggar girl. Or the river of credit he's currently swimming in will be dammed!" He laughed, the combination of his forced humor and his wife's cries of delight from the other room making quite the juxtaposition.

A soft chime sounded from the entryway's vaulted ceiling. Jeeves rolled past us toward the front doors.

"Now what?" Talbot said with exasperation. "The whole point of living in this gated community is to *avoid* unwanted visitors showing up on your doorstep!" He staggered after the robot. "Who is it, Jeeves?"

We didn't have much time.

Taking Wanda by the elbow, I held an index finger to my lips and backed away, heel to toe, steering us toward the living room and the young Mrs. Talbot. She'd quieted down considerably, lying on her back now with her arms out to the sides, chest heaving as she caught her breath. Her eyes were closed, her Link interface dangling from the fingers of her right hand. No longer online.

"As good as the real deal?" I said, taking a seat beside her.

Her eyes shot open and she sat up, pulling her flimsy excuse for a robe tight about her. The faux-leather of the sofa squeaked beneath her as she scooted away from me.

"Who the hell are you?" Not the most welcoming folks, these Talbots. "What are you doing in my house?" Her glassy eyes flicked from me to Wanda with obvious distrust. "Are you home invaders or something?"

"You get those often?"

Her lips parted without sound.

"Edgar sent us. Your son."

"Why? Who are you people?"

"He's a detective." Wanda sat down on the other side of

Mrs. Talbot. We had her surrounded. "A good one. Your son said he was in some kind of trouble. Know anything about that?"

"No, I..."

"Were you the cause?" I nodded toward her Link device. "He rebuffed your advances, so you had to come up with the next best thing. But like they say, hell hath no fury. Right?"

"I don't appreciate what you're suggesting—"

"Trust me, we got more than an earful a minute ago. And I'm pretty sure if my lovely assistant were to hack into that gizmo of yours, we'd see your stepson's face plastered onto some virtual super-stud's body. Isn't that about the shape of things?"

The woman actually blushed. Some people still did that? But no, it wasn't from shame. The way she grit her teeth and trembled made it clear she was in the middle of a full-on rage storm.

"Get out!" she shrieked.

"You're making friends all over town, Madison."

I looked up to find Detective Stankic waddling into the room in all his foul glory and sporting an ugly bruise on his jaw. Bellincioni came up beside him, her arm in a sling. I could tell she wanted to put my ass in one too. A pair of beat cops in uniform waited at her heel like well-trained police dogs.

"You're done here, dick." She motioned the two uniforms toward me. "Cuff him. His secretary, too." She smiled, and even though she looked happier than I'd ever seen her, those eyes just kept on twitching.

"They're wanted felons? In my *home*?" Mr. Talbot gasped. "Jeeves, you're getting a complete security overhaul, you miserable piece of scrap!"

The robot retreated, rolling backward a meter or two.

I got to my feet so the uniform could cuff my hands behind my back. No reason to make her job any more difficult than it already was. Working with Stinkin' and Blinkin'? Fate worse than death.

"You like playing with fire, Mrs. Talbot?" I said.

She scowled hideously at her husband. "I want these people out of my house. All of them. Right now." She kept a hand on the robe at her throat. Diamonds perched on her fingers like sparkly sparrows.

"Don't you worry, Mrs. Talbot," Stinkin' said. "We've got a nice cramped cell for Madison here. And his little errand girl, too." He licked his chapped lips and ran his gaze up and down Wanda's figure as she was cuffed beside me. "They've interfered with their last police investigation, I promise you that."

"What sort of investigation?" Mr. Talbot demanded. "What does any of this have to do with my son?" He waved Edgar's ID card through the air like a conductor's baton.

Stankic glanced at his partner, deferring to her like a good junior detective.

"I'm afraid your son is dead, Mr. Talbot," Blinkin' said with the bedside manner of a dump truck. "He passed away yesterday evening."

Another scream erupted from Mrs. Talbot, her stepson's name yet again. But this time, she doubled over like she was in agony, clutching her Link device to her chest as guttural sobs shook her slender frame.

Call it detective's intuition, but I had a feeling she wasn't our pyro. The Hills may have been Old Hollywood, but nobody could put on an act like that.

10

So Stinkin' and Blinkin' finally had me right where they wanted me. Never mind that a killer with long-distance pyromania was still out there, itching to be caught. Never mind that I had no proof for my pyromaniac idea, other than the evidence: Someone had wanted Talbot dead. He'd burned alive right in front of me. The *how* could wait. I needed to find the *who*.

Once I got out of jail.

"We know where to find you, Miss Wood," Blinkin' said as she uncuffed Wanda and sent her on her way.

"A pity. You look real good in cuffs." Stankic leered at her.

Wanda fully extended her middle finger in his direction. Good girl.

"I'll get you out, Charlie," she promised.

"Not a chance," Stinkin' muttered as he shoved me into the waiting cell. Just as cramped as promised. Not small, but packed to the gills with fellow criminals from all walks of life. "Bail's set at a million credits. I'm pretty sure none of your low-life pals have that kind of money. So you just sit tight. One of these days, we might remember that we left you down here. Or not." He chuckled, and it was the most disgusting thing I'd heard all day.

But the day wasn't over yet. Not even halfway there.

As Stinkin' and Blinkin' sauntered off like a couple of

poachers who'd finally bagged their elusive prey, I leaned against the bars and spoke low to Wanda on the other side. She seemed reluctant to skedaddle, despite her recent proximity to incarceration herself. She massaged her wrists absently where the cuffs had bitten.

"We could've outrun them a little while longer," she said. "You led them straight to us. Why?"

"They would've caught up sooner or later. This way, they get what they want. And you're free to do your thing."

"How'd you know they wouldn't hold me?"

"Lucky break." I winked.

Truth was, I'd prayed hard that they would let her go. Yeah, me pray? My grandmother would've been proud.

"What do you need me to do, Charlie?"

"Find Douglass." The sergeant had been nowhere in sight as my two least favorite detectives dragged me into the 37th, much to the applause and rowdy cheers of their less than savory cohorts. "And I need you to look into every recent case of immolation, asphyxiation, strangulation—everything Edgar Talbot mentioned. See if there's some kind of connection, I don't care how insignificant."

"Got it. But what about you?" Her eyes glistened as she clutched the bars. I covered her hands with mine.

"Hey, I'll be fine. Who knows, I might even pick up some new clientele in here." I looked over my shoulder and raised my voice. "Everybody's innocent, right?"

"Damn straight!" more than a few replied. Others murmured agreement. A few flipped me off.

"If only I'd remembered my business cards..." I lamented.

"You don't have any business cards, Charlie," Wanda reminded me. I winked at her and she almost smiled, sniffing as she looked away. "I hate seeing you in there. It ain't right. You're the good guy!"

"If you say so. I'm sure Stinkin' and Blinkin' are pinning Talbot's murder on me at this moment."

"They can't!"

"Not with your help."

"Right." She nodded and wiped her nose across the back of her sleeve, real quick. Hoping I wouldn't notice. "I'll connect the dots."

"That's my girl." I patted her hand. "You're the brains behind this operation. Always have been. I just slug people I shouldn't and wave my gun around." Which reminded me. "Any chance you could head back to the Hills and pick up my .38?" During our hasty departure, I'd left it at the guard station.

"Sure thing, Charlie." She composed herself, taking a deep breath. "I got it covered. Won't be long."

"I'm not going anywhere."

I watched her leave, heels striking a confident rhythm, legs as gorgeous as ever, pumping right along. She wouldn't let me down.

Instead of culling my twenty-odd surly roommates for potential clients, I closed my eyes and feigned napping on my feet, a skill I'd never perfected. Didn't help that sleep was the farthest thing from my mind. I needed to sort out this mess that had landed on top of me.

Edgar Talbot had been convinced that someone was trying to kill him. Rachel the tailor, also the girlfriend, was equally convinced that Talbot's evil stepsister—no, step*mother*—was out to get him. The stepmother had her own issues, no doubt about it. Infatuated with her stepson?

Oh yeah. Probably a card-carrying member of the guy's fan club. Rejected by him? Most likely. Intended to kill him? Not so sure about that. She'd been overcome by grief at the news of Edgar's death.

George Talbot, on the other hand? Not so much in the way of grief. His first question after Bellincioni had relayed the news: "Will the tabloids get a hold of this?"

His only concern was the potential scandal. He'd also been concerned about his son's love life, the *slumming* Edgar was up to in his free time. Was it George who'd somehow managed to keep Rachel's identity out of the gossip rags? Was he afraid he wouldn't be able to do so much longer? Worried about the embarrassment when news broke that Edgar was dating a girl outside the Hills? Perish the thought.

He wouldn't have killed his own son over something so trivial. It was ridiculous, even to think it. And yet...

"Hey, Madison!" shouted the cop on duty down the hall, kicking back at his desk with a bag of donuts and a glowing Slate on his lap. "You've got a visitor."

Wanda back already? How long had I been mulling things over?

Glancing at my cheap wristwatch, I noted that only ten minutes had passed. My girl was efficient. I smiled as I looked up.

But my smile faded quickly. Because it wasn't Wanda Wood, faithful assistant extraordinaire, heading toward me.

It was Edgar Talbot, back from the dead.

Only he looked a hell of a lot younger. A teen who, if he'd been born outside of the Hills, would've been plagued with a pimple-ridden complexion like the rest of us at that age—not the perfectly tan skin he sported, along with fashionable attire that could have come straight from Edgar's own closet.

"Mr. Madison?" The kid approached my cell and stopped a meter or so away from the bars. Keeping his distance, like he thought I was contagious or something.

Or he thought my cellmates were. He might've been right about a few of them.

"That's me." I stifled a yawn. Maybe I was more tired than I thought. Hadn't gotten any sleep last night. Probably why I was seeing things right now.

He kept his hands in his pockets and his chin high. Sixteen years old or thereabouts. Attitude to spare. Heir to an empire?

"Can I help you?" I said.

"I may be able to help *you*, actually." He glanced at the cop on duty, completely immersed in whatever was on his screen. Online poker, more than likely. Good way to supplement a measly income. Or blow it. "My name is Edward Talbot. I believe you were at my house earlier today?"

"That I was. You see everything?"

"Heard it, too." He cleared his throat quietly, politely. The kid had been groomed for more sophisticated environs. "I've seen enough Link mysteries to know who the prime suspect in this case should be. And it's obviously not you."

"Right." I nodded. "It's the robot butler, of course."

He frowned, confused for a moment. "No, not Jeeves. *Me.*" His eyes bulged intensely. "I have the motive, you see. With my brother gone, out of the way, if you will, I stand to inherit my father's entire fortune. I am now the sole heir."

"Were you two close, you and Edgar?"

He shook his head quickly. "Nothing in common, really."

Besides their looks and fashion sense.

"Your mother's out of the picture?"

"Yes. She passed away several years ago."

"Smothered? Set on fire?"

He scowled, taken aback. "No, nothing of the sort. She died of heart failure."

"And your stepmother, she doesn't stand to inherit anything from dear old daddy?"

"Nothing. It's all in their prenup."

Interesting. "So she didn't marry him for his money."

"No, she did not." Edward grinned mischievously. "She was hoping for...something else. But that unfortunately never happened."

A relationship with Edgar Talbot, popular playboy. But he hadn't been interested. Maybe he'd flirted with her at first, but his sights were set on a young tailor in town. A commoner outside the castle walls. So, young Mrs. Talbot was left with nothing—besides a lifestyle most women like her would kill for.

And an excellent Link connection.

"Still not sure how I can help you, kid." I shrugged. "In case you haven't noticed, I'm currently indisposed."

His chuckle was well-engineered, but it still sounded fake.

"Like I said, Mr. Madison. I'm here to help *you*." He pulled his ID card out of his breast pocket. "Shall we get out of here?"

II

The kid was right about being Suspect Numero Uno. He had the motive. But how had he pulled it off? And if he had, somehow, managed to set his brother on fire with some kind of remote detonator, why was he springing me from my cell? And paying my million-credit bail?

Stinkin' and Blinkin' must have found somebody else to harass; they were nowhere to be seen as Edward Talbot and I took our leave. A few of the uniforms cast us a curious eye, but nobody made a peep as we exited the precinct and hoofed it down the street toward my office building.

Where was Sergeant Douglass? No sign of him, which also struck me as odd.

Until I stepped into Wanda's office and found him sprawled out on the futon couch in our client receiving area. The big man was out of uniform and just as surprised to see me as I was to see him.

"Unpaid leave of absence, lad, but just for a week," he explained, grunting as he hauled himself to his feet. Grabbing my hand in a vice-like grip, he shook it vigorously. "That's what I get for goin' up against the likes of Bellincioni. She's in the Captain's pocket." And the captain was in Ivan's, more than likely. "Who's this dapper whippersnapper?" He frowned at Edward standing behind me.

"My generous benefactor." I stepped aside, ushering

Edward in from the hallway. As I shut the door behind him, I noted the damaged doorframe. Stankic had made quite an entrance earlier. "Meet Edward Talbot. He had a million credits to spare."

"Money well-spent." Talbot shook the sergeant's paw. "Mr. Madison is trying to solve the mystery of my late brother's murder. As far as I'm concerned, he doesn't belong in jail."

Sound reasoning there.

"Good to see you, Charlie." Wanda smiled over the top of her Underwood/Slate combo. "I did like you asked. Sergeant Douglass was a big help."

"We've got a list here of every death by asphyxiation and immolation in the city, goin' back two years." Douglass shook his head as he returned to his seat with a grunt. "Nasty stuff." He cursed under his breath. "Only one connection that—"

"The tailor shop?" Edward said hopefully.

"What?" Douglass scowled. I couldn't blame him. The kid's comment had flown in from left field. "No. Ivan and his cronies—none of 'em were charged, of course, things bein' what they are in this town. But almost every victim, one way or another, is connected somehow to the mob. Hell, even some of the victims themselves were members of Ivan's organization!"

"The brotherhood," I muttered. Bratva.

"Not my brother," Edward said. "No way."

"He's right," Wanda said. "No connection to Edgar Talbot." She graced me with an apologetic look. "Guess we're back at the starting line, Charlie."

Maybe not.

"What made you suggest the tailor?" I faced Edward.

"Didn't my brother tell you about what happened? That he was almost strangled to death?"

"He might've mentioned it."

Edward loosened the knot on his tie. Then he cinched it viciously tight with both hands, enough to bring some blood-red color to his face.

"It was his tie," he grated out, strangling himself in front of us. Weird kid.

"Okay?" I didn't know what else to say.

He loosened it again and let it sag from his open collar. "The thing tightened on its own, like it had been programmed to do that. Would've killed him if I hadn't been there."

"You saved his life?"

He shrugged. "We didn't hang out together or anything, but that doesn't mean I wanted Edgar to die. I took out my blade and got that tie off him as fast as I could." From inside his jacket, he withdrew a folded pocket knife. A deactivated laser cutter glowed where a blade should have been.

"Put that thing away," I said before show and tell could begin. Rich boys and their toys. "Let me guess. Edgar bought that tie at his girlfriend's shop."

"Where else? That's where he bought all of his duds. He had it bad for that girl, no doubt."

Douglass cleared his throat. "You seriously think his necktie...was programmed to *kill* him?"

The fabric, something in the weave of the cloth, could have included some kind of microscopic fiber designed to constrict—

"Remote-controlled," I murmured.

"What?" Douglass scoffed.

Wanda's brow wrinkled.

"Yeah, that makes sense!" Edward nodded eagerly. "I mean, when I found him, there was nobody else there strangling him. The tie was tightening all by itself. Somebody had to make it do that, right?"

The same with Edgar's suit. Nobody had struck a match. Maybe it had some kind of remote-activated incendiary trigger—

"Let's not get ahead of ourselves." I strode toward the door separating my office from Wanda's and opened it a crack. Then I shut it. The place needed to be professionally cleaned. Add that to the list of repairs.

And rent was due at the end of the month. If only my young benefactor hadn't blown his fortune on my bail, I might've been able to milk him for a few hundred credits more. As it was, I wouldn't have felt right about it. I couldn't ask him for his brother's fee on top of everything else.

"Wanda, dig a little deeper into those mob deaths. Find out how many of the victims bought their shirts and ties at that tailor shop. If any."

She glanced at Douglass. "I don't think I can, Charlie. That-uh...would involve hacking into the shop's financial records—"

"You may need to step outside during this part, Sarge," I advised.

He smirked. "And miss my only chance at a glimpse behind the curtain here? No way. Besides, I'm off duty."

"Good enough?" I raised an eyebrow at Wanda.

She nodded and went to work, fingers flying across the keys of her Underwood.

"Always knew you were more than just a pretty face, Miss Wood," Douglass said.

She graced him with a friendly wink.

"You can really do that? Hack into the shop's records?" Edward stared at Wanda as she made the magic happen.

"Everything's online, kid," she said. "Nobody keeps hard copies anymore. Other than Mr. Madison." She flashed me a quick smile.

"Guilty." I always appreciated the old black and white and stored in a fireproof filing cabinet. "Ones and zeroes in the cloud? Not for me."

"Careful, Charlie," Wanda said, her gaze fixed on the screen of her Slate. "You might start sounding like you know what you're talkin' about."

"No chance of that," Douglass said with a chuckle. He shared my affinity for old-school filing methods and had the only desk in the 37th without a computer on it.

"Doesn't look promising." Wanda shook her head. "I can't find anything customer-related here. Textile shipments received, rent paid, taxes due. But nothing specific about any of the customers or what they've purchased."

I wasn't surprised. After my last encounter with the young tailor, it was clear that her shop valued its customers' privacy. Could there have been some old filing cabinets in that back room? Keeping that kind of information off-Link was a good idea if Rachel had something worth protecting.

Or hiding.

"Did you happen to...?" I gestured toward my armpit where my holster usually resided.

"Sorry, Charlie," Wanda said. "Didn't get to it. Wasn't expecting you back so soon."

Me either.

"I'll take care of it. Be back in a bit."

I'd take the Talbot heir apparent home and pick up my Smith & Wesson from his friendly neighborhood beefcakes. Then I planned to see a tailor about a certain necktie—and a fashionable flamethrowing suit.

12

Edward was as chatty as a used car salesman as we rode through the afternoon gridlock in the back of a cab. We had plenty of time to kill, and he had plenty he wanted to say. The point he kept coming back to, oddly enough, was how he should have been the prime suspect in his brother's case, and why weren't the cops after him?

"They should be, right? I mean, it makes sense they should be. Are their detectives really so inept?" He threw up his hands in exasperation.

I remained silent on that point.

"I mean, at least *you* have me in custody." He grinned, but his eyes were flat, lifeless. "Hypothetically speaking, you could take me straight to the cops, and they could throw the book at me."

"Might not be that simple."

"Explain." I had his undivided attention. By all appearances, he was living out some kind of fantasy. Too much time spent Linking up mysteries.

"Well, there's no evidence of foul play, for one thing."

"People don't go around bursting into flames, Mr. Madison. Not without some kind of trigger. And I doubt your office was designed with that in mind."

Not sure what he meant by that, but I nodded anyway to show I was listening.

"Which brings us back to the tailor shop." Suddenly irritated, he turned toward our cabbie. "Cut across third. It's faster." He grinned at me again. "Neil—my driver—he does it all the time."

"You head into the city often?"

"Every now and then. For the essentials, you know." He gestured broadly at his attire. "Can't order everything off the Link. Where's the fun in that? Besides, one-size-fits-all usually fits nobody as well as it should. I have a very unique physique."

I hadn't noticed. "Where's your driver?"

"What?"

"You took a cab to the precinct earlier?"

He nodded, staring back at me without much of an expression.

"Was Neil otherwise occupied?"

He shrugged. "I'm not like other people from the Hills, Mr. Madison. I appreciate living a little from time to time. Spending too much of my life behind those walls—it can get rather claustrophobic. Trapped in my father's town car behind bulletproof windows is just as bad."

I nodded toward his trendy suit. "So you have your own tailor in town?"

"Yes, I—"

"Not Rachel."

He blinked. "I'm sorry, who?"

"Your brother brought her to dinner one night, at your house. Made your father irate, the way he tells it. I'm sure you remember her."

"I was out with friends that evening. I'm afraid I missed all the hoopla." He flashed another soulless smile. "But boy oh boy, did I ever hear about it. Dear Stephanie—that's our unrequited stepmother, by the way—sank into a deep depression afterward. I'm sure that's what Dad was the most upset about. She wouldn't tickle his fancy anymore, if you get what I mean."

"He should try the Link."

Edward guffawed at that, slapping his knee like a hillbilly. "Turn right here," he ordered the cabbie. "Just another little shortcut. It'll keep us out of that mess on Broadway."

"From your driver."

"What?"

"This shortcut."

Another tight grin. "That's right."

"You wouldn't be steering us away from the Hills? In no real hurry to get home?" I had to wonder. The kid seemed to be having so much fun, after all. "Because the last I checked, we're going in the opposite direction."

"We'll get there, Mr. Madison. Don't you worry. But in the meantime, I'd like to hear more about your theory. You know, regarding my brother's death. You mentioned a remote control device, something that could have triggered the fire in Edgar's suit. That's a pretty cool idea, don't you think? I've never seen it done in any of the murder mysteries. And I truly doubt any of those flat-footed Neanderthals in uniform would think of something like that."

"Yeah." *Cool*—seeing Edgar engulfed in flames, kicking and screaming on my office floor? Not so much. "I was just spitballing, kid. I have no idea what really happened."

"Right, right, but let's say that's how it did happen. Hypothetically. And that I'm the prime suspect." That again. The kid was stuck in some kind of bizarre feedback loop.

"What would connect me to that tailor shop? And what motive would the tailor possibly have to be in league with me?"

In league. Maybe I was wrong about the Link. He was reading mystery novels from over a century ago. Or watching old films on TV. Televisions still existed for those who couldn't afford the Link's monthly surcharge or didn't want to Link up. A local station run by older generation newscasters showed fights from the Coliseum, news stories, and old movies. Sherlock Holmes, perchance?

"Hypothetically? You'd both have something to gain from your brother's death. You and his girlfriend, Rachel. Maybe you see a future together. Heirs to the Talbot throne?"

"Does she run that tailor shop alone?"

"Two-woman operation. Her and her sister." Not counting the holo-grandpa.

"Did you meet the sister? Find out about her background, whether she would know how to weave remote-controlled fibers into a suit? Or a necktie?"

I watched my hat as I turned it over in my hands. "Listen, Edward. I get it. You're a mystery buff. And you're a smart kid. Maybe you've always wanted to be a detective, like Sherlock Holmes or somebody."

"Who?"

Wrong about that, too. "I can see now why you paid my bail."

"You can?" He looked disappointed.

"You've got some interesting ideas—"

"You know they have merit. I'm just connecting the dots here. The remote control was your idea, and a brilliant idea it is. Way to think outside of the box on that one!"

"Thanks." I cleared my throat, keeping an eye on the streets we passed, having a pretty good idea where we were headed. "So you wanted to bounce your ideas off me, see what stuck. Fine. I'll give it to you straight: there's no evidence of foul play. Doesn't matter if we've got a feeling your brother was murdered. If there's no murder weapon, there's no murder."

"Oh, but there is, Mr. Madison. I'm sure of it." He turned toward the driver and ordered, "Pull over."

The cab veered toward the curb with a splash of acid rainwater. Across the street sat a quaint storefront Wanda and I had visited earlier. The place looked empty now. No motion-activated hologram to be seen.

"Don't you want to know?" Edward said.

I nodded. "Of course I do." I'd been planning to head over here anyway—after dropping him off at home. And picking up my gun. I felt so naked without it. "But if these sisters killed your brother, then this is the last place you should be."

He threw open his door.

"Coming, Mr. Madison?" He struck off across the street brazenly, with all the teenage overconfidence in the world. "Time to solve this case, detective!"

13

I didn't have the infallibility of hindsight. I needed to use every angle, every possibility to my advantage. Right here, right now.

So I kept the eyes in the back of my head—figuratively speaking—wide open as I joined Edward out front of the dark shop. The glowing vidscreen mounted inside the glass door said they were closed for lunch, but that couldn't be right. According to my watch, it was creeping closer to 1600 hours with every second that passed.

"Looks like they cleared out." Edward pressed one hand against the window and leaned forward to peer inside.

"Looks that way." I watched him. "So now what?"

He smiled. "We go in there, of course. I assume you have a lock pick on you."

Any self-respecting P.I. would. "You think we should break and enter."

"I think we should gather evidence, don't you? That's what detectives do, right?"

"We ask questions. Stake out places. Take photos on occasion. We don't break the law." Not as a rule, anyway. Bending it was more like.

"C'mon." He beckoned me to follow as he turned down the alley running alongside the shop. "Let's try the back door."

I looked the alley over. The dumpster halfway down would be an issue, depending on who was hiding behind it.

Paranoid? No, never.

Careful.

Without my .38, all I had on me were a pair of fists. Not that Edward posed much of a threat. He'd go down easy with a sucker punch to the gut. Or a right hook across the glass jaw, if I felt like bruising his pimple-free face. But if he'd invited friends to this party, I didn't like my chances.

"Mr. Madison?" Edward stood beside the dumpster. His confused look said it all. He was used to commoners obeying his every beck and call.

Why disturb such a rosy worldview?

"Right." Keeping my hands out of my pockets, I entered the alleyway.

"I think we have enough probable cause to break inside anyhow," Edward said as he continued onward, his voice echoing against the brick walls on both sides. No effort to keep his voice down.

"If we were cops, maybe. But even then we'd need a warrant."

"Good thing we aren't police," he cast over his shoulder with a mischievous grin.

He sure was having a good time. His life of privilege must have bored the living hell out of him. The death of his brother provided just the diversion he needed.

Pathetic.

"You got a phone?" I said as I caught up with him at the shop's rear service door, a dented solid steel monstrosity that had seen better days.

"You don't?" He fished out his wafer-thin device from a

back pocket.

As a rule, I didn't carry any kind of tech other than my ID card. Kind of hard to get around that with the Federal citizenship mandate. Never know when you might run into a Blackshirt demanding proof of who you are.

"Call my office. See what Miss Wood has been able to find out." Let her and Douglass know exactly where we were. That we hadn't made it to Talbot Manor. That I was still unarmed.

"I don't think so." He slipped the phone back into his pocket, keeping an eye on me as he did so. "She can't help us. Everything we need is right behind this door." He rapped on it twice, quickly. Like a signal. "Paper files showing who purchased what and when. Those dead Russian gangsters, probably. My brother, too, of course. And don't forget the remote-controlled fibers you mentioned. I'm sure they're all inside." He stepped back from the door. "Go on, Mr. Madison." He gestured at the locking mechanism. "Work your private eye magic!"

I wasn't sure there would be any magic to work. Not my variety, anyway. The lock was electronic. No pick in the world was going to get through that. Nothing short of an EMP would persuade that door to open against its will.

"Pretty high tech for a tailor shop," I muttered, running my hand across the keypad. Custom job. No security company insignia to be seen. Wanda might have been able to hack her way in, but not yours truly. "We're not getting in there. Not like this." I curled my fingers into a fist and pounded twice, hearing the impact resonate the length of the door. "Open up. Police!"

Edward had that mischievous look going again. He liked

what he saw.

"I don't think they heard you, Mr. Madison. Yell louder."

"They?" I faced him.

He shrugged, grinning expectantly.

"Who's inside, Edward?"

The grin faded, replaced by a curious frown. "What?"

I took a step toward him. He backed up a stutter-step.

"You said *they*. Who are *they*?"

"The tailor—that girl Edgar was dating. And her sister. They run this place, right?"

"What are their names?"

"You mentioned a Rachel. I don't know her sister's name. Do you?"

"Never met her."

"Me either." Another tight grin. "Do you think we're working together? The sisters and me?" He was getting excited again. "That's it, isn't it? Oh wow, this keeps getting better and better! So now you think I brought you back here to... What? *Kill* you?"

I took another step toward him. He kept his distance, but he didn't run away.

"Why would I want to kill you, Mr. Madison, when we're having so much *fun*?" He laughed, and it almost sounded genuine. Maybe a little insane, to boot. "Don't we make a great team? I'll be your savvy sidekick, and you—"

"Goodbye, Edward."

I turned on my heel and strode up the alley toward the street. With any luck, the cab would still be waiting, right where we left it. The kid could call his own driver for a pickup. He was no longer my concern.

Sure, he'd covered my bail, and it cost more than a pretty

penny. But I didn't owe him anything. I'd let him tag along, and he'd had his fun playing detective.

But playtime was over. I had a real job to do.

As I stepped out of the alleyway, two things became clear as crystal. First off, the cabbie hadn't waited around, so I was plum out of luck in that regard. I'd have to hail the next one that came by or hoof it back to my office, half a dozen kilometers away. And the second thing?

I knew my face would be bruised for a week or two after meeting Detective Stankic's fist head-on.

"Funny seeing you here, Madison."

He chuckled as I fell back against the tailor shop's front window, dazed by the sudden blow and shaking my head sharply to keep my eyes focused. Too bad for me, they didn't see Stankic's next punch coming until it was too late, plowing right into my solar plexus. I dropped to one knee, fighting for breath.

"Naw, not really funny at all, is it?" he said.

14

Detective Bellincioni had her Glock out, pointed at the general vicinity of my chest. Sling on one arm, twitchy eyes blazing. A real sight to behold.

"Forget him." Stankic belched. "We're even now."

"Not yet we're not," she seethed. Her gun muzzle shifted toward my shoulder. About where her partner had accidentally shot her yesterday.

"You're going to gun me down? Right here in front of God and everybody?" I got to my feet, keeping my hands where they could see them. "I don't think so."

"Yeah? Why the hell not?"

"Because your killer's waiting inside." Maybe. "The girl responsible for Edgar Talbot's death? Right in here." Fifty-fifty chance, anyway. "Don't believe me? Go get yourselves a warrant. Search the place. Check the records. Look for customers no longer among the living. Russians, from Ivan's organization, not to mention Talbot himself."

Blinkin' scowled at her partner. "How hard did you hit him?"

"He always talks gibberish, far as I'm concerned." Stinkin' jabbed his chubby finger into my chest. "This ain't your case no more, Madison. Got that? Your client is *dead*. Poof! No more case. So leave this to the professionals."

"Let me know when they arrive."

Stinkin' glowered at me. "You've still got charges against you." He got up in my face, smelling like the sewer having a very bad day. "You go in front of the judge next week for assaulting an officer of the law, and I'll be piling on top of that you withholding evidence and interfering with—"

"Can't interfere with something that isn't happening."

"What do you think we're doing?" Blinkin' snapped.

"Following me." I hadn't broken eye contact with Stinkin', but I tried not to breathe in too deep. "You're more interested in seeing me behind bars than catching a serial killer."

Stankic guffawed with a blast of foul breath. "So now it's a *serial killer* is it? Where the hell do you come up with this crap?" He composed himself, wheezing. "Naw, we don't want you behind bars, Madison. We want you out of *business.*"

I clenched my jaw. "Ivan put you up to this?"

As far as I knew, no one had ever seen the reclusive kingpin. But his influence was felt all over town, as brooding as the storm clouds we knew so well. People who made a habit of helping those who needed it? Not all that favorable in his sight. Ivan the Terrible decided who lived and died in this city, and he expected the rest of us to fall in line. Or mind our own damn business.

Stinkin' cursed, shoving me back against the window but not hard enough to crack it.

"We're through here." He nudged his partner, and after reminding me not to leave town, the two of them got into their unmarked sedan and took off, splashing gutter water in their wake.

Always a pleasure.

Movement from the corner of my eye snagged my attention, and I turned toward the storefront. Inside, the hologram tailor was smiling and waving at me like a friendly neighbor, beckoning me to enter. The vidscreen beside the door had switched to OPEN.

Absently, I reached for the revolver that wasn't there and straightened my lapels instead. Judging from my reflection in the window, my nose wasn't bleeding yet. But there was already some discoloration and swelling in the early stages around my eyes.

I counted myself lucky. At least I hadn't been shot. Not yet, anyway.

I glanced over my shoulder for any sign of Edward. None at all. Good riddance. Either he was on his way home, or he was waiting for me inside.

Was he an obsessive mystery nut or an accomplice in his brother's death? Time to find out.

The sound of sleigh bells jangled from the ceiling speaker as I stepped into the shop and let the door swing shut behind me. The old man looked like he might have recognized me—something in his programming, probably intended to appeal to repeat customers. Well-designed. High tech. Just like that lock on the back door.

"Mr. Madison." Rachel emerged from the rear of the shop, and her great-grandfather's image dissolved on cue. "You're back?"

"So it would seem."

"Things didn't go well, I take it." She winced at my face. Not the usual reaction it got from the ladies. "At the Talbots."

"No, the Talbots are a great bunch. One of them paid my

bail, if you can believe. He might be around here someplace... This?" I gestured at my bruised face. "Just a mistake."

"A mistake," she echoed.

"I forgot how pigheaded some cops can be. The funny thing is, they don't seem all that interested in your boyfriend's murder. They'd rather see me pick up my marbles and go home."

The reference was lost on her. Not surprising; I'd picked it up from my grandmother, long ago. One of many clichés from a bygone era.

Rachel's gaze drifted toward the rotating holographic displays. Tuxedos at the moment, something a groom and his pals might wear at a wedding.

"You talked to Edgar's stepmother?" she said quietly.

"Stephanie, right? One strange lady. Fixated, you might say. But she's no killer."

Rachel snapped her focus back to me. "They're a powerful family. The cops are crooked. There's only so much someone like you can do to help."

"Edgar was murdered, Rachel." I took a step toward her, toward the door behind her. "And I think you know who did it."

She looked away again.

"Leave," she whispered, tears springing to her eyes. "Please."

"Your sister is very talented. The holograms. The lock on the back door. Real impressive stuff." I paused. "How about neckties that strangle men to death? Suits that spontaneously combust, resistant to whatever a fire extinguisher can throw at them?" I took another step toward her. "I can understand targeting Ivan's crew. They're a blight on this town. If your sister wants to play vigilante with their sorry asses, fine by me. But why Edgar? Why did he have to die?"

I was close enough to kiss her now. She hadn't moved a centimeter. Her glassy eyes shone with the light of the holographic displays around us as she smiled sadly.

"He was...getting too close," she said. "He would have found out, eventually."

"About your sister?" I glanced at that back door. What sort of person hid behind it, listening? Hell, she was probably watching us right now via hidden cameras.

Was Edward back there with her? Were they *in league*?

"They were bad men, all of them," Rachel said quietly, clenching her jaw. "Nobody misses them. They did horrible things, hurt good people." She stopped herself.

"Somebody in your family?" I watched her. "Did one of Ivan's crew hurt someone close to you?"

She nodded slowly. "They had to pay for it."

"But not Edgar. He wasn't one of them."

"He would have found out!" she insisted. "He would have tried to stop me, but there are more of them out there, and my father's soul won't rest until they're all *dead*!"

Crazy had entered the building. It was like something in Rachel's mind had snapped, and she'd turned into another person—one not nearly as pleasant to be around.

"I need to speak with your sister," I said.

"You *are*!" she screamed into my face, lunging at me and wrapping something around my head.

No—around my neck, crossing it over my throat. A tie? What the hell?

"Stop." I pried off her arms, and she dropped back onto her feet, stumbling away from me. She stared with wide, unblinking eyes and clutched something in her hand. "Listen, Rachel, I can see you're upset..." I pulled off the tie.

Tried to.

It wouldn't come off. Instead, it constricted as Rachel pressed the device in her hand. A remote control. The fibers in the tie responded, cinching tightly, doing their best to strangle me.

I really hated being right.

15

Blood vessels in my neck throbbed. My face flushed hot. My eyes felt too big for their sockets.

I clawed at the tie, trying to get a finger in between the fabric and my throat. A fingernail, even.

No dice. Too tight, and getting tighter by the moment.

The shop started to capsize like we were out at sea during a squall. I dropped to one knee, the same knee I'd taken outside the shop, right after Stinkin' had knocked the wind out of me.

"Rachel," I rasped. My tongue felt swollen, too thick for my mouth. "You...don't want to do this!"

She squeezed her eyes shut, the remote in both hands as she hunched over the device, trembling.

"Rachel's not here," she said.

Not creepy at all. I dealt with split-personalities all the time.

If only. Then maybe I would've known what to do with her.

Presented with a limited array of options, I charged straight for her, slamming her though a holographic display of silk dress shirts and up against the wall. I pinned her there with my shoulder, one hand struggling in vain against the killer necktie, the other fighting for the remote. Not that I knew what I'd do with the thing once I got hold of it. I just knew I'd feel a hell of a lot better with it out of her hands.

Problem #1: I was having some difficulty breathing. Pretty sure I was running on the last scraps of residual oxygen in my lungs.

Problem #2: Rachel or whoever she was at the moment was well-armed with talons painted a lovely shade of cherry, which she proceeded to dig into my arm.

But I didn't give up. As far as I knew, this was my last-ditch attempt at staying alive.

"Get Rachel for me."

My last words before the room tipped upside down, and I hit the floor with her remote clenched in my right hand. I fell hard, striking the back of my head, wishing I knew what button to press on the stupid device, now that I had it.

So I pushed them all. Nothing.

"Rachel was a *fool*," she spat, looming over me. The holographic displays glowed behind her like a high-tech aura all her own. "She let that rich bastard into our lives. Even went to his house for dinner! What was she thinking? He would have found out, and our work would have been over before it was finished!"

She dove for the remote with both hands, tearing at me with her claws.

I rolled over, and she fell onto my back, whaling at me with her fists, shrieking furiously like something not exactly human. I couldn't see much of anything. Could've been because my vision was fading; could've been because my face was planted into the industrial carpet. Either way, I had no idea what buttons on the remote I was pressing, and it didn't hit me until later that I could've been setting any number of Rachel's customers ablaze or asphyxiating them—her next targets.

But at the moment, they were the least of my concerns.

The tie loosened its hold on me enough to get my finger in, then two. I yanked and gasped, coughing, fighting for breath as I tore it free and hurled it across the room. Rachel's evil twin, who happened to share the same body, grabbed a fistful of my hair and jerked my head back, sinking her talons into the side of my face as she proceeded to bash my nose into the floor.

I twisted sideways and placed my elbow firmly into her abdomen. The blast of her breath into my ear told me I'd been right on target. Good ol' solar plexus.

Rolling to my feet, I backpedaled toward the front door right as it swung open.

"Wow, Mr. Madison," Edward said, wide-eyed. His gaze darted from me to Rachel on the floor, struggling for breath. "You hit a girl?"

"Tell me you called the police," I rasped. My voice wouldn't be back to normal for a while.

"You mean those two losers who roughed you up outside?"

He saw that? Where had he been hiding? Sneaky devil.

"No way. I called your secretary. She's on her way with Sergeant Douglass."

"Assistant."

"What?"

"Good call." I tried to clear my throat as I focused on the girl. She was scowling up at me, her gaze twitching toward the device in my hand. "Got a name, Miss?"

"Uh...isn't she *Rachel*?" Edward said.

"Not exactly."

"Lorraine." She jumped to her feet, quick and catlike. "Rachel's my sister. How do you know her?"

"Are they twins?" Edward looked confused.

Couldn't blame him any. Except...

"Thought you didn't see her when she came over for dinner."

He shrugged and grinned. One weird kid. As much as he seemed to like the idea of being the prime suspect in his brother's murder investigation, he was now equally fascinated by the prospect of a girl with dissociative identity disorder.

"So, did you do it?" He stepped toward her, but I pulled him back. No idea how many killer neckties she had on hand. Or something worse. "You killed my brother?"

"He would have found out," she repeated, grinding her teeth. Arms folded, she seemed content for the moment with just standing there, facing off with us. "No one could know about it. Not yet."

"Not until you got rid of them all." I weighed the remote in the palm of my hand, half-expecting her to lunge for it. "Those thugs who killed your father."

Her sister, too, I had a feeling. But who was this person really, standing before us? Rachel or Lorraine? For whom had the survivor's guilt been too much, fracturing her mind into two distinct identities?

"They will pay." She nodded resolutely. "All of them."

"Good enough for me," Edward said. "She did it." He was already on his phone as he opened the front door and stepped outside. "Hello, Neil? I'm going to need you to pick me up."

16

That was the last I saw of any member of the Talbot clan—in the flesh, anyway. Whenever I stopped by to check in with Mr. Newspaper, one of them always seemed to be on some dark corner of some sleazy tabloid: George, Stephanie, or Edward. Flavors of the week that didn't interest me much.

Even though Sergeant Douglass was on unpaid leave, he still carried a fetching pair of steel bracelets, which he fastened onto Rachel/Lorraine's wrists as soon as he and Wanda arrived on the scene. He made a call, and a pair of uniforms showed up in under ten minutes to escort him and the girl to the 37th for processing.

I'd given him the shape of things, and he'd scribbled everything down on his tablet. An actual tablet, made out of paper and cardboard, which he wrote on with an actual pen. Old school. That was Douglass all over.

"You did good, lad," he said, leaning on the squad car. He'd be sharing the back seat with Rachel/Lorraine, but he seemed to be in no hurry to cram himself inside.

Hard to tell who the girl was at the moment. She alternated between sobbing and pleading, "I'm sorry, I'm sorry." Didn't sound like she was talking to anybody present. Ghosts, then. Her deceased family members. She was in her own world, apologizing for not being able to avenge their deaths as fully as she would have liked.

Maybe the thugs deserved it. Most likely they did. But Edgar Talbot sure hadn't, and that's why she had to go away. Get some serious help.

As much as it felt like an open battlefield at times, this town was a civilized place. Nobody was innocent, but that didn't mean they should be killed off by anybody with a grudge. Talbot had gotten himself caught in the middle of a bizarre vendetta. I wouldn't have been able to wrap my mind around it if I hadn't been on the receiving end of that killer necktie. No way I'd be forgetting that experience anytime soon.

"You'll be wanting this," I rasped, handing over the remote.

"Aye..." Douglass glanced at the girl. "I'm sure the forensics crew will find some pretty crazy stuff in that back room. Looks like a mad scientist's laboratory or some such." He shook his head and cursed quietly as he pocketed the device. "How do you think she knew when her targets were wearin' the killer threads, anyhow?"

"Some kind of sensor?" Triggered by their body heat, maybe. "Who knows? I'm just glad she won't be frying any more of my clients."

"Don't expect Stankic or Bellincioni to thank you."

"Wouldn't dream of it."

"Sometimes I wonder if they're even interested in law and order. Good news, though." He brightened a bit, as did the sky on the west side of town, charcoal clouds burning off for a glimmer of rusty sunset. "I made a few calls and found out the judge presiding over your hearing will be Atherton. She won't take any guff from the likes of Stankic or Bellincioni. From what I've heard, she has no patience whatsoever for their ilk. She's more interested in seeing justice served than in playing their games. What a concept, eh?"

"She's a good one." That was a small miracle, and I'd take it.

"One of the few." He grinned at me, his lumpy face contorting comically. "Long as we do somethin' about it, evil can't prevail, eh lad?" Always the optimist, ol' Douglass.

"Something like that, Sarge."

He saluted crisply and climbed into the back of the car. The uniform behind the wheel flashed the blue and red lights and released a warning shot from the siren before entering the stream of early evening traffic soon to be congesting the city streets.

"Want me to hail a cab, Charlie?" Wanda stepped off the curb, fingers poised to whistle hard enough to be heard two streets over.

I shook my head. "Let's hoof it."

"You sure?" She looked me over with a sympathetic frown. My black eye and clawed face wouldn't earn me anything else for a while.

"I've had worse," I said, holding out my arm to her. "Shall we?"

She smiled, and I kid you not, it was the most gorgeous thing I'd seen since her last one. She took my arm and gave it an affectionate squeeze.

Back to the office with the doorjamb in need of repair and the carpet that needed to be cleaned. Scratch that. Replaced. After another client or few who paid in actual credits.

"You've had some crazy cases in the past, Charlie," Wanda said. She whistled low through her teeth. "But holy cow, this one was a real doozy! A remote-controlled killer with a split personality? Speaking of which, I did a little research on that tailor shop, and what Rachel told you was true. Both her father and her sister were murdered a few years back. No suspects named. It's like something from an unsolved Link mystery."

"You watch that stuff?" I kept an eye on her as we dodged puddles of bubbling rainwater with other passersby.

"Don't have to. I get to live the real deal. Which reminds me..." She stopped and pivoted to face me as we reached the street corner. "Thanks for letting me tag along on this case. I enjoyed myself. And seeing you in action was kind of a treat."

I gave her a wink. "Maybe we'll do it again sometime."

"If you're lucky."

"Next time the cops are after me." Knowing Stinkin' and Blinkin', that wouldn't be too long.

Unless they decided to give me a breather after solving this case. If it was true they were in Ivan's pocket, then the Russian Devil would like knowing that no more of his henchmen would be suffocated or burned alive. Not by their wardrobe, anyhow. As a rule, he didn't much like folks helping the downtrodden in our unfair city, but maybe he'd rein in my two favorite detectives for a little while. I could use the break.

"You're okay with pulling sidekick duty every now and then?"

"I'm a busy girl, you know. I can't just drop everything and go on adventures with you all the time." She smiled up at me. "Once a week? Maybe."

"I'll see if I can work you into my schedule."

"Hey now, Charlie. I'm the one who organizes that schedule, remember."

I knew that full well. She was the brains behind this two-person outfit, and I wouldn't have had it any other way.

"So, can you say it yet?" We crossed the street along with a bustling crowd of foot traffic.

"It?"

"You know what I mean." Another squeeze on my arm.

"You know it, Sweetheart." I squeezed her back. "This case is closed."

The Unusual Clients

DEATH DUEL

I

Some things you see during wartime, you never forget. Mandroids stomping through trenches with meter-long bayonets, lopping off the heads of six men with a single sweep. Skewering as many with one robotic arm while gunning down another half dozen with a machine gun welded to the other. Inhuman. Inhumane.

But I wasn't on the Eastern front anymore. The war had simmered down to a cold variety, with both the United World and the Eastern Conglomerate pausing to lick their wounds, preparing for the next round when they'd come out swinging. We were stuck in a stalemate now. Pieces discarded from the global chessboard were men and women, tens of thousands who'd given their lives fighting for what they believed was right.

What did I believe? Standing in the alley behind Howard's Tavern late that night, I had a few ideas. But they sounded ridiculous to those present.

"A *mandroid*?" Detective Stankic guffawed, nudging his partner in crime, Detective Bellincioni. I called them Stinkin' and Blinkin'—not because I had anything against his Serbian ancestry or her dark Italian roots. He was a slob with an affinity for garlic and onions and sauces that stained every tie he knotted around his mottled throat. She had a nervous tick that caused her to blink one long-lashed eye more often than the other. "Really, Madison? That's the best you've got?"

I stared him down. Then I pointed at the gaping hole in the victim's chest. Bigger in diameter than a baseball. The man's body lay on its back on the rain-slick pavement, his eyes and mouth open wide like he'd gotten the biggest surprise of his life before his heart quit on him. He'd been impaled, straight through. That much was obvious.

"Or maybe a cyborg," I said. "We're not looking at the work of an all-natural human here."

"A *cyborg*?" Detective Bellincioni spat, indignant at the derogative term. Her teeth flashed, but she wasn't smiling. She looked ready to bite my face off. "You mean a *veteran*, don't you?"

I winked at her. She cursed me with the extensive vocabulary of a seasoned sailor. She'd served her time in the war and returned without any missing limbs, same as yours truly: Charlie Madison, private investigator. No mechanical parts whatsoever.

"You've got no business here," Stinkin' grumbled. He thought it wise to get up in my face and plant a grimy sausage-finger into my chest. "This is a police matter. Go chase down an ambulance or something."

"Nah, that stuff's for lawyers," said Blinkin'. "Madison likes to sneak around in the shadows and take pictures of guys stepping out on their girls. Ain't that right, Madison? You private *dicks* are just glorified stalkers."

"Thought your kind went out with the buffalo, Madison," Stinkin' added. He stabbed that finger of his into my sternum a few times. Checking if I was still alive? Or whether I thought it wise to deck a cop? I was warming up to the idea, consequences be damned. "Hasn't the Link already made you obsolete?"

I tipped my hat to them with my middle finger and left them to their corpse. Sergeant Archibald Douglass, a mountain of a man, stood between two squad cars at the end of the alleyway. Rotating blue and red strobes on their dashboards cast him in an eerie light. Hands stuffed into the pockets of his long overcoat, Douglass shrugged broad shoulders at me as I approached. I shrugged back.

"Not sure why you called me down here, Sarge." I nodded toward the two detectives behind me. "Our city's finest seem to have everything under control."

"Those two?" Douglass scoffed and folded his brawny arms, glaring at Stankic and Bellincioni as they smoked and bickered and nudged the body with the toes of their scuffed shoes. "They contaminate every crime scene they come across. Tell me, lad, what did you notice?"

"Besides that awe-inspiring hole?"

"Aye. Besides that."

"Clean cut guy. Young—early thirties. Healthy." No signs of addiction around his eyes, teeth, or fingernails. "Married." Ring on his left hand, a sign of his contract and commitment to produce four strapping young citizens for our Federal government to use as they saw fit. "Upstanding fellow, by all appearances."

"He was a cop." Douglass heaved a sigh that lifted his shoulders and dropped them beneath the weight of our fair city. Wasn't easy being one of the only police not on the payroll of Ivan the Terrible, Russian mob boss extraordinaire. Times were tough, and Ivan's deep pockets were mighty tempting for those who struggled to make ends meet. "A good one."

"They're a dying breed."

He nodded. "Unlike Stankic and Bellincioni's ilk. They sent you packing, I take it."

"Wore out my welcome." My half-assed talk about a mandroid or cyborg hadn't helped matters any. But I truly enjoyed pushing Stinkin' and Blinkin's buttons. And steering them off-course happened to be one of my favorite pastimes.

"I was hopin' you'd get down here before they arrived." He lowered his voice. "I don't exactly trust 'em, Charlie."

"Think they're on Ivan's roster?"

"Wouldn't be surprised. Their cases tend to wrap up too quick, if you know what I mean. Witnesses disappear. Bodies turn up that have been worked over real good—usually it's the perpetrator of a crime. They've got their own brand of justice, these two. What's morally right or wrong seldom enters the equation."

"Vigilante cops?"

"Sometimes. When they're not coverin' their own asses." He turned his back on the crime scene. "Can't have them executing the killer before we have an opportunity to question the fellow. Find out who's behind this...bizarre display. Far as I know, Officer Bowman didn't have any enemies, but you know this town as well as I do—and its people. Like onions, they are. Layers and layers of mystery and misery." He paused. "I want you to look into this one, Charlie. Report directly to me, anything you find out."

"You can't afford my rates, Sarge."

"Consider it freelance." Emphasis on *free*, I took it. "Not like you've got a whole lot else going on now, right?"

Stinkin' had been correct about that much: nowadays the Link made it possible for just about anybody to play detective—as long as what you were after was in range of the nearest vid-cam. But for dark business that often took place off the grid, your local gumshoe came in real handy.

"Fine." I stuffed my hands into the pockets of my trench coat. "I'll ask around, see if anybody's heard rumors about an impaler on the loose."

"Maybe start with that boxer friend of yours. He's been known to associate with augmented types. What's his name again?"

"Cauliflower Carl."

Douglass snapped his fingers and grinned. "That's the one." He palmed his right ear and slurred, "What's that? I don't hear so good."

Not a bad impression of the washed-up loser. Word was Carl made his living now as a bookie, having eaten the mat too many times to win any major endorsement deals. All those years of bloody abuse in the ring had left his right ear a shriveled mess.

"He's no friend of mine, but if he knows something, I'll get him to talk." I watched Stinkin' and Blinkin' as they knelt down beside the body and prodded the hole in the man's chest with their latex-gloved fingers.

"Never seen anything like it." Douglass cursed under his breath. "If it wasn't for that video, I wouldn't believe it was possible. Maybe I still don't. Like somethin' from a comic book." He shook his head in disgust. "Good thing Julian's got that old camera mounted out here. Once our techs go over the footage, we'll have an ID for the killer. But until then, see what you can dig up—before Stankic and Bellincioni do what they do best."

2

Julian was the one-eyed barkeep at Howard's Tavern and a friend to both Douglass and myself. He'd let me in as soon as I arrived on the scene. Douglass, Stinkin' and Blinkin' had been outside with the body. When Douglass phoned, he'd advised me to speak with Julian first while he kept Stankic and Bellincioni busy out in the alley.

"When did you find the body?" I asked as Julian led me into the back office. The tavern was empty. The clientele had cleared out at the first sound of police sirens. Howard's wasn't owned and operated by the mob; it was one of the few places in town where off-duty cops and your average citizen could grab a drink without the proceeds going to fund Ivan's machine.

"Almost an hour ago. I was taking out the trash..." Julian trailed off as we reached the back room where his surveillance equipment was running: two screens, each hooked up to a camera. One mounted above the bar, giving an overhead view of the vacant tavern; one mounted above the back door that led into the alley, showing Douglass arguing with the two detectives while the dead cop lay at their feet, staring up at the moon. "I'll run back the alley footage."

"Good thing you've got a camera out there."

"The owner insisted. Said he didn't want any monkey business goin' down anywhere near this establishment. Said it was a matter of personal pride." Julian was a good guy.

Never pried into the private lives of his customers, always had a grin, a wink, or something humorous to share. I'd never seen him like this: shook up. "Never thought it was really necessary, you know?"

"First time for everything."

He cursed under his breath as his long, knotted fingers splayed over the console and the grayscale images on the alley screen jittered, reversing course. Made sense he wouldn't have the latest technology keeping an eye on his bar. These cameras and vid-feeds were old-school, nothing like the vidLinks people wore over their ears nowadays.

I didn't have much use for the Link. Machines and me hadn't gotten along real well since the war; I had no desire to rely on technology in any of its forms. Besides, all it would take was another EMP airstrike from the Eastern Conglomerate, and the Link would go the way of its much more impressive predecessor, something they used to call the *Internet*.

Julian and I both had that in common: an aversion to invasive machines. And Julian had reason not to want vidLinks in his bar. He'd lost his eye, thanks to one. Back in the war, he'd been outfitted with an eye implant to record reconnaissance for his commanding officers. Soon as the war was over, he'd had that thing removed. Problem was, he went to a surgeon while still stationed in Eurasia. The surgical standards of that operation had been primitive, at best. They hadn't been able to save his eye in the process.

So he didn't wear the latest tech to keep tabs on his patrons. Nobody working at Howard's Tavern ever had. And the surveillance cameras had only been a preventative measure; the place had never been a spot for trouble.

Until now.

"It's awful, Charlie. Never seen anything like it. Never thought anybody could do something like this."

"Were both men regulars?"

"The cop, yeah. He came in here every other night or so. But this kid?" Julian pointed at the screen now where the image had frozen. Two men stood in the back alley in plain view of the camera. The killer hadn't tried to lure the cop out of range. He stood with his face in shadow, though, an average-sized man of less-than-average build. "He's been in a few times lately. That's all."

"Drink alone?"

"Kept to himself mostly, yeah."

"Mostly?" I raised an eyebrow.

"One of the waitresses—Paige."

I nodded. I knew her. A good kid figuring out her path in life.

"Well, he took a real liking to her," Julian said. "They got along, all right. But I had to let her go yesterday. Extra help ain't in the budget no more. Times being what they are, you know. Hated to do it..."

He didn't have to explain. I'd been lucky so far, still able to afford my secretary, Wanda Wood. It was getting tough to pay the rent for both my apartment and my office, and I knew I'd eventually have to let one of them go if I wanted to keep her on as my assistant. The last thing I wanted to do was live out of my office, but maybe it wouldn't be so bad. I'd nodded off in my faux-leather desk chair plenty of times before. Sleeping through the night wasn't out of the question.

I focused on Julian. "Were they having a drink together—

this guy and the victim?"

"Opposite ends of the bar. Didn't seem to know each other." Julian shook his head slowly at the memory. "Kid ordered a beer. Wouldn't look me in the eye. Never a good sign, you know?" Julian glanced up at me from where he sat at the console. "They say eyes are the windows to your soul."

My grandmother had always told me the same thing. Whenever I got into trouble as a kid—and believe me, that happened more often than not—she'd make me look her in the eye when it came time to explain myself. Natural-born lie detectors, those almond-colored eyes of hers.

I cleared my throat. "Did you happen to see them leave?"

Julian shook his head. "Had to take a leak. When I came back, both of them were gone."

"Show me what happened."

"It ain't pretty." Julian tapped the console, and the image on the screen started moving.

Officer Bowman didn't seem to know what was going on. He looked unsteady on his feet, maybe a little tipsy. Had he taken a wrong turn and wound up in the back alley? Without a word, he turned toward the tavern door as if to reenter the bar. But that's when the killer stepped forward, his face now in full view of the camera. No attempt to hide. He grabbed the cop by the shoulder and spun him around, in a single movement plunging his fist through the victim's chest and out the middle of his back with a thick spurt of blood.

Julian cursed and shook his head, wincing, but unable to look away from the screen. I wouldn't have believed it if I hadn't seen it with my own eyes. The killer pulled his fist out and dropped the bloody hand to his side. He stared like a man in a daze as his victim swayed on his feet, stumbling forward a step, then back, before his legs gave out. He hit the ground like a marionette, strings cut without warning.

"Well, there you have it." Julian switched the view back to a live scene of the alley. "Hope it helps, Charlie."

I gestured at Stinkin' and Blinkin' on the screen, standing over the victim and shaking their heads, cursing quietly. "They'll want to commandeer that footage."

"They're welcome to it." He swallowed with some difficulty. "I'll be happy if I never see anything like that again."

3

Bidding adieu to Sergeant Douglass and ignoring the insults hurled my way by those two belligerent police detectives, I hitched a cab across town to Cauliflower Carl's home away from home: *K.O. Gym*. An appropriate name for the place, considering how all those unfortunate knockouts had ended Carl's career in the ring. Rumor had it he'd thrown more than a few of the fights, but rumors being what they are, I listened to such gossip with only half an ear—which was more than the shriveled mess Carl had on the right side of his head. You'd think he would have grown out his hair to cover it, but he shaved himself bald, skin white as a maggot's, and he never wore hats. Dark-eyed and broad-jawed, he had the look of a bona fide Scandinavian Neanderthal about him.

I found him ringside, shouting at one of the two men sparring in the illuminated ring. The place was dark and empty otherwise, as I figured it would be. This early in the morning, only those with sleep disorders or hopped up on some kind of narcotic had reason to be awake. Carl was the poster boy for insomnia: pasty pale with bruises under both eyes, he hulked around like the love child of Bigfoot and the Missing Link.

What was my excuse for being out and about at such an ungodly hour? I owed Douglass, plain and simple.

Once upon a time, Charlie Madison was no private

investigator. He was a down-and-out veteran, fresh from the battlefield. The war was over, so they said, and I'd been sent home. Sergeant Archibald Douglass had been in Howard's Tavern for a drink one night, and he'd noticed me drowning my sorrows. His drink of choice: Scotch, of course, him being a son of Scotland who refused to forsake his brogue. Mine: domestic beer. I'd had too much to drink by that point, and I'd probably said too much—enough for him to know I lacked any real direction in my life.

We became friends, the cop and the veteran, and after a few weeks of hanging out at Howard's every night, he planted an idea in my head that started growing like a fungus: Sure, the war was cold, but that didn't mean there weren't battles to be fought on home soil. After being ordered to lead the men in my unit to their deaths, there was no way I'd ever work for the government again; so becoming a cop was out of the question.

"Why not a private eye, Charlie?" Douglass had said, his eyes looking like a light bulb had clicked on in there somewhere.

"They still exist?"

"Sure they do." He'd shrugged his bulky shoulders in a good-natured sort of way. The man had the build of a pro rugby player a couple decades past his prime. "Would suit you perfectly. You've got classic gumshoe written all over you! And you could do some real good in this town—the kind Ivan's machine wouldn't see comin'. Work in the shadows, you see? No ties to the corrupt politicians and police commissioner, no ties to the mob. It would be perfect, just what this city needs. A real lone ranger!"

I wasn't sure about the reference, but I'd nodded anyway.

It sounded like a change of pace, if nothing else. "You really think I could make a living at it?"

"I think you'd succeed at just about anything you set your mind to." He'd clapped me on the shoulder and grinned. "That's what I really think, Charlie."

He'd managed to guide my life back on track when I'd lost my way, and I sure as hell owed him for that. And thanks to Belinda, his assistant who'd recommended a girl fresh out of stenography school, Wanda had been by my side ever since—a real godsend. Photographic memory, effervescent personality, and legs that wouldn't quit. To say she was the brains behind my business was no joke. The rest, as they say, was recent history.

So there I was, standing a couple meters away from Cauliflower Carl on a Wednesday morning at 3AM, watching him half-coach, half-berate the sweat-drenched, wild-eyed kid in the ring who appeared to be his protégé. If not, he was the only one out of the two combatants who paid Carl any attention. The other one looked stoned out of his mind, shuffling side to side with a dead look in his eyes. Both fighters were middle weights, all lean muscle and no fat, in their early twenties at most. Size-wise, either one could have been that killer on the surveillance footage from Howard's, only they weren't.

The killer had shown his face, and it didn't belong to either one of these guys.

"Keep your dukes up, dumbass!" Carl shouted as the kid he was coaching advanced on his opponent. The one with the dead eyes blocked the kid's first two blows easily and sent him back on his heels with a jaw-crushing uppercut.

"Hey, I remember that look," I said right before the poor

kid ate the mat. "You wore it a lot toward the end of your career, from what I recall."

Carl cursed, turning sharply to face me. "Madison," he muttered, returning his attention to the kid—now out cold. His opponent stood over him and stared mutely without an expression on his face, glistening with sweat. "I don't seem to remember inviting you here."

"Back door was unlocked. Figured that was all the invitation I needed." I nodded toward the fighter who'd delivered the knockout blow. "He's got a mean uppercut. Too bad he's so short on personality. Could be a real star."

"Go cool off, Edgar," Carl said as he reached for a pail of water. As the victor left the ring, staggering like a zombie into a dark corner of the gym, Carl tossed the pail's contents onto the unconscious kid left behind. "You too!" Carl shouted.

The kid sputtered and jerked upright into a sitting position. He glanced at me without recognition and rubbed his jaw.

"Yeah, sure, Carl," he mumbled and followed his opponent into the shadows.

"Show's over, Madison. You wanna see more, you'll have to pay—and get past Ivan's security at the Coliseum."

"Is that where these boys are headed?"

"In due time. Sure as hell wouldn't survive at this stage."

I narrowed my gaze. "You ever heard of the phrase *conflict of interest*?"

He scowled. "What're you gettin' at?"

"Oh, I don't know. You coach these guys, then you organize the bets laid on them?"

He grinned, and it was the ugliest expression I'd seen all day. "Good thing we live in a free country."

Or one where the Federal Government couldn't give a damn about local affairs. Oddly enough, the Blackshirts seemed to have no problem with Ivan the Terrible running this town. The mayor and the district attorney weren't much more than puppets in his little Russian/North American theatre.

"Granted, my eyes can play tricks on me sometimes," I said. "But as much as I hate to admit it, technology doesn't lie too often." As long as it wasn't tampered with. But even then there were traces, digital fingerprints left behind that any tech wiz worth their byte could follow straight to the source. "God knows I've seen a lot in my day, but you wouldn't believe the video I saw over at Howard's tonight."

"You gonna make me guess?"

"Tell me, Carl. What would it take to punch your fist straight through me?"

He blinked like he was waiting for the punchline—pun intended.

"Beat it, Madison. It's past your bedtime, and you're talking gibberish."

"Right here." I took a step toward him and tapped the middle of my chest. "What kind of performance-enhancing cocktail would you have to give a death duel fighter to make him punch a hole all the way through his opponent?"

"Ain't even possible." He scoffed. "Sure, a strong enough fighter can break ribs, mess up the wet works. Maybe send his opponent flying across the ring. But no bloody *hole* like you're talking about. That's only in the comics." He paused, looking me over with obvious contempt. "And I don't know what the hell you're talking about *death duels*. That sort of stuff doesn't happen in this town, not at the Coliseum anyway. Where'd you hear that kind of crap?"

I shrugged. "Guess I was misinformed."

"Yeah. Guess you were." He half-turned like he was going to leave, but something I'd said had piqued his interest. Otherwise, he wouldn't have halted mid-step to face me. "You're pulling my leg, right? You don't have any video of a fighter taking somebody out like that."

"I don't. But the police do, by now. They're running facial recognition on the killer. No chance it could be one of your prospective meal tickets?" I nodded toward the shadows where his two fighters-in-training had disappeared.

"Screw you, Madison." He stalked off.

"No thanks, Carl." I remained ringside in the glow. I wasn't through with him yet. "So, no idea what could cause a man to develop a fist of iron?"

Carl's heavy footfalls stopped abruptly. "What did you say?"

"What kind of dope or biotech should I be looking for?"

"Fist of iron..." he mused, stomping back my way like a perturbed bull.

I held my ground, crawling my right hand toward the shoulder holster concealed under my coat. I hadn't ever shot Carl before, but there was always a first time for everything. My snub-nosed Smith & Wesson .38 would take out one of his kneecaps nicely.

"You know, I might've heard something...not too long ago," he said. "A new 'roid hitting the streets."

"Now we're getting someplace."

"Don't count on it." He halted once he'd emerged from the shadows. "I'll tell you what I know, but you've gotta promise to do something for me first."

"Is that how this works?"

"*Quid pro quo*, Madison."

"Didn't realize you spoke French."

"It's Latin, dumbass. Means I get something if I give you something. Got it?"

"You're not as stupid as you look, Carl."

He cursed under his breath but kept his distance. As a rule of thumb, it was best to stay out of his reach. "I want Yevgeni's number," he said.

Of course he referred to Yevgeni Sokolov, one of Ivan's lieutenants who ran the Arena, infamous boxing ring at the Coliseum—Ivan's casino castle on the west side of town.

"And here I was assuming you were already in with Yevgeni, providing him fresh meat." I clucked my tongue, shaking my head with disappointment. "You really are just a washed-up boxer with his best years behind him. Stick to being a bookie, Carl. It's what you do best."

"Hey, I see all kinds of raw talent in here, Madison. You don't even know. Yevgeni should be busting down my door—!"

"But he's ignored your pleas for attention, is that it?"

"I just need to talk to him, let him know he should take me seriously."

"Nobody takes you seriously, Carl."

"Screw you!" He turned on his heel and lumbered away.

This time, I followed him a few steps into the dark. "What makes you think I can even get it for you?"

"Word on the street is you helped him a while back. Something about his wife stepping out with his brother. Yevgeni hired you to track down the bitch." Carl slowed his pace. "You want to know about this 'roid or not?"

Sure I did. And it wouldn't cost me anything. I was pretty sure the number I had on file for Yevgeni was out of date.

"All right. I'll have my secretary call your office in the morning."

"Can't you just link up and get it yourself?"

I tapped my naked ear. "No access." I didn't even carry a phone.

"You're gonna wake up one morning extinct, Madison."

"So they tell me. But enough small talk." My patience was wearing thin. "What have you heard?"

"Never seen the stuff in action." He shrugged. "Some fighters, they juice. Everybody knows that. If laws against doping were enforced, maybe it would be a problem. But they ain't. So it ain't."

Couldn't argue with that logic.

"From what I hear," Carl said, leaning toward me, "this new stuff coming out of Little Tokyo, it's supposed to increase bone density and strength by a factor of ten, whatever that means. Dulls pain receptors, speeds up tissue recovery."

"Sounds perfect for a boxer."

"Some fighters at the Arena are able to break through solid slabs of granite. That's what they say, anyhow. Hard to imagine."

"Martial artists have always done that sort of thing."

"Not like this—unscored blocks. No weak points. Ain't natural." He paused. "From what I've heard, that is. Ain't seen it myself yet. But if you get me in touch with Yevgeni, then maybe—"

"Little Tokyo, you say?" I would have to call my friend Sanitoro from the yakuza Emerald Tiger clan. If this new steroid was real, and if it was coming out of Little Tokyo, then he would know about it. "And Yevgeni's already gotten his hands on the stuff?"

"You didn't hear that from me."

I had, actually. "See you around, Carl."

"Yevgeni's number." He pointed at me. "Don't forget. You owe me now."

"Sure. You have my word."

He cursed mildly. "From anybody else, that might be a joke." He chuckled in the dark. "See you around, Madison."

4

The sun was struggling to peek through slate-gray clouds in the east by the time I hoofed it over to my office building. Our fair city was enjoying what you might call a respite from the acid rains that had a way of eroding buildings a little at a time and washing them out to the polluted sea bit by crumbling bit. The streets were still wet from the last onslaught. But for now, the air was cool and damp, and none of that cold, oily stuff was drizzling out of the sky. For the first time in weeks, I might've laid money on the sun breaking through and shining light into the darkness.

I took the stairs up to my office on the eighth floor—my daily cardiovascular regimen. I had to take care of my body; it was the only one I had, after all. But that wasn't the only reason. The lift may not have been in the best working condition. Getting trapped in that thing once had induced more than enough claustrophobia to last me a lifetime. I'd had to talk down my fellow passenger, a senior citizen who was sure we'd run out of oxygen before help arrived. While I might have shared that concern, I couldn't let her know it. I had to keep her calm, distracting her with questions regarding her grandchildren and whatever else she felt like rambling on about. We ended up having a pretty nice time together, all things considered.

What can I say? I've got a soft spot for the older generation. They were from a different era, back when times were better, whether they realized it or not. This wasn't the future they signed up for.

Considering how early it was—not even 5AM—I was surprised to find Wanda at her desk as I unlocked the front office door and stepped inside.

"Morning, Charlie," she said brightly, sorting through files on her Slate. She had the thing slaved to an old Underwood, modified so that when she banged on the keys, they tapped against the Slate's touchscreen with rubberized tips. Quirky? Sure, but that was Wanda all over. I wouldn't have had her any other way.

"You're up early." I shut the door—frosted glass with black lettering that spelled out CHARLIE MADISON, DETECTIVE for any passersby in the hallway outside—and shrugged out of my coat.

"Couldn't sleep," she said, keeping her eyes on her work. She didn't look like she'd rolled out of bed: dressed to the nines, as always, with just a little too much makeup. Some girls needed the face paint. Wanda didn't. Thick, curly blonde hair bobbed against the shoulders of her blue dress, close to the color of her sapphire eyes. But no category of blue could really do them justice. "Figured I'd get these files organized for you."

She didn't need her Slate to do that, or any computer for that matter. The girl had perfect memory, what they called total recall. The files on her machine were for my benefit. Not that I ever sorted through them on that thing. I had my own system: sheets of note paper stuffed into folders. But as Wanda always reminded me, it was important to have those files backed-up in case of fire or flood. So she diligently entered my chicken-scratched scribbles into her Slate. But were any of my notes to be seen, scattered across her desk top? Of course not. She was typing them all straight from memory.

Yeah, that was Wanda.

"I'll have some fresh notes for you shortly." I hung up my coat and hat and ran a hand over my slick hair, as opposite to hers as possible: close-cropped and dark. Maybe a little grizzled on closer inspection. I didn't allow too many people to get that close.

"New case?" She glanced up at me with those gorgeous eyes.

I gave her a wink. She'd get the details once I had them sorted out. "Get Sanitoro on the line. Need to ask him about something."

"And if he's busy? You know, extorting some poor shop owner or killing somebody—the usual?"

Cute. "Tell him I want to know about an iron fist."

"Real mysterious, Charlie." She picked up her phone—an over-the-ear Link model—and voice-activated the thing to connect with Sanitoro.

I didn't really know how the technology worked, but from what I'd heard, there was a lot of virtual reality involved. The Link was like the Internet from a couple generations ago, but only half as impressive. Sure, the virtual interface was really something, incorporating both audio and video components, and it could take you anywhere and let you see anything. But it had its limits. Bandwidth was a major issue; cost was another. Even so, United World citizens didn't seem to mind. Folks across the globe could spend time together in the same virtual environment if they'd saved up enough credits to pay for the experience.

Most entertainment these days was Link-based, and it was equally pricey. You and your significant other could collapse on the couch after working all day, plug in, and spend your evening in the same virtual world or light-years apart: one in a bloody shoot 'em up while the other wiled away the hours on a moonlit beach with an exotic sexual partner.

Of course, there were citizens who'd become addicted to all that the Link had to offer, and they went so far as to completely neglect their real-world lives. Living in squalor, slowly starving to death. We called those unfortunate freaks *zombies*.

"Some kind of weapon?" Wanda continued to fish for details.

"Could be. I'll take it in here." I opened the door to my dark office. As an afterthought, I added, "And if you get a chance, send Carl Hayes the private number for Yevgeni Sokolov."

"Hayes—" Her eyebrows knitted as she searched her memory banks. "Any reason you're doing that washed-up old boxer a favor?"

"I've got a bad reputation...for keeping my word."

She smirked and tapped the phone mounted over her ear. She had the device routed through the intercom on my desk so I never had to wear her gizmo if I didn't want to—which was most of the time. I had to make an exception when there was no other option, but thankfully those occasions were few and far between.

Machines and me had no reason to get along. I was better off without them. Most people would be, honestly, but they were so attached to their gadgets, they couldn't imagine their lives without them. My grandmother always used to say it had been the same in her time, that the turn of the century hadn't marked the end of technology as many doomsayers had suggested. In many ways, it had signaled the birth of a whole new world where people stared at screens in the palms of their hands all day long.

With the Link, they didn't have to do that anymore; everything was right in front of their eyes. And rumor had it a subdermal plug was in the works that would be routed through the customer's visual cortex. Citizens would be lining up in droves to take the first step toward turning themselves into cyborgs.

I wouldn't be counted among them.

"Charlie, I've got him," Wanda's voice came through the intercom.

I turned away from the window behind my desk where I'd been standing in something like a trance, staring at the damp street below through slats in my venetian blinds. I switched the intercom over to the line with the blinking red light—dated technology that I knew and understood.

"Madison," Sanitoro's voice came through the speaker. He never sounded happy to talk to me. But he never sounded annoyed, either. He had one of those grim, deep voices that you couldn't help but take seriously. His reputation backed it up.

"Thanks for taking my call," I said, easing into my faux-leather desk chair. "Hope I haven't caught you at a bad time."

"It is 5AM," he said in that inscrutable tone.

Was he an early bird or a late sleeper? I had no idea. "This won't take long."

"Your assistant mentioned *tetsu no ken*." He paused, always one to rub in my ignorance of the Japanese language.

Most of it, anyway. "*Fist of iron.*"

"Right." Straight to business. I couldn't help but smile briefly. "What would you know about a new steroid?"

"Very little. Our house does not include purveyors of narcotics."

The Asada crime family, with which Sanitoro was affiliated, preferred extortion over the narcotics and prostitution trade Little Tokyo's other yakuza clans were infamous for. With blackmail came true power—the power to control others. Or so they believed.

"How did you learn of this drug?"

"We've got a dead cop, and the killer might have been high on the stuff," I said. What else could explain what I'd seen? The man in that video footage had been no cyborg. He must have been pumped full of illegal performance-enhancing 'roids. And I couldn't get over the drug's name; it would have taken nothing short of a *fist of iron* to punch straight through another man.

"Not surprising. From what I have heard, *tetsu no ken* is being produced by House Fire Dragon. They are not known to be discriminating with regard to their clientele." Sanitoro paused. "That is all I know."

"But you could find out more." My turn to pause. "Easier than I could."

Little Tokyo was yakuza territory, and as a rule, Anglo citizens such as myself weren't exactly welcome across the border. Ever since the Great Diaspora back when the Eastern Conglomerate started expanding their borders, encroaching into what had once been the sovereign nations of Japan and Mother Russia, a steady stream of immigrants had flowed into the Unified States. Most of them came down through the Alaskan oil fields and were put to work there. Of course the government welcomed them with open arms, always in favor of increasing the population. When you were up against China and her allies in a global conflict, numbers sure as hell mattered.

But not all of the new citizens liked the idea of being assigned backbreaking work in order to fuel their mighty protector's war machine. Many filtered south. Due to prevailing anti-Asian sentiments, the Japanese were not welcomed the same way as the Russians. Ignorance ran deep in some folks, and it didn't matter to them that the Japanese had been on our side during the war. They were forced to create their own townships—slums really, just outside of major cities.

Most Anglo citizens who valued their lives avoided Little Tokyo. Tensions were on the rise among the Japanese youth, dissatisfied with their second-class status. They'd fled their homeland to be free, not to live their lives trapped in ghettos. Many perceived Anglos as the enemy, and where bottles and rocks were hurled, bloodshed often followed.

Not saying I was afraid to cross the border or anything. I just usually had one hell of a time finding a cabby brave enough to take me.

"You believe the killer to be Japanese?" Sanitoro said.

Not based on what Julian had showed me. "If a super-steroid caused the damage I saw, then I'd say the Fire Dragon clan is expanding its reach outside Little Tokyo."

A moment of silence. "If so, the Russian Devil could be involved."

"Or one of his lower-level lieutenants." I thought back to my recent conversation with Cauliflower Carl. "A 'roid like that might be popular among fighters in the Arena."

"As a rule, the yakuza and the Russians do no business together."

I knew that full well. "Which is why I thought you might like to help me out. I'm sure the Emerald Tiger clan could teach Fire Dragon the error of their ways."

"If such is the case, I will get to the bottom of it. Leave this matter to me, Madison." With that, Sanitoro ended the call.

"Thanks," I muttered, reaching to switch off the intercom.

"Got somebody else for you, Charlie," Wanda's voice came through the speaker. "Sergeant Douglass, line two."

"You don't say?"

"You're Mr. Popular this morning. Oh—" She stopped herself abruptly, returning to her all-business tone. "And we also have a prospective client waiting for you, Mr. Madison. Just walked in. I told him you'd be with him in a moment."

A paying client? Wouldn't that be nice. It could offset this pro-bono work I was doing for ol' Douglass.

"What's up, Sarge?" I said as I switched over to his line.

"We've got a match, lad," Douglass said, out of breath by the sound of it. The guy seriously needed to increase his cardio. "The tech team identified our killer via the Link—ID, home address, the works. We're getting set to raid his apartment. Thought you might like to know, maybe tag along with us."

"Stinkin' and Blinkin' on the way to grab the guy?"

"I'm hoping to beat them to it. No tellin' what they'll do. Cop killers don't survive long in this town."

"Not always a bad thing."

"As a rule, no." He fell silent.

Maybe he was thinking about the way that victim had been impaled. There was more to this story, and we wouldn't know anything about it if those two overzealous police detectives got rid of the killer in an act of vigilante justice.

"I want that perp in here for questioning, Charlie. He wasn't born with the ability to kill a man that way. No sir." Douglass paused. "You find out anything from that has-been boxer?"

"I'm following a lead, Sarge. I'll let you know as soon as I have anything solid."

Wanda buzzed in, something she never did in the middle of a call. "You are needed in the front office, Mr. Madison."

I didn't like the sound of her tone. Was our prospective client making her nervous?

"Gotta go," I told Douglass. "Paying client."

He chuckled on the line. "Don't let 'im get away, lad!"

I switched off the intercom and checked the bulge of my holstered .38 through my suit jacket. A reassuring tic. I'd never had to shoot somebody in my office before, but if that somebody was making a move on Wanda, all bets were off.

"Sorry to keep you waiting," I said as I stepped into the front office.

That's where I stopped, rooted to the floor. Because staring me in the face from where he'd halted mid-feverish-pace...

Stood the killer from Julian's video.

5

"Mr. Madison?" he said, wringing his hands as he took a step toward me and stopped. Beads of sweat stood out on his forehead. "I-I'm sorry for barging in here like this."

"Not at all." I sidestepped nonchalantly toward Wanda's desk. Not out of some chivalrous attempt to protect a woman from a killer with superhuman punching abilities—not that I wasn't chivalrous when I needed to be. But at the moment, I liked the odds of two against one—particularly one as unpredictable as Mr. Impaler there. "What can I do for you?"

"I've-uh heard about you." The guy hadn't blinked since I first laid eyes on him. His clothes were clean, but rumpled—a white tank and khaki trousers, scuffed shoes. Not the same attire he'd worn in the surveillance footage. Then it had been a suit. Not a fancy one, but it had done the job. He'd looked respectable enough. No one would have glanced at him twice. Now? He had the wild look of an asylum escapee. "Good things. I've heard good things."

"Then you've been talking to the wrong people."

"No, I mean—from what I hear, you...help people. Right?"

"Sure. People who can pay." I raised an eyebrow.

"Right." He nodded quickly and reached into his back pocket.

My hand slid toward that bulge under my arm.

"Whatever your rates are, I can pay you." He produced his ID card from a well-worn faux-leather wallet. "I sure as hell need your help, Mr. Madison. There's nobody else I can go to."

Not exactly the case. Maybe the cops were out of the question with so many of them in Ivan's pocket, but there were still good ones to be found if you looked hard enough. Sergeant Archibald Douglass, for one.

Even so, I was in no hurry to call Douglass and tell him not to bother ramming down the door of this guy's apartment. If the sergeant was right that Stankic and Bellincioni would sooner off the man standing before me than question him, then I needed to find out all I could while I had the chance.

But if either one of those calloused hands of his curled into a fist, I'd have my .38 out and a round through his knee before he could move another muscle.

"We'll worry about that later." I gestured for him to put away his wallet. "For now, just tell me what seems to be the trouble."

He paused with a frown, but he did as he was told. "Figured you'd want me to pay up front."

"No charge unless I can be of service. That's how I run my business."

"That's why he's in debt," Wanda said with a little smile. And in that instant, the mood in the room relaxed by a wide margin. She had that magical way about her, always knowing what to say and when to say it to put folks at ease.

"What's your name, for starters?" I watched him glance from me to Wanda and back again without a single blink. He looked unsure of himself, to say the least.

"Enoch," he said quietly, turning his gaze to the middle-aged industrial carpet covering the floor.

"Have a seat, Enoch." I nodded toward the futon couch we had up against the wall. A potted palm on one side and Wanda's lily on the other gave the front office something of a lived-in look. That's what we were going for, anyway.

"Sure." He nodded again and rigidly seated himself on the edge of the cushion.

I sat on the corner of Wanda's desk and kept one foot on the floor, just in case I needed to move fast.

"Take a deep breath, Enoch. Then tell me what's going on."

He glanced up as he tried to follow my directions, but the breath he took shuddered his chest, and his shoulders remained high and tight. He didn't have a whole lot of meat on him, but what he had was solid muscle—the lean, wiry type.

"Mr. Madison," he said at length, breaking his staring contest with the carpet and fixing his gaze on me. "I think I might've killed somebody."

I was pretty sure he had. But I wanted to hear his side of things. "What makes you say that?"

"Somebody...I don't know who. They sent me a video, like from a security camera or something." He touched his ear in the way some people did when they weren't wearing their Link interface. Like a ghost limb, something amputees experienced after they'd had an arm or leg blown off in battle. Felt like the limb was still there, and even after they'd been outfitted with a prosthesis, vets often still thought they were going to reach out with a flesh-and-blood hand to touch a loved one. "I couldn't believe it at first—that I could do something that horrible. Kill somebody, I mean. But then I saw...how I did it."

I glanced at Wanda. This was the first she'd heard details of the case, and she was listening with rapt attention, soaking it all up like a data sponge.

"So you're saying you don't remember doing it? Or why you would have done it in the first place?"

"I have no idea who he was—that guy...I killed. I know the video wasn't a fake."

"What makes you say that?" Nowadays any kid with a Slate could doctor just about every video ever recorded. Put themselves in a classic old film. Borrow a golden-age actor for their own idiotic production. But Julian's footage had been analog in nature, and I doubted his antique tech would have allowed Enoch's face to be digitally replaced. Then again, what did I know?

"Last night, when I got home..." He trailed off, turning his right hand over before his eyes. As the fingers curled slowly into a fist, I reached into my jacket and curled my own fingers around the grip of my revolver. "I had blood on my hand. A whole lot of it. But I couldn't remember where it had come from. I scrubbed it off, and there were cuts in my skin. You can't even see them now." He flexed out his fingers, holding up the back of his hand for me to take a look.

"Cuts? From what, do you think?"

"The guy's ribs, maybe." He hung his head, plenty shook up. Reminded me of some of the new recruits we'd had on the front lines during the war. More than a few were always left rattled by their first kill. The ones with souls. Didn't matter that they were up against an enemy who wanted to overhaul their entire way of life. They'd been raised to value humankind in all its forms. "I don't know. But it made sense. The video, I mean. It explained what I couldn't remember."

"What's the last thing you recall—before arriving home with a bloody mitt?"

"Working." He shrugged.

"Where?"

"The Coliseum. I'm one of the janitors over there. I vacuum floors and clean toilets for a living." He smirked at the glorious sound of his career choice. "It pays the bills, you know?"

"Sure." I graced him with a pensive frown. "So, one minute you're cleaning up after some mogul's mess, and the next, you're walking in your front door? No memory at all of what happened in between?"

He shook his head, fixing me with his unblinking stare again. "I know it doesn't look good—that I don't have any kind of alibi." He paused. "Listen, I know I killed that man. But I don't know *why* and I can't for the life of me figure out *how.*"

"If you saw the same footage I did, I'd say the *how* is fairly obvious."

"It's not possible, Mr. Madison!" he said without skipping a beat. "Look at me. I weigh a buck fifty on a good day. There's no way I could punch straight through somebody like that."

I heard a short intake of breath from Wanda, who sat back in her chair abruptly.

"I wouldn't have the strength, for one thing," Enoch continued. "And I sure as hell have never had any kind of training for something like that."

"Never taken martial arts?"

He shook his head.

"Do you box?"

"I'm no fighter, Mr. Madison. My parents raised me to turn the other cheek."

Religious types? When my parents were killed in that freak auto accident, my grandmother became both my mother and father. Part of living under her roof had entailed joining her for Sunday services every week. An hour of Sunday school followed by another hour or two listening to the minister. She'd always advised me to turn the other cheek too. I'd had to learn to fight on my own with all the other boys whose parents dragged them to church on Sundays—behind the chapel during overlong prayer meetings.

"Working at the Coliseum, you get to see plenty of fights."

"Sure, now and then. But my shifts are staggered. I never know when I'm coming in until that morning—I get a ping." That was a shorthand way of saying his employer messaged him via Link. "And I almost always work the casino."

I didn't envy him. "Those fat cats don't know how to keep a tidy litterbox."

"You're telling me." For the first time, he almost smiled. "So, what do you say, Mr. Madison? Can you help me?" He stood up quickly but didn't advance, wringing his hands again like he was still trying to rub off Officer Bowman's blood. "I'm not asking you to prove my innocence. I know you're not a miracle worker. But can you find out who's done this to me—whatever this is?"

I held his gaze for a moment. "Do you have your phone with you?"

He reached into his pocket for the flimsy device—an over-the-ear model like Wanda's. Handing it to me, he absently scratched at his ear lobe.

"Have you made or received any calls since that video came through?" I weighed the thing in my palm.

"No. Nothing. I just...I came right here."

I faced Wanda. "Think you can trace whoever made that call?"

"I'll give it a shot," she said without pause, pinching the device from my hand.

"I'll check with Julian, see who's had access to that footage since the murder." I turned back to Enoch. "You have any enemies I should know about?"

"Does this mean you're taking my case?" Hope kindled in his bloodshot eyes.

"Answer the question."

"No. Nobody." He faltered a bit. "Besides that guy I killed, I guess. But I don't know why I would've done that. Unless he was out to get me or something, and maybe I just...fought back."

That's not how the scene had gone down. Not judging from the footage I'd seen. Enoch had killed that off-duty cop without hesitation. If anybody had been confused by the situation at the time, it had been Officer Bowman.

"Anybody follow you here?" I said.

"I don't think so."

"Did you tell anybody you were headed over here?"

He frowned slightly. "No, Mr. Madison. Like I said, I've got nobody to turn to."

Good enough for me. "All right. Here's the deal. You're going to sit tight in my office." I pointed him toward the door. "Take a few deep breaths while you're waiting. Try to settle down. We'll find out who might've sent you that video, and we'll go from there."

"Thank you, Mr. Madison." He shuffled awkwardly toward my door, like he wasn't sure I meant what I'd said.

Was he a killer? Sure. That much was clear. But it was just as obvious that he had no clue what was going on. And that made two of us.

"Go on in. Make yourself at home."

He nodded, glancing at Wanda as he left the front office. I shut the door behind him. I hesitated, debating whether I should lock it. The guy could punch his way out of anything, after all. I left it alone.

"So he's your new case." Wanda nodded toward my door. "The one you wouldn't tell me about."

I gave her a half-hearted wink. "Now you know about as much as I do."

"Did he do it?"

"You'll see for yourself. You've got his phone." I narrowed my gaze at the device. "Whoever sent him the footage—there would be some kind of timestamp, right?"

"I'll make a tech wiz out of you yet, Charlie." She slipped the device over her ear and waited for the external aural-neural connection to come online. "Here we go."

"Brace yourself."

She stared into space as the video played for her eyes only. She flinched at about the right time. Seeing Enoch's fist plow through that cop would elicit that reaction from anybody not desensitized to gore. I'd seen plenty of eviscerated corpses during the war, and after a while I'd been able to glance over serious carnage without feeling the urge to empty my stomach contents. But this murder on home soil, in the alley behind my favorite watering hole... It was too bizarre to gloss over.

"He acts like a machine," Wanda said quietly. "He just walks away after...punching his fist through that poor guy."

"Poor guy was a cop." I nodded as her eyes flicked toward mine. "Friend of Douglass."

"A good one, then."

"Yeah." They were few and far between these days. This town needed all the good cops it could keep. Far too many had been lured into corruption by the depths of Ivan's filthy rich pockets. "So when did Enoch receive that video?"

"Timestamp says 4AM. He opened it immediately."

Why would someone have waited four hours to send him the footage? By then, according to Enoch's story, he'd already found himself in his apartment and washed the blood off his hand—the blood he couldn't remember plunging his knuckles into.

"How about the source?"

She shook her head slowly. Didn't look promising. "Maybe if I had your police friend's equipment. But from what I can tell, whoever sent it knew how to keep out of sight."

"That's possible?" Everything I'd heard about the Link made it out to be a digital Big Brother—seeing all, hearing all, knowing all. Even though I did my best to remain off its grid, the Link still had plenty on me. Wanda made it a weekly ritual to let me know just how much.

"With the right equipment, you can make yourself pretty much invisible online. Filters, pass-image protocols, false fronts. Heck, I'd set you up with an awesome cyber alias if we could afford it."

"When we get some paying clientele, I'll be sure to make it

a priority." I reached for my coat and hat. "You'll be all right here with our guest?"

She removed Enoch's phone from her ear and blinked up at me. "Me and a cold-blooded killer? I'm sure we'll get along fine."

I reached back for my office door. "Got that double-barreled derringer handy?"

"Always." She patted her thigh where she kept the weapon holstered alongside her garter. Or so she'd told me, once.

"Good girl." I opened my door half a meter. Enoch stopped mid-pace, wringing his hands again. "Seriously. Take a load off." I pointed him toward my desk chair. "And under no circumstance do you open this door. Understood?"

He nodded without much conviction in the gesture and stiffly sat down in my chair. The faux-leather creaked around him as he leaned back.

"You take one step out this door, and my secretary puts a bullet in your kneecap. Got it?"

"Do all of your clients receive this kind of hospitality?"

Finally, some attitude from the guy. Maybe he was a human being, after all.

"Only murderers." I shut the door and faced Wanda. "He takes one step—"

"I shoot him. Got it." She smiled and smacked her signature wad of chewing gum. "And I don't tell nobody we've got a guest—not even the cops."

"Especially the cops."

Something didn't sit right with me about the timestamp on that video footage. By 4AM, it should have been confiscated by the police. Julian wouldn't have had it on his antiquated recording equipment anymore—not unless he had a backup. By why would he have sent it to Enoch? Was Julian holding out on me? Did he know more about that guy in my office than he was letting on?

Wanda had mentioned a certain level of tech skills and equipment required to pull off the anonymous transmission. A cop could have utilized the precinct's technology at his or her disposal once the footage was in evidence. But what would have been the motive?

What sort of mess was Enoch mixed up in?

"You believe him, Charlie?"

"He's not arguing with the evidence. He needs the pieces put together is all. So do I." I passed our futon couch and potted palm on the way to the front door. "I'll be at Howard's. Call me if our guest starts to misbehave."

"You want to take this?" She held out Enoch's phone. "Easier to stay in touch that way."

I gave her a wink. "You know better, sweetheart."

"Can never hurt to try," she muttered as I stepped out into the hallway and shut the door with a smile tugging at the side of my face.

I had a feeling she'd never give up her mild-mannered quest to bring me into the late twenty-first century. But there was only so much she could do with a guy who secretly wished we'd all go back to using the rotary phone. I might have mentioned that to her on more than one occasion, just to see her roll those beautiful blue sapphires.

6

Expecting Howard's Tavern to be as vacant as it had been earlier, I was surprised to see a young woman exiting the establishment as I entered. What made it more interesting: she was the last person I would have expected to be there.

"Hey now, don't hurry off." I caught her by the arm as she passed me, satchel held close, her eyes focused on the pavement.

She shook her arm free and cursed me, but her fervor dimmed as sudden recognition sparked in her emerald-green eyes. It was Paige, the pierced, tattooed, good-looking brunette who'd served me drinks at Howard's plenty of times.

"Sorry, Charlie. I..."

"Heard you got canned."

She shrugged, glancing up at the sun's efforts to pierce our city's cloudy canopy. "I get it. The place isn't doing the kind of business it used to."

"Think that'll change now?"

"Now?" Her gaze returned to meet mine.

"Because of the murder."

She took a subconscious step back, like I'd flashed her a grisly photo.

"Nothing like morbid curiosity to boost your clientele."

"Yeah, maybe," she said quietly. Readjusting the cloth bag strapped over her shoulder, she moved to leave. "Listen, I've gotta—"

"How well did you know Enoch?"

She froze in place. "Who?"

"Janitor over at the Coliseum. Came in here from time to time. Julian said the two of you were friendly."

"I get paid to be friendly. Was paid—that's what waitresses do, right? Whore ourselves out for tips?"

"That's what I'm looking for, Paige. A tip." I stepped toward her, but not in a threatening way. I wanted her to know I needed whatever information she had. "I think Enoch's in trouble—the kind that's going to get him killed soon if he doesn't get help."

"What do you expect me to do? So I served the guy a few drinks. What about it?"

"You know him, then."

"I've got a good memory. He took domestic beer. Looked like the weight of the world was on his shoulders. Maybe I felt sorry for him." She shrugged again. "That's it."

"Did you know he was involved in the murder last night?" I glanced at her bag. "Did you see the video?"

"What video?"

"Where are you going with that?" I reached for her satchel.

She slapped my hand away, but I grabbed her wrist and pulled her close. "The cops want him dead, Paige. He killed one of their own. But I think there's more to the story, and you're going to tell me about it."

"Or what, Charlie?" She cussed me out. "You gonna rough me up?"

As a rule, I was no brute when it came to women. Not because I was sexist. It's the way my grandmother raised me. *You never lay a hand on a woman unless it's out of love,* she'd planted into my impressionable young mind. That had been around the same time as our talk regarding the birds and the bees—just as unforgettable, but a whole lot more awkward.

"Give me five minutes." I released her wrist. "That's all I'm asking for."

"And if I tell you to go take a flying leap?"

I nodded at her bag. "I'll tell Sergeant Douglass you were tampering with a crime scene."

"I was just clearing out my locker!"

"Sure you were." I folded my arms. "So how about it? Help me help Enoch, or spend the rest of the day down at the precinct."

She shook her head slowly, doing her best at staring me down. I admired the effort.

"You spend too much time around that cop, Charlie. You're starting to act like one yourself." She turned on her heel and slammed through the tavern's front door.

I took that to mean she was giving me five minutes. I followed her inside.

The place was dark, deserted. No sign of Julian, so he must have been in back. He never left the front door unlocked unless he was on the premises. No cops in sight, so they'd already packed up and left. I considered checking the back alley to see if they'd cleaned up after the corpse, but I decided to postpone such overweening curiosity until later. Right now, the girl across from me in the booth was my top priority.

"How'd you learn his name?" she said, keeping a hand on the satchel at her side. "Enoch."

"About that." I set my hat down on the table between us.

"He came to see me."

"Good," she said quietly, and there might have been a tear in her eye before she glanced away.

"Let me guess. You sent him."

"You've got a solid reputation. When you're not being a jackass." She glared at me for a moment.

"Reputation isn't worth squat in this town when cops are in the picture. He killed one of them, Paige. A good one."

"I know."

"So you saw it—the footage."

"Julian hadn't erased it yet."

"I would have thought the cops—"

"Yeah, they took it. All of his equipment is gone. But Julian keeps a backup in a separate location."

"Back near the lockers?"

"Maybe."

If I was a cop, I would've told her she couldn't leave with it. That she was interfering with an investigation. The usual. But I wasn't. And I cared about only one thing: finding out what the hell was going on before Stinkin' and Blinkin' took care of matters, and everything got swept under the rug, nice and tidy.

Douglass never asked me for favors. This was one of those rare occasions I could do something for somebody who'd already done so much for me. Simple enough, really: find out the how and the why of a bizarre, back-alley murder before the killer was exterminated by dirty cops. All in a day's work for yours truly.

Except the killer was sitting in my office. So the truth of the matter: Charlie Madison, private investigator, was himself interfering with a police investigation. And if Stankic and Bellincioni ever got wind of that, there would be nothing Douglass could do to pull my ass out of the frying pan—or the fire.

"Why'd you send it to him?"

"What?" She frowned slightly.

"The footage. Why send it to Enoch? Did you think he wouldn't remember?"

Glasses clinked at the bar. I looked up to find Julian headed our way with a bottle of whiskey in one hand and two tumblers in the other. He didn't look like he wanted to roust her out. If I had to guess, there were no hard feelings between him and Paige. Julian was a stand-up guy, and if he'd had to let her go, the reasons were solely financial.

"Figured you could use a drink." He set the tumblers down and filled them, splashing a few drops onto the scarred tabletop.

"Thanks, but not while I'm working." Booze dimmed my detective senses. I never minded a buzz after my cases were through, but I tended to avoid the stuff while I was casually interrogating.

"I know." Julian winked with his good eye. "This one's for me." He tossed back the tumbler and left the bottle, returning to the bar.

"Thanks, Julian," Paige said, fingering the glass he'd poured her. She stared at the amber whiskey and seemed unwilling to allow herself to enjoy it.

"Not a bad boss?" I nodded toward the barkeep across the tavern.

"Julian?" she said quietly. "He's the best."

"You wouldn't want to get even with him for letting you go?"

"Hell no." She scowled at me and tossed back the drink. She winced as she swallowed.

"Sending that video to Enoch implicates Julian. Don't ask me how. I'll let the D.A. figure out that part—it's what Stevens does best. You know. Making connections. Sometimes they stick, and people go away for a very long time. Doesn't always matter if they're guilty." Not in this town.

"Listen, I don't know what you're talking about. Yeah, I took the backup, okay? But I didn't send it to Enoch. Why would I do something like that?" Her words came out in a rush. The whiskey was already working its particular brand of magic, so to speak.

"Why would you take it in the first place? Plan to sell it online to the highest bidder? I'm sure stuff like that is popular all over the Link. What's that game all the cool kids are playing now? *Carnal Bludgeon Seventeen* or something?" I never understood the draw of violent games. Probably because I'd seen enough flesh and blood torn apart in battle. The real deal is nowhere near as much fun.

"I..." She dropped her gaze, fiddling with her empty glass and making no move to refill it. "I wanted to show him."

"In person."

She nodded.

"That might've been rough."

"He doesn't know." She looked up fiercely. "He still thinks he's a freakin' *janitor* over there!"

"The Coliseum?"

"He has no idea what they're making him do every night. Maybe he does clean up the place sometimes, I don't know. But that doesn't send you home like a zombie with blood all over your hands."

"It's happened before? He's come home bloody?"

"He's a fighter, Charlie. I know he doesn't look it. He weighs barely more than I do, and he doesn't have a violent bone in his body."

I pointed at her satchel. "That video proves otherwise."

"I've got to show him—to prove it to him."

"That he's a murderer? He already knows that, Paige. Somebody's already shown him—sent it right to his Link." Or his phone. Sometimes I had trouble distinguishing the two.

She rested one hand on her bag. "Wasn't me. I wouldn't even know how. I mean, this thing is analog. It would have to be digitally converted before it could be transferred via Link."

"Sounds like you know your stuff."

"It's basic tech, Charlie—if you're not a Luddite."

Touché. "If it's true what you're saying, then why is Enoch pretending to be a janitor?"

"He's not. Pretending, I mean. He honestly believes it." She shook her head sharply and cursed. "They're messing with his mind over there. I don't know how else to explain it. Lately, for the past couple weeks, he comes home like he's sleepwalking, and half the time he doesn't seem to know I'm even there."

"You two living together, I take it?"

"None of your business."

"Fair enough. But I'm sure D.A. Stevens will want you on the stand—assuming Enoch lives long enough to see a trial."

"What are you getting at?"

"The cops are out for blood. They don't care about due

process. And if it's true what you're saying, that Ivan's crew is using Enoch as some kind of hit man—"

"That's not what I'm saying at all. Haven't you been listening?" She leaned forward in the booth, her eyes wide. Ferocious. "He's *fighting* in the Arena. They're filling his veins with drugs and turning him into some kind of...*killing* machine!"

Far-fetched? Maybe if I hadn't seen that video. Or if I hadn't already learned about *tetsu no ken*. If the Fire Dragons were dealing with Ivan's organization, then it stood to reason a humble janitor at the Coliseum could be used as a guinea pig in the Arena. Something that despicable wouldn't be too low for the Russian Devil or any of his vodka-soaked lieutenants.

"I don't care what this shows, Charlie." She clutched the bag beside her. "Enoch's not a killer. Not in his heart. He's a good person, and he needs our help."

"All right. Then hand it over."

She pulled the satchel closer.

"Listen, Paige, I can't have you or Julian getting caught up in this mess—"

"I'm already caught up in it." Tears glistened in her eyes. "Can't you see?"

"Sure I can. You love him. That's why you're going to do exactly as I say." I beckoned once with my hand. "Trust me. There's no way Enoch can avoid prison time for what he's done. But I'll do whatever I can to keep him alive. And I promise you I'll get to the bottom of this."

Something she found in my eyes caused her to nod slowly. Without breaking my gaze, she slid the satchel toward me.

"Be careful, Charlie," she said, relinquishing her grip on the bag. "There are dangerous people in this town."

She was right about that—and they were the ones in power. Telling Paige to enjoy the whiskey, I swiped my ID card over the scanner and swung her satchel over my shoulder. PAID flashed on the small table-mounted screen.

"It was on the house," Julian said as I approached the bar. "She's family. What's mine is hers."

"Then consider it a donation toward my own tab." I patted Paige's bag. "Is this it? No other backup file of that alley footage?"

He shook his head. "That's it. Cops took everything else."

"And I don't need to ask why you would've forwarded this video on to Enoch?"

"Who's Enoch?" He looked genuinely curious.

"Never mind." I turned to leave, but one more question elbowed its way to the front row of my thoughts. "The cops who took your surveillance equipment. Was it anybody in particular, or just flunkies in uniform?"

"Well..." Julian squinted up his good eye as he did his best to remember. "Sure, yeah, it was that cop you know."

"Douglass?"

He shook his head. "No, the other one. You guys don't really get along too well, from what I've seen." He chuckled quietly, seeming more like himself again. "That Serbian detective."

"Stankic."

"Yeah, that's the one. He confiscated everything. Looked like a fat rat who'd stumbled upon a storehouse of cheese, carrying it all out of here."

"Alone, eh?" Usually Stinkin' and Blinkin' were

inseparable.

Julian nodded. "In a hurry." He narrowed his eye at me. "Why, Charlie? You think he's dirty?"

"What cop isn't these days?"

He gave me a knowing look. "Stankic told me to call him if anybody came around asking about the murder. Gave me his card."

"How friendly."

"I tore it up and flushed it."

"Good man."

Saluting the barkeep, I kept a hand on the satchel and headed for the door. I glanced back at Paige and found her leaning on her elbows in the booth, staring at the tumbler she slid back and forth in its own sweat puddle. Whiskey sloshed in the glass, but she was in no hurry to drown her sorrows in the stuff. She looked lost. Didn't even seem to notice me leaving.

Love could do that—take your heart in a vice and squeeze the life out of it. Leave you a hollow shell, broken up on the inside where nobody could see the cracks. Or so I'd been told.

Love and me, we'd never hit it off. Sure, there were people I cared about, and I could name them off on one hand. But as far as there being somebody to have and to hold till death did we part? Never been that lucky. A cynic might have said romance was for suckers. I left that level of disenchantment for the unbelievers.

I squinted in the sunlight as I stepped outside. My eyes were unaccustomed to such celestial glory piercing our city's gray ceiling. It was more than welcome, but my eyesight would take some time to get used to it, fleeting as it was likely to be. Pausing a moment, I turned my face up toward the warmth and closed my eyes, knowing better than to think a few seconds would make a dent in my pale complexion. But that moment was a real respite, taking me back to the days when, as a kid, we had no idea what acid rain was or what the viscous stuff could do to the world as we knew it, collapsing the facades of both buildings and people alike.

"Mr. Madison."

I cracked open one eye to find two men standing before me. Like yours truly, they hadn't received the memo that it was going to be a sun-shiny day. They too wore hats and overcoats. But unlike me, they'd thought ahead and packed shades—the black, wraparound variety favored by yakuza muscle. They also sported the telltale tattoos, climbing up the sides of their necks and across the backs of their hands, that denoted their clan affiliation.

With the sun in my eyes, the ink work looked like twisting flames.

7

"That's me," I said, wondering why emissaries from the Fire Dragon clan were waiting outside Howard's Tavern. Had they heard I was sticking my nose where it didn't belong, asking about *tetsu no ken*?

"Someone wishes to speak with you." They parted to reveal a black hybrid sedan humming at the curb, gleaming under the sun like polished obsidian. The rear door slowly levitated without a sound, rotating on well-oiled hinges. At first glance, the backseat appeared vacant.

"Oh, I never get into cars with strangers." I kept one hand on the satchel and slipped the other into my suit jacket. Curling my fingers around that snub-nosed .38 always brought on a certain confidence boost.

"You will want to join this stranger," came the voice of Katsuo Sanitoro from inside the vehicle.

"Right." Ducking my head, I stepped past the two yakuza goons and climbed into the backseat. Sitting across from me was a well-built Japanese man in a tailored suit. He wore his long hair pulled back in a tight braid. The signs of his own yakuza affiliation were tattooed up the side of his neck—the fangs and maw of a roaring tiger—and he wore a pair of those slick wraparound shades to cover his eyes, even as he sat in the car's dark interior. "A little theatrical, don't you think? You could have just called me."

"You do not carry a phone," Sanitoro said.

I almost chuckled. People these days tended to have scant patience for folks who preferred living offline.

"I assume you're here to update me on the Fire Dragon situation. Speaking of—" I glanced back at the two men standing shoulder to shoulder outside my door, which had dropped silently back into place. "Aren't they—?"

"Yes, they are of House Fire Dragon. As a sign of good faith, they have accompanied me into the city." Sanitoro paused to watch traffic pass us by on the busy boulevard. "*Tetsu no ken* may have originated with their clan, but it was never their intention to associate with the Russians. One of their members has gone rogue. He is *ronin* now, without the protection of his clan."

"So he's the one selling that special sauce to Ivan."

Sanitoro shook his head slowly. "Sokolov. At the Arena."

"For the death duels."

"Such fights do not exist, as you well know. If they did, the Blackshirts would shut down Sokolov, and there is nothing the Russian Devil could do about it."

"Blackshirts would need proof. Maybe an insider." I'd never seen a death duel myself, only heard the rumors: that there were cyborgs in that basement boxing ring who tore their opponents apart to the roaring approval of their adoring fans—both in person and online.

"Are you volunteering for the job, Madison?"

"Me? Work with the Feds? Not on your life." After our illustrious United World government sent my squad to be butchered by mandroids on the frontlines, I vowed never to work for the UW ever again in any capacity. "So this renegade Fire Dragon—what do you plan to do about him?"

"End him, of course," Sanitoro replied as if he were

discussing the lunch menu at a local bistro.

"Of course." I scratched at my neck. "Well then, I won't keep you." I slid toward the door, expecting it to rise as it sensed my proximity. It didn't budge.

"I am told the cop-killer is hiding out in your office," Sanitoro said.

I hesitated, knowing better than to deny it. Word on the street was that Ivan the Terrible had eyes and ears everywhere. Safe to assume Katsuo Sanitoro wasn't one to be outmatched in that regard. But why was he keeping track of what went on in my office?

Sure, I might have been his favorite Anglo. Once upon a time, I'd done his family a favor, and they'd never forgotten it. As a token of their appreciation, they gave me a fancy silver watch with jade inlays and a radio transmitter. Gotta love Japanese technology. If ever I had need of Sanitoro, he'd be there to help me—whether or not I wanted him sticking his nose in my affairs.

"The cops are out for blood. His blood, to be exact," I said. "But I need him alive if I'm going to get to the bottom of this."

"*Tetsu no ken* is a dangerous steroid. It causes severe psychosis, blackouts, murderous rage."

"You're saying I should get back to my office."

"I am saying I will take you there."

Sanitoro's driver took us through traffic like a wasp with a singular target in sight, weaving around other cars like they were stationary obstacles to be passed. The two beefy Fire Dragons sat on either side of me, pinning me in the middle with every sudden shift to the right or left. By the time we reached my office building, I felt something like a tenderized protein.

Saluting Sanitoro, I climbed out of the car as the door rose upward and then dashed straight for the lift inside. As a rule, I usually took the stairs up to my office, but I didn't have the luxury today. I had to make sure Wanda was all right, that Enoch hadn't gone berserk on her in my absence.

I found him right where I'd left him.

"You all right, Charlie?" Wanda rose from behind her Underwood and approached me with a few lines of concern creasing her brow.

"Fine." I caught my breath as I shut the office door. Sure, I'd taken the elevator, but I'd also run down the hallway at full-tilt. Not something I did every day. "Just wanted to check on things here. Make sure you're all good."

"You could've called. If you carried a phone." She winked up at me.

Right. And Sanitoro could have let me borrow his, if I'd thought of calling Wanda instead of dashing straight to her desk in a frenzy.

I collected myself, restoring the calm, cool demeanor I was usually known for. Turning away from her, I pressed a button on my fancy watch and muttered into it, "All clear."

Had Sanitoro known I would react on gut-level instinct to protect Wanda? Had he wanted me to?

Maybe he figured I'd try to convince him not to kill the Fire Dragon renegade, otherwise—or request an opportunity to question the guy before Sanitoro's *katana* sliced off his head. As much as Sanitoro seemed to be my friend, maybe he didn't want an Anglo involved in yakuza affairs. Plain and simple as that. So he'd used Enoch's potential psychosis as a diversion.

And I'd played right along, like a chump.

"Our guest behaving himself?" I hung up my coat and hat on the free-standing rack.

She shrugged. "Not a peep. I heard him pacing around every few minutes, but other than that, he's been a perfect gentleman. Both kneecaps intact."

I winked at her.

"What's in the bag, boss?" She nodded toward Paige's satchel.

I opened the bag for the first time and withdrew the only item inside: an old-school videotape.

"I think I might've seen one of those before..." Wanda giggled. "In a museum."

I gave her half a grin and opened the door to my office. Enoch jumped out of my chair at once and strode toward me.

"Mr. Madison—!"

"Keep your shirt on, kid." I set the tape on my desk and held up the satchel. "Does this look familiar?"

He frowned, confused, and shook his head.

"Belongs to a sweet girl named Paige," I said. "Mouth like a sailor, spunk like you wouldn't believe."

"No, I..." He stared at the bag as though it was something from a former life.

"She wanted to show you this." I tapped the videotape. "Because she's worried about you. Hell, she might even love you. I've got a feeling she does."

"I don't know...anybody named Paige." He was wringing those hands again.

"Well, she seems to know you pretty well. Said she's seen you come home more than once with blood on your hands. Said you're not a janitor at all, though you might have started out that way." I paused, looking him over. "Did one of Ivan's lieutenants see promise in you? A guy named Yevgeni Sokolov by chance?"

No spark of recognition flared in Enoch's eyes. He looked just as bewildered as ever. "Is that a tape of...what I did?" He shook his head then and stared at the floor. "I can't really believe it happened anymore. The details are all fuzzy, like somebody's erasing the whole thing from my mind..."

Convenient.

"Paige says you sometimes don't remember her, that the two of you are involved. That you live together."

He blinked at me. His lips parted, but for a few moments there were no words exiting them.

"She's the girl," he said hoarsely.

"How's that?"

"There was a girl in my apartment yesterday. A brunette. Green eyes. Gorgeous."

"That would be Paige."

He cursed and ran both hands over his face. "I chased her out. Probably scared the hell out of her. Had no idea who she was or how she'd gotten into my place."

If Sanitoro was right about *tetsu no ken*, then Enoch's psychosis was going to get a whole lot worse. He was obviously suffering from memory lapses. I hadn't seen any signs of murderous rage yet, not even on the video footage from Howard's when he'd impaled Officer Bowman. If that stage of the drug's side effects came next, Wanda and I wouldn't be able to stop him—short of putting a few rounds in his knees. Maybe in his chest, to boot. But if he stopped doping—or getting doped against his will, if that's what was going on—wouldn't he eventually even out? Recover his lost memories?

"I don't know what's happening to me, Mr. Madison." There were tears in Enoch's eyes now. "Who's doing this to me? Why?"

I'd seen enough actors in my day to know this kid wasn't playing. He was honestly scared to death. He wasn't in control of himself, and he had no idea who was.

Neither did I, but I had a feeling I'd be going to the Coliseum next to squeeze some answers out of Yevgeni. Problem was, I didn't have a whole lot to go on. If Sanitoro killed off the Fire Dragon renegade, there wouldn't be any more *tetsu no ken* crossing the border. But Yevgeni might have already gotten one of his chemists in on it, attempting to replicate the supply he already had on hand. Assuming Sokolov was the guy on the receiving end. I had no proof at all, nothing solid to tie the Arena manager to this dangerous 'roid. And I had no real evidence that Enoch was even on the stuff.

"Charlie," Wanda's voice came through the intercom on my desk. "I've got Sergeant Douglass on the line. He says it's urgent."

"I've got to take this," I said. Before I shut my office door, I locked eyes with Enoch and gave him what I hoped was a reassuring nod. "Give me an hour. I'll have some answers for you."

He nodded mutely and sank back into my chair, the look in his eyes hopeful but unsure whether I'd be able to make good on my promise. Hell, I wondered that myself.

Reaching Wanda's desk, I slipped her phone over my ear. "What's up, Sarge?"

"No luck, lad. The guy—Enoch Wilson, that's his name—wasn't at the apartment. Must've cleared out. But we ransacked the place good and turned up a few details I figured you might like bein' privy to."

"As long as Stankic and Bellincioni don't mind."

"They can go take a flyin' leap, far as I'm concerned." He cursed under his breath. "They're out lookin' up the girlfriend, a woman named Paige Harris. Waitress over at Howard's Tavern—until yesterday. Coincidence? I think not."

I made a mental note to call Julian next, to warn Paige the cops had her in their sights.

"Wilson's parents—here's where it gets interesting. They're living in one of the priciest elder care facilities in town: Seven Oaks. And guess who's paying their monthly bills? That's right, their beloved son."

"On a janitor's salary?"

"So you've been doin' some digging of your own? Good. According to Wilson's records, he's bein' paid handsomely by one Yevgeni Sokolov." He paused. Of course, Douglass knew Sokolov and I were acquainted. "But it's no janitor salary. The guy makes more than I do! And after gettin' a good look at the dump Wilson calls home sweet home, it's clear what he's spending all his credits on."

"Mom and dad." I glanced back at the door to my office. A son looking out for his aging parents, providing the best housing and care money could buy. How could that be the same guy who'd plunged his fist through Officer Bowman? "How clear are those records, Sarge?"

"Black and white, Charlie. Bill statements. Wilson printed them out. Looks like he wanted everything organized, and at the front end of things, that's the case. But his life must have taken a turn for the worst recently. The place was already in shambles, and his records for the past few weeks are all out of order."

"Like somebody tossed the apartment before you arrived?"

"More like Wilson's gotten heavy into drugs or booze. It reminded me of a case from just a few months ago. A fellow diagnosed with a bipolar disorder. Half his place was all neat and tidy, and the other was a sty." Douglass paused on the line. "With that guy, there was a clear demarcation: east versus west. Maybe some kind of OCD thing. With Wilson, the line is just as clear. But we're talkin' about a timeline. Two weeks ago, his orderliness took a serious hit. That's when his meticulous records lose their coherence—unrelated papers and receipts stuffed into files willy-nilly. That's when he must have suffered some kind of serious psychotic break, I'm thinkin'."

Two weeks. That lined up with what Paige had told me about Enoch's bizarre behavior. "Papers in files? Kind of old-fashioned."

"You're one to talk." Douglass chuckled.

He had a tendency to organize his workload in obsolete ways as well. Unlike the desks of all his compatriots in the Precinct 37 bullpen, the desk of Sergeant Archibald Douglass was piled high with towers of manila file folders. These weren't cold cases. They were his current assignments, which he refused to trust to an unreliable computer. According to him, all it would take was another EMP strike by the Eastern

Conglomerate, and the Link would be out on its ass. Maybe I subscribed to the same idea.

"Why would he wait two weeks to kill somebody? And why Bowman?"

"I was hopin' you'd figure out that part, Charlie." Douglass heaved a sigh, and a gust of breath blasted into the receiver. "I went to Bowman's residence. Broke the bad news to his wife—his widow. Worst part of the job, I'm tellin' you. They always seem to know, as soon as they open the door. Truth is, they probably expect the bad news day in and day out. None of 'em would ever admit to it, but I'll wager there's some relief in knowin' they won't have to worry anymore. That their loved ones are in a better place."

"You really believe that?"

"Have to, Charlie. It keeps this life from seemin' like a pointless waste of time."

"Well, when you put it that way..."

My grandmother had always spoken of Heaven in the way a career office grunt talked about retirement. It was out there, this wonderful paradise, just beyond her grasp, but she'd get there someday. When I was a kid, she had me believing my parents were already there, waiting for me in a perfect world without pain, death, or sorrow.

As a kid, it was easier to believe. I hadn't been chewed up and spit out on the battlefield. Hadn't seen the horrors that humankind is capable of. Hadn't committed a few of them myself.

"Let me guess: Bowman and Enoch Wilson didn't know each other. The Mrs. had no idea why her husband would've been in that alley behind Howard's."

"Who interviewed her? You or me?" Douglass grunted

like he was shifting his girth in an uncomfortable chair. "No, she'd never heard Bowman mention Wilson. But she did shed a little light on the situation. Said her hubby had a weak bladder. Couldn't wait if the restroom was taken, even when the two of them went out together. Said it drove her nuts the way he'd sneak out back of a restaurant to piss behind the dumpster."

So that mystery was solved—somewhat. "Wrong place, wrong time?"

"Looks like it to me. Wilson finally snaps, and Bowman's there to take the brunt of his psychosis."

I shook my head. "Still doesn't explain his ability to impale the guy with his fist. According to Cauliflower Carl, that shouldn't be possible. Even if he was on the most powerful performance enhancer preferred by your local 'roid-rager. A man's hand wouldn't survive that kind of impact." Yet Enoch's was completely intact, by all appearances.

"So we're lookin' for a guy with a busted hand." Douglass cursed. "I want Wilson brought to justice—and not in a body bag. We've gotta find out how he was able to do what he did—and if we're goin' to see any more cases like this in the near future. If there's some new 'roid on the street, we need to know about it before Ivan starts injecting it into all of his hired muscle!"

I decided to tell him what I'd learned about *tetsu no ken* and the Fire Dragon renegade, as well as Sanitoro's offhanded remark that the *ronin* would be killed.

"I still don't know what you see in that Sanitoro fellow, Charlie. He's no better than the Russians. Thugs are thugs."

"He owes me." Or he seemed to think he did. "And when

you're up against Ivan the Terrible in a city like this, it pays to have someone equally dangerous on your side."

"Someday you're gonna tell me why you and Sanitoro are so friendly."

"Maybe. If there's nothing better to do." I reached for the phone, slipping it off my ear. "I'll check in with you later, Sarge. Give me an hour."

I handed Wanda her phone and grabbed my coat and hat. Sure, the sun was shining now, but I had a feeling the light of day was about to darken a bit.

"Where you off to, Charlie?"

"Guess." I gave her a wink, knowing she'd been eavesdropping on my conversation with Douglass.

"Sokolov?"

"About time, don't you think?"

"Charlie, you can't go in there alone."

"You volunteering to come along?"

She shook her head. "Can't. I'm babysitting for somebody."

"You be careful." I nodded toward my closed office door. "If he starts going bonkers, you get the hell out of here."

"What happened to *shoot his kneecaps*?"

"They're not the priority. You are." I looked her in the eye. "Stay safe."

She nodded. Swallowed. Serious now. "You too, Charlie."

8

With Enoch's financial records in the hands of Sergeant Douglass, I had what I needed to put the squeeze on Yevgeni Sokolov. I had no proof that he was doping his fighters with *tetsu no ken*, and word on the street about his death duels was only hearsay, but I did have a solid connection between him and Enoch Wilson.

Yevgeni was signing Enoch's paychecks, and they weren't for janitorial work.

I hailed a cab out in front of my building, and I was in luck. It happened to be one of the newer models with a phone/vidLink combo. Swiping my ID card across the pay scanner, I told the driver where to take me.

"Coliseum, eh?" He raised his bushy grizzled eyebrows in the rearview mirror. A pudgy Saudi, he didn't look or smell like he'd left his seat for the past twenty-four hours. "You got connections?"

"You could say that." I punched in Julian's number and picked up the receiver, deciding to forego a face-to-face. The dial tone pulsed a full ten seconds before the barkeeper answered.

"Howard's Tavern. Sorry we're closed—"

Damned recording. I slammed the receiver home.

"Hey—careful with the merchandise, mister!" the driver barked.

I debated having him take me back to Howard's. But

Paige was a big girl. She could take care of herself and then some. Would she tell the cops she'd sent Enoch to see me? That would go over real well.

I had a feeling she'd keep that under her hat. Like most of our fair city's populace, she knew better than to trust the police. If she really wanted me to help Enoch, she would send detectives Stinkin' and Blinkin' in the opposite direction, as far off-track as possible.

She hadn't sent the footage to Enoch. Couldn't have, according to her. But she'd told him about me—obviously before he'd forgotten who she was and chased her out of their apartment. What was going on in his mind? What was that drug doing to him? Assuming he was messed up by *tetsu no ken*, what had it done to his fist to make it withstand the trauma of breaking through a man's chest?

"Let me off here," I said, glancing out the window at the busy intersection.

"What? We ain't even close!"

To the Coliseum? No, we weren't. This was the nicer end of town, the coastal west side, and I'd caught sight of Seven Oaks Nursing Home in the distance. The leafy trees and manicured lawns were a stark green contrast to the urban concrete and plasteel surrounding it. Not that all the foliage was genuine or anything; the real deal wouldn't survive more than a few hours under acid rains. But the artificial life made the place look inviting, and it settled the nerves of its residents: the aging, those on their way out who remembered what this world was like before air purifiers and oxygen generators. Back when trees lined the streets and rustled in the breeze.

Grumbling to himself, the cabbie pulled to the curb,

cutting off two lanes of traffic in the process. He flipped off the half dozen or so motorists he'd offended as I stepped out and slammed the door shut behind me. Leaving the cab to burn rubber as it rejoined the lunch rush, I pressed a button on my fancy watch and waited for the miniscule red light to blink.

"You find your *ronin* yet?" I said.

"He is not your concern, Madison," came Sanitoro's voice, as clear as it would have been on a solid phone connection. But this was a private radio frequency, completely outside the bounds of the Link and impossible to hack. Japanese technology at its best.

"If he gives you the name of his Russian contact, I'd be most interested."

"He is no longer able to speak."

Losing one's head tended to put a real damper on one's conversation skills. "What was his name, if you don't mind me asking?"

Silence. The red light was still blinking, so Sanitoro was still there. But he wasn't saying anything. Had I overstepped?

"Hiroki Nakano," he said at length. Then the light stopped blinking. Over and out.

Sure, it would have been better if I'd had the opportunity to question Nakano and find out more about *tetsu no ken*, but I was smart enough to know where I stood with Katsuo Sanitoro. When it was a yakuza matter, always best that I minded my own business. We were something like friends, Sanitoro and I, but I knew better than to press my luck.

I let the cuff of my trench coat drop over the watch face and continued my leisurely stroll toward the Seven Oaks entrance. The winding path had an uncanny calming effect on me. I knew I'd never be able to afford such a place once I reached senior citizenship and could no longer care for myself. If my luck held out, I'd remain healthy to my dying day and end up passing away in my sleep. Or my luck would eventually run out, and some scumbag with a grudge would take me out when I least expected it—some weak moment when my private eye radar wasn't fully functioning. Truth be told, resorts like Seven Oaks were for aging relatives of local politicians and celebrities, not to mention those same politicians and celebrities after they aged out. Not your local lowly gumshoe.

A matronly nurse at the front desk smiled as I stepped inside and the automatic glass doors slid shut behind me with a whisper of air. The place smelled like home. Not like chemicals or human waste, as the city institutions usually reeked. This place was filled with the aroma of fresh-baked apple pie, and my mind was instantly assaulted with images of roaring fireplaces and thick, soft blankets, and reading into the wee hours, enraptured by a good book.

Something in the air? Most likely. The neuro-chemicals mixed in with the O_2 ensured that residents would enjoy what the nursing home promised in all of its brochures: Seven Oaks was a quiet, peaceful place to rest on your way out of this life.

"May I help you?" The middle-aged nurse smiled up at me as I approached her desk. She was the only one on duty, but a formidable presence. Shoulders like a linebacker underneath those crisp white scrubs.

"I'm with the Journal," I lied with a charming wink, fishing through the pockets of my coat for my ID card, which I flashed briefly. I tended to do better with it when folks didn't get a prolonged view. For one thing, the guy in the photo wasn't me. It had belonged to a Mr. Richard Jenkins, once upon a time. Poor guy had fallen asleep in a public bathroom just when I'd been in need of an alias. Fate? I liked to think so. "We're doing a piece on elder care in the city. Of course Seven Oaks was at the top of our list."

She smiled warmly and dipped her chin with what appeared to be sincere modesty. "We do have quite the reputation. But I'm afraid Mrs. Anderson is out at the moment."

Anderson. Right. The administrator. I glanced at the nurse's name tag. "Actually, I'm going for more of a human interest story, Janice. I'd like to share with the public what your residents think of Seven Oaks. Straight from the horse's mouth, if you will."

Her eyebrows knitted together slightly. "I see. Well, most of our guests are currently being served lunch in the dining hall. You've caught us at a very quiet time."

"Of course." I leaned toward her. "Any married couples on the guest list?"

"How's that?" Her eyebrows rose.

"With the piece I'm doing, I'd like to focus on the *till death do we part* angle."

"Angle?"

"Sure. Listen, everybody knows what a solid reputation you've got here. Highest level of care in the city and all that. But what our readers would really get a kick out of is a story about a couple mated for life. Know what I mean? Spending their last years together in peace and harmony." I nearly gagged on my own saccharine tone, but I kept the façade going strong.

"Some have only months left." She nodded pensively. "I suppose there wouldn't be anything wrong with introducing you to a few of our couples. They do so enjoy having visitors. But I wouldn't mention you're with the press. That might make some of them nervous. And with Mrs. Anderson out, I wouldn't want any sort of disturbance—"

"Neither would I. If I notice any of them getting agitated even in the slightest, I'll be out of your hair." I graced her with another winning smile. An old girlfriend once told me I had a grin disarming enough to charm a rattlesnake. She might have exaggerated some.

"Of course. I'm sure nothing of the sort will occur. You seem like a very nice man, wanting to write such a story. And for the *Journal*, no less." She beamed. "I'll say this for the EMP bombardment from those E.C. bastards—pardon my language."

"No worries. They really are bastards."

"It certainly brought back the good ol' black, white, and read all over!" She giggled at her little newspaper humor, gesturing for me to follow her as she rounded the corner of her desk and waddled down the wide hallway—gleaming linoleum with a few abandoned wheelchairs parked sporadically along each side.

"Even with the Link, our circulation hasn't taken much of a hit." My long strides kept pace with her quick-footed gait.

"Back when we lost the Internet, everyone thought that would be the end of it all. Technology, that is. I for one said good riddance to all those smart-phones and e-readers, silly time-wasting gadgets and gizmos. I've always been a fan of the written word on the printed page. Call me old-fashioned, but that's the only way to read."

"As a card-carrying reporter for the Journal, I thank you for your patronage." I half-bowed as I walked, which earned me another fit of giggles from the kindly nurse.

"Mr. Jenkins, you certainly have a way with words!"

She led me into the dining hall where groups of residents in a variety of robes—each suited to his or her particular taste, whether that be flannel or fleece—sat at lunch, clustered five or six to a table.

"No loners?" I said.

"We encourage them to socialize during their mealtimes. They can sit in their rooms all day long if they like, but when they eat, they need to interact."

I noticed a few tables toward the edge of the room where couples had gravitated, two to a table, speaking quietly to each other as they ate. One pair in particular drew my attention—the only couple who shared Enoch Wilson's darker skin tone.

"What's their story?"

"The Wilsons?"

Bingo.

"Oh, they're a delightful couple," she doted. "You'll want to speak with them first."

As a matter of fact, I did. "Have they been here long?"

"Just a few weeks, actually. They love Seven Oaks."

"Where were they staying before?"

"At home." She beckoned me to follow as she navigated a course around the backs of chairs and smiled at the residents she passed, patting them on the shoulder. Some smiled back as they munched on what looked like potato salad. Others were in their own little worlds, staring into deep space. "Their son brought them in, said they were having difficulty taking care of themselves. Accidents, you know. Mr. Wilson had already slipped and broken his hip, and his son paid for his hip replacement—can you believe that? Such a fine young man—" She stopped herself, glancing back at me. "Listen to me go on. I know you're not interviewing *me*!"

"That's quite all right." More than. She'd already corroborated the fact that Enoch was covering his parents' medical bills. "So he's paying their rent, so to speak? The son?"

She dipped her chin bashfully. "Well, I'm sure Mrs. Anderson wouldn't want me sharing something like that. Privacy concerns, you know. But I really don't see the harm. They're such a nice family, the three of them. So much love for each other. I mean, look at them." She halted a few meters away from the Wilsons' table. "Married fifty-odd years, and they still have something to talk about!"

"That's the stuff." I nodded.

She beamed up at me. "Seven Oaks is such a wonderful place, Mr. Jenkins. I wish every senior citizen in the city could afford to be cared for here."

"No, you don't."

Her eyebrows did that knitting thing again.

"Then this place would be just as overcrowded as the city hospice."

"Oh, I suppose you're right." Her smile faded, and she gestured for me to follow as she approached the Wilsons' table.

She introduced me as a fine young man, a reporter for the Journal named Mr. Jenkins. Incorrect on all counts, but that didn't matter. The Wilsons grinned up at me and welcomed me to their table. Mr. Wilson offered some of his potato salad while Mrs. Wilson asked about the Journal's circulation these days. I did my best at declining and deflecting while Nurse Janice excused herself, returning to her abandoned station.

"I'm actually a friend of your son," I said, once she was out of earshot.

"Oh?" Mrs. Wilson raised her eyebrows.

Her husband glanced at her, then returned his attention to me, wiping his mouth with a cloth napkin. "Is Enoch all right?"

"He's working hard, just wanted me to check on you. Make sure everything's going well over here."

"Of course it is." Mr. Wilson scoffed, shaking his head. "How could it not be? We've never had it so good. Enoch, he's makin' real money now. Makin' a name for himself in this godforsaken town. That's what he's doin'."

"We never dreamed of living in such a fine place, Mr. Jenkins," Mrs. Wilson said with a warm smile.

"Only the chosen few do." I gave her a wink.

"So you work with Enoch, you say?" Mr. Wilson was testing me. Sharp old codger. Nurse Janice had said I worked for the Journal. No way Enoch would have told them he did the same; no way he'd be raking in a fortune working for any periodical, online or otherwise.

"Just friends," I said. "I've never seen him so busy—"

"It's the economy." Mrs. Wilson nodded grimly. "Even inventors have to work double shifts to stay out of the red."

"*Investors*, Mother," Mr. Wilson gently corrected her. "Our Enoch's no inventor."

"Of course not!" She chuckled. "Is that what I said?"

I smiled at them both and figured it was time to bid

farewell for now.

"But you only just got here!" Mr. Wilson exclaimed. "What about this article you're writing for the Journal?"

Right. That. "I'd like to interview you both—at a later time, if you'd be amenable to it. This was an introductory visit. Next time, I'll do better at scheduling. Won't be during your midday meal."

"You stop by anytime now, Mr. Jenkins," Mrs. Wilson said, taking my hand in both of hers. They were warm and soft, covered in wrinkles like parchment. Like my grandmother's, God rest her soul. "Any friend of Enoch's is a friend of the family. We'll be right glad to have you back."

"You tell Enoch to keep his nose clean." Mr. Wilson shook my hand with a strong grip as I rose. "And remind 'im to stop by himself too. Been more than a week since we seen 'im last."

"Will do." With a nod and another friendly smile, Mr. Jenkins the local journalist excused himself and took an alternate route to the nearest exit, hoping to bypass Nurse Janice.

My small talk reservoir was all but depleted.

9

By the time I exited Seven Oaks and made it back to the street, the sun had already vanished behind a bank of expanding cold steel clouds. There would be more rain within the hour, and the sidewalks would clear. Not that I found myself overwhelmed by foot traffic at the moment. As it was, mine were the only pair of shoes hoofing it down that particular block.

I remained on my own until twenty minutes later, when I passed a narrow alley between two high-risers. That's when the short hairs on the back of my neck pricked upward, standing at attention. My own innate radar system: I'd picked up a tail.

And from the smell of things, I had a good hunch who it was.

"Thought you'd be over at Howard's, badgering the clientele." I turned on my heel to face detective Stankic.

The man looked even worse in dreary daylight than he had last night. Sallow and obese, he drew on a stump of cigar and squinted at me like his surroundings were too bright for him. His kind fared better in the shadows where stained, rumpled attire and corpse-like flesh were easier to hide.

"Where you headed, Madison?"

"No place special. Beautiful day—at least it was. Figured I'd take a walk."

"Guess I'll join you then." He shuffled alongside me like a

hippo crammed into a cheap suit.

I thrust both hands into my coat pockets and remained where I stood. "Lose your wheels?"

"My partner." He shrugged, spewing smoke as his flat feet came to a halt.

"You two get into another fight?"

"Difference of opinion. She's at Howard's. I'm here."

"Stalking me."

"Had no idea you'd be out this way." He picked at his bulbous nose. Not a habit he would have mastered in finishing school. "Going to the Coliseum, I take it?"

"Nothing escapes you, Detective."

"The Arena, maybe catch a fight?" He chuckled quietly, and it sounded like he was gargling gravel. "They've got a good lunch special going today."

"You must be a regular."

"Not really. Day fighters are like daytime strippers. Not the choicest meat, but they can be mildly entertaining. C'mon." He shuffled ahead, beckoning me to follow with haggard effort. "We could both use a break."

Why this sudden congeniality? As a rule, Stinkin' was never anything more or less than belligerent, yet now he was inviting me to join him for lunch. It didn't take a crack private eye to tell when a picture was hanging askew. The man wanted something. Or he knew something.

Either way, I figured it was in my best interest to play along. I could be congenial enough when the situation called for it. And besides, Stinkin's change in behavior had my curiosity piqued.

Curiosity had killed all the cats, according to public opinion. More likely, it was the acid rain. Either way, a detective's curiosity can be just as dangerous. Sure, asking *why* can lead to solved cases more often than not. But it can also get you into a heap of trouble.

Maybe Stankic was in Ivan's pocket. Maybe he knew Enoch Wilson was hiding out in my office. Maybe he was waiting to ambush me. The way he'd been lurking in that alley should have been a big clue. I could have played it safe, told him to take a flying leap. But I didn't.

And that made all the difference.

"Mr. Stankic," greeted one of the two gladiator-sized Russians standing guard out front of the Coliseum, a giant edifice modeled after its Roman namesake where Christians and other undesirables were torn apart for the amusement of the masses. Clad in extra-extra-large tuxedos, the glorified bouncers stood on either side of the massive front doors under a regal purple canopy that extended out to the sidewalk.

Ivan's security was tighter than the Prime Minister's, and these two were just the icing on the cake.

"Hey boys," said Stinkin' as he shambled across the strip of spotless red carpet beneath the canopy. He jerked his head my way. "The dick's with me."

The muscle in monkey suits nodded politely and heaved open the doors, one standing off to the right and the other to the left. It wasn't that Ivan couldn't afford to install automatic doors. These two oversized gentlemen decided who got in and who didn't. And thanks to Detective Stinkin's influence with the hired help, I was getting inside without a hitch.

I'd seen plenty of casinos back when I was younger and prettier, in the days when I'd had a little extra money to burn. But none of those places held a candle to the Coliseum—an expanse of plush, red-carpeted, gold-inlaid opulence filled to the brim with folks from every walk of life. They huddled around games of dice, cards, and chips, while half-naked dames sauntered about selling cigarettes from trays slung below their gilded bosoms. The place had real class; too bad it was owned and operated by such a soulless tyrant.

A full stage showcased the big band providing a musical backdrop loud enough to keep anybody from thinking straight about their personal finances. Bad economy these days? Sure as hell not in here. This was where the rich got richer off each other, the last bastion of excess in a crumbling city. In the old days, these people would have partied all night and slept away the mornings. Not anymore.

This was the only place they could pretend times hadn't changed.

"This way," said Stinkin', leading me through a haze of cigar smoke. We passed tables with stakes as high as a million credits, open only to high-roller types: the ones who'd made a killing off the weapons trade during the war. "Been here before, Madison?"

"Once or twice."

"How'd that go?"

"Might've lost my shirt."

Stankic chuckled, and it sounded just as disgusting as before. He led the way out of the chaos of the casino and into a quieter hallway lined with elevators. He made his way straight to the second one on the left, even though there didn't seem to be any particular reason to pick that one. Nobody else was waiting around to use any of the lifts, and they all appeared to be ready and waiting on our level.

The mirrored doors slid open with a well-oiled whisper, and Stinkin' dragged his feet inside, one at a time. I followed.

"You really seem to know your way around," I said as he pressed BASEMENT LEVEL on the touchscreen.

"I've lost my share of shirts." He gave me a knowing wink. I hoped to God I'd never have to see that expression on him again. Made me feel a bit like a two-credit floozy. "But I ain't a full-time loser."

"Of course not. That would be too much work."

He muttered something unintelligible under his breath. I couldn't tell if he was belching or cursing me quietly. After descending over a dozen levels into the ground, a ding sounded and the doors slid open to reveal the yawning mouth of a dark hallway. Minimal lighting. Not inviting.

I didn't move to exit the lift. Neither did he.

"Almost there." Stankic tapped BASEMENT LEVEL again, and the doors slid shut. We continued to descend. This time, the touchscreen didn't keep track of the floors.

"Don't tell me you have your own secret lair down here." Only one thought ran through my mind: I was glad those goons out front hadn't frisked me. My Smith & Wesson .38 sat in its shoulder holster, right where it belonged.

"You think I'd still be working as a cop if that were the case?" He guffawed. "Hey, I've laid some good bets, don't get me wrong. But I ain't livin' in the lap of luxury or nothin'."

He watched me close for a few moments, probably hoping to see me squirm a little. He'd have to wait a whole lot longer to see any signs of fear creep into my body language. Was I a little tense? Sure. Anything could have been waiting for us so deep under Ivan the Terrible's base of operations. But I'd escaped enough horrors in the war to keep a solid poker face when necessary.

"We're heading down to the Arena, Madison."

Of course we were. "Time for a lunch hour death duel?"

He snorted. "Right. That's why you're a private dick. Can't tell rumor from reality." He shook his head at me in disdain, showing his true colors. I had a feeling his congenial façade would disintegrate completely, given time. "You'll see for yourself. Might want to check any of your moral proclivities at the door, though. Trust me when I say you've never seen anything like this."

He was right about that. The fights Ivan's TV station tended to broadcast were the fit-for-public-consumption variety, filmed at one of three main rings upstairs, adjacent to the casino. Sure, the boxers were shot full of 'roids and often beat each other nearly to death, but there weren't any actual fatalities. Not onscreen, anyway. Federal restrictions keep such fare from the mainstream viewing public. Paid viewing sites were all over the Link, from what I'd been told, but the Arena's fights were never shown there. Nor anywhere else. To see an Arena fight, you had to be there in the flesh.

It was special that way. Secretive. And so the rumors had circulated about death duels—fights to the death witnessed by our city's fattest cats, men and women who'd made a killing (literally) on arms deals during the war.

How did Stankic fit in with that bunch? No idea. Far as I knew, city cops didn't make squat, which was why so many of them were tempted by Ivan's deep pockets. But once the Russian Devil had you on his payroll, you belonged to him. He owned your soul, and you'd never get it back until he killed you—or you died of what appeared to be natural causes.

"After you," Stinkin' said as the elevator doors slid open.

Unlike the previous basement level, this one wasn't dark and lifeless. Jittery fluorescents washed the concrete in a sickly white, devoid of any natural hues. No windows down here, no warm incandescents. I stepped out into the narrow hallway and glanced both ways.

"Left or right?"

"Follow the grunts, Madison."

Echoing faintly from somewhere down the left end of the hallway, I heard what sounded like clanking noises, metal striking metal, along with human groans and an audience vacillating between cheers and jeers. As we headed closer to the point of origin, the artificial light grew stronger and the sounds louder.

A bell clanged, signaling the end of the third round as we stepped into the top tier of the Arena. In the ring, two fighters took a breather, seated on stools in opposite corners. Glaring at each other as their lungs expanded and retracted.

The subterranean boxing ring was packed wall to wall with people. Private boxes above held revelers sporting all manner of glitz and glamor, and the seats below carried the same species. But those who preferred to sit were few and far between. Most were on their feet with a drink in one hand and something smoldering in the other: cigars, cigarettes, joints. A murky haze hung from the ceiling like a cloud of secrecy.

"Real life of the party," I said, turning toward Stankic so he'd hear me over the noise of the wealthy rabble. "Don't these people know what time it is?"

"Always party time at the Coliseum, Madison. Some of

these schmucks probably haven't been outside for weeks." He jerked his head for me to follow as he lumbered down the steps toward one of the back rows.

Season ticket holder? I was seeing a whole new side of ol' Detective Stinkin'.

"What's your name, Handsome?" said a middle-aged woman showing off a well-maintained body in a tight gold-sequined dress. "Where you going?" She latched onto my arm as I passed her seat, pulling me around to face her. "The party's right here!"

"I'm sure it is, ma'am." I took off my hat and nodded to her escort, a tall graying fellow who seemed oblivious to her inebriated demands for attention. "But you see, my acquaintance has seats farther down the aisle, and it might be rude to ditch him."

"*Acquaintance*, huh?" She frowned at Stankic's elephantine backside as he struggled to sidle down the row to the far end. "That sack of crap?" She lowered her voice conspiratorially, her breath heavy with gin. "You know he's a cop, right?"

"Not a very good one," I confided.

She laughed out loud and gave me a shove in Stinkin's direction. "Go on, get out of here. Fourth round's about to start."

I gave her half a smile and followed Stankic.

"What was that all about?" he grumbled, leaving the stadium seat behind him untouched. No room for his girth, so he'd be standing regardless. "You in the market for a sugar momma?"

"Did yours retire?"

He cursed and nodded toward the ring. "What did I tell

you?"

I don't know what I was expecting, exactly. Maybe blood and guts, teeth flying beyond the first five rows. Behind Howard's Tavern, I'd made an offhanded comment to Detective Bellincioni about a potential cyborg killer, and she'd nearly torn my face off. I knew full well that plenty of veterans didn't return home in one piece. Most found work as machinists in the factory district. These two had decided to duke it out in the Arena during their lunch break.

Both men looked to be around my height—two meters or so—and well-built, the muscles in their shoulders and biceps straining as they hurled their prosthetic fists at each other. Each boxer wore a helmet and breastplate, making them look more like ancient gladiators than the throwbacks to 20th century fighters Ivan usually televised. The faux-leather loincloths added authenticity to the whole bizarre display before us.

"It's a little weird." I caught sight of Yevgeni Sokolov boozing it up in his private box with half a dozen other Russian locals. Men in tuxedos served by a rail-thin blonde carrying a platter of martinis. "So, this is a death duel."

"Only nobody dies. Not usually, anyway." Stankic guffawed, then groaned as one of the cyborgs planted his mechanized fist into his opponent's face. The helmet absorbed most of the blow, but the guy staggered back, dented and bleeding out of both nostrils. "He'll stay on his feet if he knows what's good for 'im."

"Got some money riding on that one?"

"None of your business." He kept his bloodshot gaze riveted on the ring. "You hungry?" He fished into his back pocket and tugged out an overweight wallet. "The fried rat here is to die for."

"As tempting as that sounds..." I winced at a sudden flurry of clanking. The fighter with the dented helmet was returning with a storm of body blows intended to weaken his opponent. Problem was, the other guy looked adept at fending off every hit, meeting metal with metal. Sparks flew, and the crowd went wild.

"You know where Enoch Wilson is."

I kept my face straight as my stomach turned over. Having Stinkin' whisper in my ear wasn't something I'd wish on my worst enemy. He smelled bad from a distance. It was even worse up close and personal. Imagine the sweet smell of a dead cat smothered in onions and garlic, and you might get the idea.

"Enoch who?"

"Go ahead. Play dumb, Madison. It's what you do best. Hell, maybe it ain't even an act. Maybe you were born that way." Stankic leaned away, his eyes never losing their focus on the fight below. "You're interfering with a police investigation, you know that. And if Douglass is in on it, you're endangering his sorry career along with your own. Maybe if you're lucky, you'll both share a cell over at the Twin Towers."

"I should've known this was too good to be true."

"What's that?"

"You and me enjoying an afternoon together like this. It's something I've always wanted, but I've never known how to go about it. Would've felt kind of awkward asking you out."

"You know where he is or don't you?" Stankic faced me now, his pallid skin flushing violently. "I could drag you into the station, Madison. You want that? Spend the night behind bars?"

That wouldn't work at all. I'd promised Enoch I would have things sorted out within the hour. Sokolov was right up there, surrounded by his cronies. I just had to figure out how to get to him—alone.

"Listen, Detective, this has been a heap of fun, but—"

Stinkin's phone warbled loud enough to hear over the uproar around us. I glanced down at the boxing ring. Player 1 had Player 2 (crumpled helmet and bloody nose) against the ropes, and he was delivering a payload of hurt. Uppercuts sent Player 2's head jerking back. Hits to the ribs dented his breastplate. Stankic must have had his money on the guy doling out the punishment; he didn't seem concerned as he answered the call, slipping the phone over his ear.

"Yeah? I'm having lunch, for crying out loud." A short pause. "Another one?" A string of curses. "Yeah, all right. I'll be right over." He tucked the phone into his pocket and turned toward me, jabbing a thick finger into my chest. "Your friend Enoch killed another cop."

"Sorry to hear that." I shrugged. "But like I said. Don't know the guy."

He did his best to stare me down with his nostrils flared like a raging bull. Then he shoved me aside. "Get outta my way." He stormed down the row, knocking into well-dressed spectators right and left.

"Like I said!" called out the woman who'd caught my attention earlier. She nodded toward Stankic's retreat as he exited the Arena. "A real sack of crap!"

Couldn't argue with that. I gave her a full smile and held her gaze as I sidled her way.

"Change your mind?" She took my arm and leaned into

me as soon as I was in range.

"All by myself now."

She stuck out her plump lower lip. "So I'm second fiddle."

"I wouldn't say that."

She perked up again, gasping as Player 2 started to fight back. There was no clinching with these guys. Maybe their prosthetic forearms and hands wouldn't allow it. Go try and hang onto your opponent, and you end up taking off his head by accident.

"Say, you know where I can find a payphone around here?" I said.

She looked up at me in astonishment, auburn eyes rimmed in mascara failing to blink. "What are you, like a hundred years old?"

"I carry my age well, don't I?"

"Yeah, I'd say." She snickered, releasing my arm and dipping two fingers into her pronounced cleavage. "Here, take mine." She handed me her phone as she took another sip from her half-empty martini glass.

"Thanks." I half-turned away from her as I slipped the device over my ear. As soon as the thing made contact, I subvocalized the number to my office.

"Charlie!" Wanda picked up after the first warble. "Damn it Charlie, I sure wish you'd carry a phone!"

"We've been over this—"

"He's gone. Flown the coop. I don't have a clue where he went, but he sure made a mess of the place."

"Our...guest?"

"Who else?" She paused. "Where the heck are you? Sounds like you're at a ball game."

"Something like that." I glanced back at my benefactor

and gave her a wink. She toasted me with her glass and downed another swallow, attempting to smile seductively the whole time. Wasn't easy, but she almost pulled it off. Caught a dribble from the corner of her mouth with the back of her hand and licked it off. Watching me watch her. "I think it's time to bring in Douglass."

"He's not going to be happy about this," Wanda said.

No. He wouldn't be happy at all that I'd kept it from him—Enoch lying low in my office. If Stankic was right that Enoch had killed another cop the same way he'd slain Bowman, then Douglass was likely to blow his top.

"Did he come after you?" I spoke low, shielding my mouth with one hand, hoping to cut out some of the ambient noise. "Are you all right?"

"I'm fine, Charlie," Wanda said. "But you're not gonna like it. Your office is in shambles. Looks like he threw a temper tantrum in there before he plowed through the wall."

"How's that?"

"Didn't even bother opening the window. Would've been easier, don't you think? Nope, he punched right through the wall and took the fire escape down."

First time for everything. "Did he say anything?"

"Not in words, but he sure sounded like he was in a whole lot of pain. I pulled out my gun and aimed it at the door, waiting for him to come bursting through like some kind of monster in a rage. But by the time I got to that big hole in the wall and peeked out, he'd already hit the streets below, out of sight." She paused to laugh quietly, but without much humor. "The guy's a real superhuman."

"He may have killed again."

"Another cop?"

"Yeah." A pattern was emerging. "Get Douglass on the line."

"Sure thing, Charlie."

My lady in waiting nudged me with her hip, swaying side to side with a goofy grin on her face. I held up my index finger. She clucked her tongue and returned her gaze to the fifth round below.

"You don't want to keep me waiting, buster," she said.

I glanced at her escort. Husband? Boyfriend? Martini half-finished in one hand, smoking half a cigar, he completely ignored her shenanigans. I wondered what it would take for him to notice her flirting. I hoped I wouldn't find out.

"Charlie—was just about to call you," Douglass said as he came on the line. "We've got another one, sorry to say. Impaled straight through the chest, same as Bowman."

"Fresh kill?"

"How's that? Can hardly hear you, lad. Sounds like you're at a football game."

"If only, Sarge." I cupped both hands over my mouth like I had the plague. The woman beside me raised an eyebrow at me. I shrugged at her. For some reason, that made her smile. "Time of death?"

"Close to midnight."

The same as Bowman. "Also a cop?"

"Give the man a gold medal," Douglass said without humor. "You guessed it, Charlie. Another good one, he was. It's like he's targeting them, this Wilson fellow."

"Or somebody's using him to do their dirty work."

"Aye, the thought had crossed my mind. That video—the guy looks like he's sleepwalkin'. Like his brain's stuck in second gear."

"Like he's drugged." I watched the two men in the ring and wondered what their faces looked like beneath those helmets. Had they each been given a shot of *tetsu no ken*? Doubtful. Neither one had punched through his opponent—yet. "Listen, Sarge. I've got to tell you something."

"Did you talk with Wilson's parents? I'd like to know how their son is paying—"

"He came to me for help."

"Wilson? You know where he is?" Douglass didn't sound happy. No surprise there.

"I can't tell you everything right now, but trust me on this. Yevgeni Sokolov. I've got a feeling he's your man."

Silence. I wondered if the woman's phone had died, but then I heard Douglass clear his throat. "Ivan's lieutenant," he said at length.

"Yeah." I watched Sokolov through the glass window of his box. Those guys in there hadn't stopped laughing and joking around from the time I'd arrived. They barely paid any attention to the fight. "I think he's trying out a new 'roid on Wilson, one manufactured by the Fire Dragons."

"Yakuza scum," Douglass muttered.

"One of them, a Hiroki Nakano, was bringing the stuff across the border from Little Tokyo. It's called *tetsu no ken*."

"My Japanese is a little rusty, lad."

"Means *fist of iron*, Sarge. The stuff is supposed to increase bone density, dull pain receptors, speed up tissue recovery." So Carl had told me. "The perfect 'roid for a fighter. I have a feeling Sokolov's been doping Wilson with the stuff. That's how he was able to kill Bowman. Maybe that other cop as well."

Douglass cursed under his breath. "Still doesn't explain the *why*."

"Working on it."

"And nothing explains why you've been keepin' me in the dark. You had Wilson in your damned office, and you didn't even contact me?" I'd never heard him so irate. No, I take it back. He'd been furious at plenty of other miscreants before, just not me.

"He's a cop-killer. Soon as he's brought in, he's dead meat. I figured you wanted me to get to the bottom of this. I needed him alive."

Douglass sighed begrudgingly. "All right. Fine." It wasn't. But he knew I was right. "Where is he now?"

"Time's up!" The woman snatched the phone off my ear, severing the connection. She dangled it in midair before stuffing it down between her breasts. "Come here, you." She linked arms with me, pulling me close. "You're not going anywhere, mister."

10

The wording may have been sinister coming from another pair of lips, but she just wanted to have a good time, by all appearances. So for the moment, I played along, keeping an eye on Sokolov.

Two cops dead, killed the same way. Good cops—Douglass had vouched for them both. And as one of the last honest policemen in the city, his word was golden as far as I was concerned.

According to Wanda, Enoch had left my office in agony. What was that all about? He'd seemed like a nervous wreck when I last left him, but he hadn't been in pain.

Then there was Stankic. Somehow he'd known Enoch sought me out. Had Paige divulged that much to Bellincioni? Unlikely. Stinkin' had been playing a hunch. If he'd had anything solid on me, he would have dragged me in on the spot. We wouldn't have played our chummy little charade, delving into the bowels of the Coliseum.

So there I was, fairly certain Yevgeni Sokolov was drugging Enoch with *tetsu no ken* and forcing him to kill. Two cops so far. Would others turn up? What leverage was he using against Enoch? According to Wilson, he was only the janitor. But that didn't hold water. The financial records, his parents' level of care, the blood on his hands that Paige had witnessed—none of that lined up with janitorial work. The blackouts he'd experienced, the amnesia—forgetting who his own girlfriend was and chasing her out of their apartment—all signs of heavy drug use.

If Sanitoro hadn't killed that *ronin* Nakano, I might have learned more about *tetsu no ken*. As it was, I had to go on what Sanitoro had told me about the side effects: severe psychosis, blackouts, murderous rage. Enoch had left Wanda untouched, thank God, but from the way he'd left my office, it sounded like he'd been dealing with some major anger issues.

Sokolov was shaking hands with the men in his private box. Preparing to leave? The fight wasn't even over yet. Unless Yevgeni had his own secret exit, he would have to pass by me on his way out of the Arena.

I had two questions for him: Why was he paying Enoch Wilson so much to vacuum the carpet? And why was Yevgeni in business with Hiroki Nakano? The big question, why the hell he was drugging a janitor to kill honest cops, would have to wait until a later date. At the moment, I was on Sokolov's turf, so to speak. Several levels underground. No way out unless I played nice.

I could do that. I wasn't suicidal.

"What do you say we get out of here for a bit?" the woman stage-whispered into my ear, up on her toes as her warm, alcoholic breath entered my ear canal.

"I don't even know your name."

"Call me Jane." She shook her platinum-blonde mane.

"I'm no Tarzan."

She squeezed my bicep. "Oooh, I beg to differ."

Yevgeni strode out into the open on the main floor, heading straight toward the ring. As if on cue, Player 2—despite all the abuse he'd received up to that point—plowed his mechanical fist into his opponent's chin with a sudden burst of power and speed that shattered Player 1's helmet, sending it upward in pieces as the man's head jerked back. Broken teeth lurched from his upturned face, eyes wide with surprise as his body tipped over and hit the mat with a resounding thud.

Half the audience roared with approval. The other half stood with shoulders slumped, stunned into silence. They couldn't believe Player 2 had come out on top, but I had more than a hunch it was all part of the show. Always great entertainment when the underdog wins in the end.

Sokolov ducked under the ropes and leapt into the ring. With a confident grin plastered across his face, he gripped Player 2 by the prosthetic forearm and, with some effort, hoisted it into the air over his head.

"We have a winner, my friends," Yevgeni said in his thick, Russian-coated accent. His high cheekbones nearly eclipsed his eyes, only dark slits as his bleached teeth stole the show. "Thank you for joining us here at the Arena. Please return this evening for a fight unlike anything you have ever seen before!"

"Rain check." I patted Jane's hand on my arm and moved to slip past her and her escort before the exiting tide became a force to reckon with.

"Where do you think you're going?" Her grip tightened. Her smile vanished.

"I need to speak with Mr. Sokolov."

"And what business do you have with Yevgeni?" said the man beside Jane, the fellow who hadn't seemed to notice I even existed—until now.

Glancing at Jane's hold on my arm, I returned my gaze to

the tall, grizzled man with the cigar who was now blocking my access to the main aisle. Neither he nor the woman seemed to be in any hurry to leave the Arena, even as spectators filed by, laughing uproariously or cursing their bad luck.

"Which fighter carried your wagers?" I changed the topic.

"We never lay bets," said Jane.

"We only watch," said the nameless man.

They were starting to creep me out—just a little. "Ever wonder if it's rigged?"

"The fights?" said Jane.

"Of course they are," said the man. "That's all part of the fun."

Nonchalantly, I attempted to slip my arm free of Jane's hold. She didn't give up easy—woman was as strong as a body builder—but eventually I emerged victorious. Taking a step back from them, I said, "I doubt everybody in the audience would agree with you."

"They can afford to lose a few thousand credits. Loaded mucky-mucks, all of them," he said, drawing on that stub of a cigar. He spoke as if he didn't identify with the wealthy masses around him.

"Why do you want to speak with Yevgeni?" Jane took a step toward me.

I seriously considered vaulting over the next row of seats to bypass this odd couple. Glancing down toward the boxing ring, I saw that Sokolov was conferring with the referee while two trainers hauled Player 1's unconscious ass off the mat.

"I'm with LinkNews 3," I said absently, going with the first alias that popped into my head. "We're working on a story about veterans who leave the war, but the war never leaves them. They can't stop fighting—"

"You're not a reporter, Mr. Madison," said the man.

How the hell did he know my name?

"Have we met?" I faced him.

"You're a private eye. The last one worth anything in this city," he said as Jane took another step toward me. Tipsy no longer, she eyed me with a cold, calculated look in those auburn eyes. "You're working on a case involving a performance-enhancing steroid, and you think Sokolov is somehow involved."

"If that's true, then you know a hell of a lot more than I do."

Jane smiled, but it wasn't seductive this time. "You're going to come with us. And you're not going to make a scene."

"Like I said before. Rain check." I launched myself over the row of seats below me and headed straight for the aisle, planning to elbow my way through the horde of well-dressed humanity surging toward the exit. Somehow, I had to make it down to the ring.

Instead, I stumbled. Nearly pitched face-first into the floor as a martini splashed across the back of my neck. The nameless man was right there to catch me, gripping my shoulders with strong hands. My legs had gone numb, useless. I was no longer in control of my own body.

As the Arena started dimming to black all around me, the last thing I heard was Jane clucking her tongue and saying to someone nearby, "Poor boy can't hold his liquor..."

II

"Time to wake up, Mr. Madison." Jane's voice, sounding like a tolerant schoolmarm.

But I was a couple meters underwater, struggling to breach the surface. I saw light glittering above me. Cold. Shivering. My eyelids blinked sluggishly, and I saw those auburn eyes staring back at me, too close to my face—unless she intended to kiss me. All that platinum-blonde hair, breasts swelling as she bent over in her tight sequined dress.

"There he is." She smiled, but it wasn't pretty. Cool and collected, she rose to her full height and placed both hands on her hips. "Ready to talk now?"

The fog dissipated, radiating out toward the edges of my vision, and I saw Mr. Nameless standing off to the side with a steel bucket dripping onto the concrete floor. Industrial shelving lined the walls in that confined space, and a single bulb dangling on a chain provided the only light. We appeared to be in a cramped janitorial supply closet. Still at the Coliseum? Or had they taken me offsite for this kinky interrogation routine?

"When you asked if I wanted to get out of there—" I clenched my teeth for a moment to keep them from chattering. The contents of that bucket had been dumped all over me, and I sat soaked and bound to a rigid folding chair. "This wasn't what I had in mind."

"You always excel at getting their hopes up," said

Nameless with a bored sigh.

"Part of the job." She shrugged. Then she nodded slowly, locking eyes with mine. "You're going to help us, Mr. Madison. Or you're going to end up in Federal prison. The choice here is very clear-cut."

So they were Blackshirts. Undercover operatives for our benevolent Federal government. Bad news for yours truly. Feds had a way of making things disappear—as well as people who refused to kowtow to their authority.

"Surprising," I said.

"Oh?"

"They haven't put either one of you out to pasture." I'd never seen agents in the field over the age of fifty.

She narrowed her gaze as half a smile crept up one corner of her pillowy lips. "Appearances can be deceiving, Mr. Madison. We can be whoever we need to be. Again, all part of the job." She cocked her head to one side. "By all appearances, you and Detective Stankic are real pals. Spending your lunch break together, taking in a fight at the exclusive Arena. But of course, that's not the case at all. You've never been anything but antagonistic towards one another."

"We have our good days."

"You hate each other's guts. Even so, circumstances can bring together the most unlikely of allies."

"Stankic thinks you may know something useful," said Nameless. "As do we."

"We just have different ways of expressing our interest," she added.

Right. These two drugged me and tied me to a chair. All Stankic did was whisper in my ear. Come to think of it, I preferred the current situation.

"Yevgeni Sokolov." Jane crossed her well-toned arms that should have belonged to someone much younger, now that I noticed. "Why did you come here to see him?"

So we were still at the Arena. Funny—I hadn't spotted any supply closets on the way in.

"He's a former client," I said with a shrug. "A while back, I scrounged up a little dirt on his brother."

"The brother who is now dead?" She raised an eyebrow.

"I had nothing to do with that."

"Not directly, no." She took the bucket away from her partner. His turn to cross his arms and look authoritative as she hefted the pail in both hands. I didn't like the look on her face. It reminded me of a kid who enjoyed ripping the wings off defenseless sparrows. "But that was the consequence of your actions. You found out that Sokolov's wife was cheating on him with his own brother. The brother ends up dead, and you get paid. That's how you private eye's operate. Outside the law. Mercenaries, really, providing your services to anyone who can afford your rates. Gangsters. Murderers. You don't care, as long as you get your payday. Sure, you might have a better reputation than most, but when all is said and done, you're still little more than a bottom-feeder."

"Well, since you seem to know all about me—"

"We know Enoch Wilson came to see you," said Nameless.

"Who?" I frowned, playing dumb.

That was a mistake. The steel bucket launched out of Jane's hands and into my face. She caught it before it could hit the floor and make such a clatter that would draw unwanted attention. But the damage had already been done. Pain exploded from my nose into my eyes, and warm blood drizzled down my upper lip.

"That wasn't very nice," I managed.

"She played basketball back in college," said Nameless with a smirk. "Her passes are quick and snappy, wouldn't you say?"

"Yeah, she's got real fast hands." I winced, spitting blood off to the side. "What do you want with Wilson? He's a problem for the cops. As far as I know, your kind never gets involved in local affairs."

"He's not as dumb as he looks," Jane said to her partner, catching and releasing the pail like it really was a basketball. Her reflexes were those of a twenty-odd-year-old, unlike her much older facial façade. What a clever disguise—flawless until now. Some kind of age-progression serum, designed to make her and her partner fit in with the Arena's demographic? Maybe it was starting to wear off. "Wilson's case is a problem for the police. The men he murdered, however, are a different matter." She paused. "They were working for us."

"They weren't Blackshirts," I said.

Nameless scowled at my use of the derogatory term. He probably preferred not to think of himself as a jackbooted fascist. "Officers Bowman and Sykes were gathering evidence on Yevgeni Sokolov," he said at length.

"What kind of evidence?"

"Obviously, that's classified," Jane said.

Obviously. "So I'm supposed to tell you what I know, but you won't be returning the favor?"

Jane tossed the bucket at me again and I flinched backward. But she caught it before it could do any further damage to my ruggedly handsome face.

"Fine," I muttered. Time to cut my losses and make the best of the situation. With any luck, I'd get out alive. "Wilson came to me for help. He doesn't remember killing those cops, doesn't remember much of anything. If I had to guess, I'd say he's being drugged. Regularly."

"By Sokolov." She watched me like a scientist monitoring a volatile experiment.

"That's what I plan to find out." I paused, glancing from Jane to her partner. A light bulb had flared to life—inside my head. "You don't care about the murders or catching Wilson. But smuggling an illegal substance across the border from Little Tokyo...that's a Federal offense." I paused. "Or maybe your bosses want the stuff. When our cold war with the Eastern Conglomerate thaws out, I'm sure they'll be able to use a few thousand super-soldiers able to punch through enemy lines." Literally.

They stared back at me without expression. Professional poker faces. I tried not to look too impressed.

"All right," I said. "I'll throw you a bone. The stuff's called *tetsu no ken*. It was carried out of Little Tokyo by a guy named Hiroki Nakano. Yakuza type—Fire Dragon clan. God-awful stuff, from what I hear. Side effects include serious rage issues, psychosis, and amnesia. Shall I continue?"

Jane nodded to her partner, and he stepped behind me. That I didn't like. I always preferred facing my enemies eye to eye.

"Hold on," I said before he could drug me again or do whatever he planned to do. How had they knocked me out the first time? No clue. Probably some fancy government tech. "I've got a question for you two."

Again, she nodded to her partner—this time, over my

head. I waited, but nothing happened. No supplemental clobbering as of yet.

"Well?" She stared at me, waiting.

"Right. So here's the thing: I'm pretty sure you Feds could throw your weight around wherever you want. So why use a couple local cops to do your dirty work? Why not drag in Sokolov yourselves if you suspect him?"

"Technically, that's two questions." Another half-smile from the she-agent. She was warming up to me, I could tell. Must have had a thing for guys with bloody noses. "You're a big boy, Madison. You know how the world operates. Sokolov works for Ivan. Enough said."

So they couldn't touch him—not without a whole lot of proof gathered at the ground level. Rumor had it that Ivan and the Feds had developed a working arrangement of sorts. I wasn't privy to such high-level information, but I had my suspicions. Word on the street: Ivan had plenty of contacts in the Eastern Conglomerate underworld. So let's say the government of the Unified States wanted to get their hands on some gently used war toys from the enemy to deconstruct and reengineer. Then Ivan was their man. In return, the Russian Devil and his associates were off-limits.

These Blackshirts, accustomed to getting what they wanted, were facing an iron curtain of resistance by targeting one of Ivan's lieutenants. But I had to hand it to them. They had cast-iron balls to break the unspoken Federal protocol and keep Sokolov in their sights. Made me almost want to help them.

Almost.

"Maybe you could get Nakano and his Fire Dragons to turn on Yevgeni. You know, rat him out?" I offered.

"Too bad Nakano's dead." The sound of metal springing against metal came from behind my ear. A switchblade.

"You people know everything." I shook my head. "How the hell can I be of any use to you?"

"Good question." Jane set the wet bucket on a shelf nearby and fluffed her hair. "Cut him loose."

Nameless did as he was told. My bonds—nylon straps—dropped to the floor. I massaged my wrists but remained seated as he joined his partner in front of me, closing the blade and pocketing it. Cool as a cucumber. I'm sure he would have taken off one of my earlobes with equal composure if he'd been ordered to do so.

"One last thing, Madison." Jane strode to the door, pausing before she opened it. She tried to stare me down. An honorable effort. "Stay out of our way."

With that, she and her well-dressed companion left, shutting the door quietly behind them. I blew out a sigh and reached for a sealed roll of paper towels nearby. Tearing it open, I ripped off a few sheets and dabbed at my face. I would be quite a sight if I tried to meet with Sokolov. Soggy and bloody, I'd stick out like a broken nose. Security would toss me out on my ass.

That wouldn't do at all. There was no telling when I'd be able to get back inside, and I had a feeling time was in short supply.

Enoch was loose. If the cops hadn't already found him and killed him, where would he go? Not his apartment—already under police surveillance. Work, then. The Coliseum.

I stood and shook out my drenched sleeves, splattering the concrete with runoff from my recent dousing. Then I noticed something: a storage locker on the far wall, in the shadows beyond the light bulb's reach. A padlock secured the door. Beside it stood a vacuum and a mop, complete with a dingy yellow industrial bucket on casters.

Slipping a hand into my soaked suit jacket, I fished around an inside pocket until I found what I was looking for: a paperclip. Probably not something they taught you in college, but since I'd been educated via many repeat courses at the school of hard knocks, I knew my way around a variety of locks. My trusty paperclip was the key. Patience was the virtue.

Less than a minute later, I'd sprung the padlock and pulled open the locker door. A navy blue jumpsuit hung inside. Scuffed work boots sat on the floor. Checking the name tag on the uniform, I shouldn't have been surprised to find WILSON. Enoch's locker. Sometimes things just fell into place that way.

Deciding on the lesser of two evils—borrowing something that didn't belong to me versus sloshing around the swanky casino in my own duds—I shrugged out of my soggy coat and tugged Enoch's janitorial threads off the hanger. The goal was to remain inside the Coliseum for as long as I could, and somehow get to Sokolov. My disguise wouldn't be as impressive as Jane and her partner's, but it would have to do. I didn't have the resources of the Federal government at my disposal.

Dragging the mop bucket behind me, I opened the door and took a quick peek outside. The hallway looked like the same one Stinkin' and I had passed through earlier. That meant I was still down on the Arena level. Good. And from the sound of things, the crowds had already cleared out.

I hoped Yevgeni hadn't been among them.

Turning right, I headed down the silent corridor. A coin toss would have been just as scientific a solution. I honestly had no idea where I was going. Long fluorescent bulbs in the low ceiling cast a morgue-like pallor over the concrete walls and floor. From the looks of things, a serious mopping was in order. Too bad I didn't plan on playing my part to the letter.

The unhurried percussion of shoe soles approached at my six. I hunched over the bucket and doused the mop, figuring that was as good a spot as any to start acting like Wilson the Janitor. I kept most of my face hidden behind my shoulder as I turned toward the wall.

"Mr. Madison?"

Enoch's voice.

12

"Feeling better?" I faced him with all the confidence I could muster. The guy had smashed straight through my office wall, and now he had me in his sights. I couldn't help there being a bit of a tremble behind my kneecaps.

"What are you doing here?" He looked stunned. Seeing me in his uniform probably didn't alleviate his confusion any.

"I could ask you the same thing. According to my secretary, you made quite an exit."

"Yeah..." He frowned, staring at his name tag on my chest. "Sorry about that. I-uh...feel a whole lot better now."

"Were you ill?"

"What? No, nothing like that. It was a headache—a bad one. Migraines, I get 'em sometimes. But they always clear up when I get back to work."

"Here at the Coliseum."

He nodded. "And it's weird, but my memories...I think they're starting to come back some." Then he noticed my nose and frowned with what looked like genuine concern. "What happened to your face? And why the hell are you wearing my jumpsuit?"

"Funny story. I might tell you about it someday." I glanced up and down the hallway. By all appearances, we were alone. No vidcams to be seen. "But how about you tell me what you're remembering."

"Paige, most of all." He shook his head sadly. "She's my girl, and I chased her out like some vagrant—"

"What else?"

"Well, I...don't think I'm a janitor here. Not really, I mean." He stared down toward the dark end of the corridor. "I've been fighting in the ring. Mr. Sokolov's been paying me to fight." He clenched his jaw. "To the death, Mr. Madison."

"Death duels." Of course they existed. Never doubted it for a moment. I knew my city, ugly as it could be.

He nodded. "Mr. Sokolov pays me enough to... My parents, you see, they need—"

"You take care of them."

"Yeah." His expression clouded. Were his memories doing the same? "If I don't fight...to the death... If I refuse to kill them—my opponents—then Mr. Sokolov says he'll cut my pay. My parents will have to be institutionalized."

No way they would receive the Seven Oaks standard of care anywhere else on this side of the continent.

"He's got you in a bind. But that still doesn't explain how you killed that cop." I decided not to mention Officer Sykes. One murder weighing on his conscience was bad enough.

"Injection." His eyes widened with sudden recollection. "I was late to work a couple weeks ago. Mr. Sokolov's men took me to his office, and I had to explain why the floors hadn't been mopped. I told him about my parents, and Mr. Sokolov promised me they'd be taken care of—if I let him test a new drug on me. He said it would help me focus and get my work done in half the time. So they gave me a shot, the trainers, and I got this surge of energy. My heart went haywire, but I felt strong enough to do just about anything." He stopped abruptly. "It's crazy, Mr. Madison, but I think that last migraine sorted out everything in my head."

Maybe. But I didn't like the sound of that, either. "Why are you down here, Enoch?" There wasn't another fight scheduled until that evening, according to Yevgeni's announcement in the ring earlier. How long had I been out of commission, thanks to those friendly Blackshirts?

I glanced at my watch. Late afternoon already.

"I don't know. I just ran over as fast as I could, and the guys out front let me in. I came down here because—" He shrugged. "This is where the headache goes away."

Something in his subconscious had driven him down to the Arena level. Had Sokolov planted some kind of homing beacon on him? Something that caused him incredible pain until he returned to where he belonged?

Far-fetched maybe, but I wasn't ready to put anything past Sokolov. If he was doping Enoch for the death duels—and to kill off nosy cops—then an implant that caused excruciating pain wasn't beyond the realm of possibility. Assuming such malevolent technology existed.

I had a feeling it did. Ivan's lieutenant could have easily acquired it from the Eastern Conglomerate's black market. Just the sort of wicked little thing our exalted enemy would have engineered to control its people.

"Yevgeni has a fight scheduled tonight," I said. "Will you be in the ring?"

Enoch shrugged his narrow shoulders weakly and shook his head. "I sure hope not."

I gave the hallway another glance in each direction. "What else is down here?"

"Storage rooms. Supply closets. And the Arena, down that way. Nothing else that I remember."

I couldn't shake the feeling that we were being monitored somehow, even though there wasn't a camera in sight. The short hairs on the back of my neck stood at attention, warning that soon this corridor could be filled with well-armed Russian security.

"We have to get out of here." I pointed down the hallway in the direction he'd come from. "Elevator that way?"

He nodded.

"Let's go." Abandoning the mop bucket, I led the way. When we reached the cold mirrored doors of the lift, I tore Enoch's name tag off the uniform and handed it to him. Figured I'd make an easier exit past any prying eyes without his name on my chest. "Hope you don't mind."

"I don't think I wore it much."

"Any idea how you went from mopping floors to killing people?" I gave him a smirk to soften the harshness of those words.

He looked a little taken aback, regardless. "I've got some of my memories, but not all of them. And they don't really seem like mine, you know? It's like I'm watching somebody else—a weird other version of me, doing things I...could never do."

Doppelgänger? I prayed that wasn't where this case was headed. Only once in a private eye's career should he or she be cursed with such a thing, and I'd already served my time. Material for a whole other story, believe me.

"Probably a side effect of the 'roid they're giving you," I offered. "Stuff messes with your head."

"You're telling me," Enoch muttered.

The doors slid open, and I stepped inside—right into the smelliest man I wished I didn't know.

Detective Stankic was alone in the elevator. His gaze fell on Enoch, and he started. Before I could unzip the jumpsuit and grab my revolver, Stinkin' already had his Glock gripped in both hands and aimed at Enoch's head.

"Don't do anything stupid now," I said, keeping my hands where he could see them.

"Madison, you're full of surprises." Stankic glanced at my borrowed uniform. "I don't even wanna know."

Disguises never worked out so well for me.

"Who are you?" Enoch had followed my lead, raising both hands to shoulder height.

"I'm the *police*, kid." Stankic smiled, revealing crowded yellow teeth. For such a large guy, you'd expect jaws to match. But poor Stinkin's snaggleteeth hadn't been given enough room to grow in properly. "I've been lookin' all over for you, kid. But you've been real busy, by all accounts. Offing a couple cops, making friends with the local lowlife." He fixed me with his bloodshot eyes. "You lied to me, Madison. That makes me kinda sore."

He tightened his grip on the gun, ready to shoot. One to Enoch's head, execution-style. Maybe two. He'd be exacting revenge for a pair of his fallen comrades, after all. Would he turn the gun on me next or leave me alone? Debatable.

"You don't want to do this." I took a step to the side, intending to plant myself right in the line of fire. Not because I was some sort of hero. I just had a feeling Stankic wouldn't kill me. Not right there, anyway. Apprehending a fugitive was one thing. He could say he fired his sidearm to protect himself. But gunning down the neighborhood gumshoe? More difficult to explain.

"Stay outta my way, Madison." He had a clear shot.

Would Enoch try anything to save himself? Move with lightning-quick speed and plunge his fist straight through Stinkin's flabby chest? Part of me hoped he would.

"You got a fight tonight, kid?" Stankic's confident sneer hadn't left his pudgy face.

"I...think so."

"You're gonna lose. You hear me? Make it look good, like you're givin' it your all. Hell, tear the guy's arms off, I don't care. But you ain't gonna win it."

What was this all about? "I don't think fighters throw death duels," I said.

"Shut it, Madison. Or I'll shut it for you."

I wasn't sure exactly how that would work, but I kept mum for the moment. He was the one with the firepower.

"You understand what I'm sayin', kid?" Stankic scowled at Enoch.

"You don't want me to win tonight." He looked uncertain whether he'd have any say in the matter. Once he was drugged, wouldn't he forget he even had this conversation?

"That's right."

"Or what?" Enoch raised his chin, staring down the weapon pointed at his face. Guy had some guts. "What happens if I don't?"

"Well, that's when things get interesting. You got that video I sent you?"

So Stankic had sent the footage from Howard's Tavern.

Enoch frowned, blinking. "Yeah."

"Then you already know what I'll be showing your dear, sweet parents if you don't throw the fight. They'll see you for what you are: a murdering freak. Might take some convincing for them to believe it's really you, but hey, I'm a cop. The older generation hasn't stopped believing in those who protect and serve this city."

"You only serve yourself, Stankic," I said. "Let me guess. You're in deep with Sokolov's crew. Hoping to overcome your losses tonight by betting big?"

A pistol whipping is never pleasant. But let me tell you, it's even worse after you've already had a steel bucket planted in your face within the past hour. I staggered back from the blow as Stinkin' cursed a foul streak straining the limits of his vocabulary.

"Madison, so help me, you're gonna watch yourself or this ain't gonna end well for you at all!"

"My parents...?" Enoch looked a little weak in the knees. "You can't, mister. Please. I didn't do it—I mean, I did, but I wasn't myself—"

"Try explaining that to anybody." Stankic chuckled, gargling gravel as only he did best. "I'd like to see you try. Can't believe your knuckles are still intact after what you did to Bowman and Sykes." He waved the gun muzzle off to the left, toward the Arena. "Go on now," he dismissed Enoch. "You'd better warm up. Gotta make it look convincing when you eat the mat later."

Enoch glanced from the dirty cop to me. I gave him a nod. Nothing he could do here.

"I'm sorry," he said quietly, backing away and avoiding eye contact. Then he trotted off like a nimble athlete, keeping his gaze on the floor.

The kid was in a tight squeeze. Sokolov forced him into winning death duels, threatening to institutionalize his parents if he didn't fight and win. Now there was a new player on the scene, threatening to tell his parents the truth if he didn't lose. It was no exaggeration to say Enoch Wilson had the weight of the world on his scrawny shoulders as he faced the near future. What would he do?

But I had my own worries. Now that Stinkin' and I were alone, I had a feeling things were about to get more hands-on.

"You're a real piece of work, Stankic." He was never interested in vigilante justice. A revenge killing had never been on his radar. "You just want to use that kid to get out of the hole with Yevgeni."

The Glock's muzzle was aimed at me now. "You're quite the speculative fictioneer, Madison. You've got no proof. Only conjecture. But I guess that's what you do best." He snorted. "People actually pay you for that? Can't believe you've lasted so long in this town."

"They say cockroaches will outlast us all. Something about their simpler bodies and slower cell cycles. You can relate to that right? You're awful slow."

"What?"

I'd already charged him before he had time to react. It was risky, sure, but I was still betting on the fact that he wouldn't shoot me. Not to kill, anyway. Besides, a shot in that hallway would have echoed like a bomb going off, bringing all manner of unwanted attention. I hoped he wanted to avoid that as much as I did.

Something in common between us? Go figure.

My right shoulder plowed into his expansive gut, throwing him off-balance. As he staggered backward into the lift, I punched him in the kidney with two left hooks, one right on the tail of the other. Stankic groaned, curling up on that side of his body. As he did so, he brought down the butt of his Glock, striking the back of my head.

The elevator light dimmed, but that wasn't due to any fluctuation in electricity. Stinkin' had gotten me good with that crack on the noggin, and I was starting to lose traction on my own consciousness.

"That all you got?" He kicked me below the belt, doubling me over. Then he gave me a shove that sent me sprawling into the hallway outside.

I hit the opposite wall and shook my head sharply, struggling to stay on my feet. Stankic had his gun down at his side now. Must not have seen me as much of a threat. I had no chance to go for my own revolver. The stupid jumpsuit was in the way, for one thing. For another, Stinkin' was hitting me again: a jab to the ribs followed by yet another pistol-whipping—right across the jaw.

The cold floor rushed up to meet me a whole lot faster than I would have thought possible, knocking the wind out of my lungs. I stretched out across it, unable to focus on anything but concrete pores in my line of sight.

"Stay down," Stankic growled into my ear with a gust of foul breath. I imagined his face flushing crimson as he bent over. "And stay the hell out of my way. Your work here is done."

"Not exactly," I managed, rising awkwardly onto an elbow. "I still need to speak with Sokolov. I've got a few questions for him. And I'm sure he'd be interested to know about Wilson throwing tonight's fight."

"What part of *stay outta my way* didn't you understand?"

He drew back his left foot, probably to kick me in the throat or something equally as pleasant. But he telegraphed that kick like a real amateur. By the time his flat-footed shoe came at my head, I was ready for it. I grabbed the dull faux-leather with both hands and gave his foot a sharp twist in midair. The crunch from Stinkin's ankle told me all I needed to know. He'd be hobbling for a while.

With an agonized roar, he fell against the wall and brought up the Glock, spastically firing two rounds that went off like grenades in that hallway.

The first shot blew out the fluorescents above us, shattering the meter-long bulbs. The second ricocheted off the wall a centimeter or two from my shoulder and banked against the mirrored elevator doors. Leaving the polished surface marred with a flash of sparks, the bullet disappeared farther down the corridor. Lucky for me, Stankic's aim wasn't the best when he had a busted ankle. Unlucky for me, the guy had no problem throwing his weight around.

Before I could get to my feet, he landed on top of my chest like a dozen bags of cement. Outweighing me by a factor of two, he nearly crushed my ribcage into the floor, squeezing out all the air I had left. I couldn't say a word—not one of the dozen curses careening through my skull. I could barely gasp for breath.

He sneered down at me in the sickly glow of the remaining ceiling bulbs. "As much as I'd like to end you, Madison, I'm thinkin' it'll be more fun to see what the Russians do with you."

Despite the murderous intent raging in his eyes, Detective Stankic decided to take the higher road that was less likely to get him suspended. Telegraphing his flabby elbow, he clocked me right between the eyes with the butt of his gun.

The lights went out before he hauled his fat ass off me.

13

No idea how long I was out, but I was sure of one thing: if I lost consciousness one more time on this case, I'd have to penalize myself for sleeping on the job. Reduce my rates by twenty percent or something.

Not that I planned on getting paid for this one. Wilson had offered, but his money was no good. I had a feeling it was about to be cut short.

Like my thoughts were, as soon as my eyes focused on the gorgeous face staring back at me.

"There we are," Wanda said, kneeling with her silk handkerchief gently swabbing my nose and cheek. "Somebody sure went to town on you, Charlie. Didn't you even bother putting up a fight?"

"Don't you worry about that." I sat up too quickly, finding myself on the cold floor of the supply closet.

That's right, folks. Not only had I been knocked out yet again, but I'd also been abandoned in the same chemical-smelly environs as before—which started pitching oddly to the left as I dropped back to the concrete.

"Easy now. Take it slow." She ran her hand through my hair. An affectionate gesture? Not exactly. "Your scalp's bleeding," she said. "Looks like you took a hit to the back of your head, as well as the front. One of Ivan's goons?"

"Somebody far less talented."

"He sure got you coming and going."

I had to chuckle at that. "What are you doing here?" I looked her over briefly. The girl knew how to dress, that's for sure: sexy but with plenty left to the imagination. In that frilly lavender number, she would have had no problem getting past those gladiators at the front gates. They had a thing for letting in the drop-dead gorgeous, no questions asked. The Coliseum's casinos did better business that way. "How'd you find me?"

She bit her lip briefly. Not a good sign. She knew I wouldn't like what she was about to say. "Well, since you refuse to carry a phone—"

"We've been over this—"

"I had to take a desperate measure." She forced a smile. "I planted a tracker."

"What? When?"

"You were in your office, talking to your client—that fellow who smashed through the wall. I called the building manager about that, by the way. Construction crew should be done with it by tomorrow morning, but it's gonna cost you."

"Figured it might."

"When I saw that footage from Howard's..." She shook her head, never breaking eye contact. Those gorgeous blue sapphires were deep enough to dive into. "I had to make sure you were safe."

"So you planted a tracker on me?"

"No, not you. Your coat." She gestured at where I'd left it earlier, still soggy and draped over the folding chair Jane and Nameless had tied me to. "When it didn't move for over an hour, I started to get worried. The tracker led me right here."

"Way down here." I shook my head, impressed. "That's

some tracker."

"Only the best for our Charlie. Tricky elevator, though. I had to press the basement level twice. Think they've got some secret stuff goin' on?"

"Secret. Illegal. You name it."

"Oh," she said all of a sudden. "Almost forgot. That video took some work, but I managed to trace it back to its source. No ID—whoever sent it was careful about that—but it came from the 37th precinct. Sergeant Douglass's station, Charlie."

"Yeah." I carefully sat up, wincing all the way. "I need you to call him—"

"Already taken care of. He's waiting outside."

I gave her an appreciative wink. "You thought of everything."

"He can't get in without a warrant, since he's not so popular with Ivan's crew. But he's ready to bust in anyway, whenever you give the word."

"If he was in the Russian Devil's pocket, I'm sure it would be different. He didn't send that footage, though. Stankic must've hijacked his station."

"Another reason not to like that guy."

As if I needed any more.

I struggled to my feet, and Wanda was right there to help me up. Slipping my right arm over her shoulders, she supported me while I grew accustomed to the change in altitude. "Thanks, by the way."

"For what?" She smiled.

"Rescuing me."

I checked my watch. Half past six in the evening. I had no idea when the death duel would start, but I knew I had to be there. To see Enoch tear his opponent apart? No thanks. I'd seen enough carnage in the war. But maybe I could turn the tables on both Stankic and Yevgeni—make it so Enoch wouldn't have to throw the fight or kill another fighter.

Would he be going up against one of the cyborg veterans I'd seen in the ring earlier? Or did Sokolov have something even more special planned for tonight's fight?

"Care to take in a show?"

"You're not going anywhere looking like that, Charlie." She cringed a little as she dabbed at my face once more with her hanky. "How'd your coat get so wet?"

"Funny story." I unzipped the janitor uniform the rest of the way down. Aching from head to toe, I shrugged out of it. "Couple Feds are interested in this case too. Gave me the water treatment."

"Fascist pigs."

Her heels clopped and shifted against the concrete floor, waiting patiently as I adjusted my wet attire. They hadn't dried a bit.

"Well, how do I look?" I held out my arms, hat in one hand, coat in the other.

"Like something the tide washed in." She looked me over with disapproval.

"Let's hope they keep the house lights low." I pulled the chain on the bulb above us, plunging the closet into darkness. No streak of light underneath the door to attract any passersby.

"Now what?" Wanda reached for me and took my damp arm like I was escorting her to a ballroom.

I nudged her toward the folding chair. "We wait."

14

The glowing face on my watch read 9PM before we heard movement in the hallway outside—and lots of it. Talkative herds disembarked from the elevator at regularly timed intervals, and the foot traffic all merged in the same direction: straight toward the Arena.

We waited until the first dozen batches of spectators had filled in some of the seats before we exited the supply closet and followed them. No security to be seen along the way. No glances cast in our direction as we filed into one of the rows in the middle with a good view of the ring below. The audience murmured with anticipation, most of them seeming to know what the night held in store. But there were plenty who looked excited, curious and anxious to see for themselves what an infamous *death duel* would entail. Would it be for real or faked? Would they be able to tell the difference?

Rumor was about to become reality.

"Welcome to the Arena," I said to Wanda as I took my seat.

She sat beside me and looked around with keen interest. "It's as big as the ring they show on TV—you know, with the regular fights."

"What were you expecting?"

She shrugged her lavender shoulders. "A dark basement. Standing room only."

"Trust me, we'll be standing soon enough." I glanced over my shoulder toward where Stankic and I had been standing earlier. No sign of Jane and her nameless partner. No sign of Stinkin', either. But I had a feeling all three of them would arrive shortly.

"Will he do it?"

I turned back to Wanda. "Enoch?"

"Do you think he'll...kill the other fighter?"

"He's got a lot riding on this fight. If he wins, Stankic shows his parents the footage from Howard's. If he loses, I doubt Yevgeni will be happy about it. Might kick Enoch's parents out of Seven Oaks."

"Nice place. I tried to get my ma in there before she passed away. Couldn't afford it."

"Most people can't."

"He must make good money doing this. Enoch, I mean." She nodded toward the ring and paused. "You think he's one of Sokolov's assassins on the side? That he killed the cop—?"

"Cops." I kept my voice low as well-dressed fat cats filed in around us. The latest batch from the elevator. "Two of them. Both dispatched by Enoch. Both working with the Blackshirts."

"Working on what?"

"Locating the drug Yevgeni is giving Enoch. It's from Little Tokyo—an experimental steroid, from what I've heard. The Feds want it."

Her brow wrinkled. "Why not go to the source?"

"The supplier? Already dead. And they know better than to go trespassing into Little Tokyo."

Little Tokyo was a sovereign state on United World soil—a city of refugees from the war. Blackshirts had no jurisdiction over what went on over there, only over what came spilling out into our fair city. When Sanitoro executed Nakano on their side of the border, the shipments of *tetsu no ken* would have ended just as abruptly as the man's pulse. Now the Feds' only hope was that Sokolov still had some of the stuff in his possession.

If he did, then Enoch would come out swinging tonight with fists like unstoppable tanks.

A bell clanged ringside, and the murmuring masses quieted down. Yevgeni Sokolov, dressed in a tuxedo even fancier than the one he'd worn for the lunch crowd, leapt into the ring and grabbed hold of the old-fashioned microphone that descended on a line from the ceiling.

"Welcome to the Arena!" he bellowed, and the crowd—more than a couple thousand in attendance—roared with anticipation. "Prepare yourselves for a fight unlike anything you have ever seen before, my friends. Even if you have attended one of our death duels in the past, you are sure to be surprised by what we have in store for you tonight. Of this, I have no doubt." He paused, grinning ghoulishly at the spectators, savoring the moment. "Now allow me to introduce a new fighter making his debut here in the Arena. This may be his first fight, but if he gives it all he's got, it won't be his last. Please join me in welcoming..." Yevgeni's voice echoed in the stillness. "*Grim Reaper!*"

The spectators were on their feet in an instant, and Wanda and I were up right along with them, applauding and cheering as a hulking figure entered the aisle beneath Yevgeni's private box. The staging area must have been back there, where the fighters prepped for battle. Unlike the veterans I'd seen duking it out at the lunch show, this one looked to be more machine than man. When he launched himself into the full light of the ring, my breath caught for a moment.

"What is he?" Wanda gasped into my ear.

The arms and legs of a mandroid had been welded into his flesh and bone, replacing the God-given variety. The only human parts of his body were his head, muscular neck, and ripped torso. Everything else had been stripped away to make room for blast-scarred metal and hydraulics, mechanized portions that had seen serious battle. The killing machine disassembled to create this monstrosity had fought for the enemy.

Grim Reaper. I had no doubt. No fighter would stand a chance against him. Not even Enoch, high on his 'roid.

Spectators cried out in awe and horror, their cheers reaching a new level of fervor. Most of the well-dressed folks in the first few rows had no clue they were in the splash zone. I'd seen enough mandroids in the war to know it didn't take much for one of those mechanical arms to tear through half a dozen men. If Grim Reaper's reprogrammed limbs decided to go on the fritz without warning, sending him flailing into the audience, there would be nothing but blood and guts left in his wake.

I grabbed Wanda by the arm. "That thing goes haywire, you make straight for the exit."

"Okay, Charlie." She winced at the force of my grip. "Where's Enoch? How's he gonna fight that thing?"

"And now," Yevgeni on the mike attempted to steal everyone's attention away from Grim Reaper. The cyborg stood beside Sokolov in the center of the ring with his massive arms raised, plasteel fists the size of basketballs clenched and ready to fight. "In his third duel here at the Arena—a crowd favorite—please join me in giving a hearty welcome to...*Enoch Wilson*!" He stretched out the kid's name like a professional announcer would have, back in the day.

The crowd went wild all over again, and Wanda craned her neck to see around the tall tuxedo in front of her.

"There he is," she said, patting my hand on her arm.

My hold on her didn't relax as Enoch trotted down the aisle looking like a lost dog in a hyperail's glaring headlight. The spotlight had shifted from the ring, glowing down on him from above. He wore the same sleeveless shirt he'd had on before and the same pair of dingy-looking trousers. Sokolov obviously hadn't allocated any of his formidable budget toward the Arena fighters' uniforms. Grim Reaper was just flesh and metal. At the very least, Yevgeni could have splurged on flashy leotards for these guys.

Mandroid arms clashed over the cyborg's head. Was he trying to applaud Enoch's efforts as the kid clambered into the ring? Intimidate him, more likely. Couldn't tell if it was working.

"Tonight's fight promises to be a real David versus Goliath match!" Yevgeni held up one of Enoch's arms as the spotlight shone down on the three of them. The drugged kid on the left, blinking in the glare. Sokolov in the middle, grinning like a freak. Grim Reaper on the right, mechanical arms raised as he stared at the audience without any expression on his corpse-like face.

"We've got company," Wanda spoke loud enough into my ear to be heard over the ambient noise. She nodded toward the end of our row where a hobbling Detective Stankic stood in the aisle, scowling viciously. Good news for us: there weren't any available seats nearby. "He doesn't look happy to see you."

"He shouldn't be." I tipped my hat to him with my middle finger.

He flashed the Glock holstered under his expansive suit jacket and heaved himself down a few rows, clutching onto the railing for support. No way he'd be moving at all if I had broken his ankle.

I'd have to try harder next time.

"And there are my Blackshirt friends." I pointed Wanda's attention across the aisle as Stankic passed them on the end of their row. Agents Jane and Nameless, dressed exactly as they'd been earlier in the day and looking like flawless fifty-somethings. Unlike yours truly, they were masters of disguise. "The gang's all here."

"To watch a man die." Wanda shook her head.

"You want to leave?"

"Of course. If you agree to come with me."

I gave her a wink. "Gotta see this through, sweetheart."

To the bitter end.

The crowd quieted down as Yevgeni ducked out from under the ropes and dropped to the floor beside the ring. Adjusting his tux, he stood there with a couple bodyguards and watched the two fighters with as much simmering anticipation as those around him. All eyes were focused on Enoch and Grim Reaper in opposite corners, facing each other. Neither one with a trainer ringside offering words of wisdom. Each man was completely on his own.

It looked ridiculous at first glance: a scrawny kid versus a mechanized man twice his size. But this kid was able to punch his fist straight through a man's body, not to mention what he'd done to my office wall. I wasn't too sure how that translated to dealing with plasteel and iron mandroid parts, but I wouldn't have long to wait and see.

Something about Enoch's face gave me pause. He didn't look like that dazed, confused kid who'd visited my office. Neither did he look like that killer zombie from the video. And he sure as hell didn't appear to be suffering the raging side effects of an experimental steroid. Instead he looked worried and out of place, unsure what to do next.

Maybe he was counting the cost of throwing the fight, allowing Grim Reaper to dole out a lethal round of punishment. Live or die, if Enoch lost the match, his parents wouldn't find out he was a murderer. But if he died, there was no way they would continue to receive the same level of care he'd been able to provide for them. And if he lived, if he fought to the finish and somehow managed to kill the mechanized man across the ring from him, what then? Yevgeni would continue to pay him well, but Stankic would go straight to Seven Oaks and show the Wilsons what their son was capable of.

It was no wonder Enoch swayed on his feet, blinking under the blinding light, willing to let his opponent make the first move.

As soon as the Round 1 bell clanged, Grim Reaper charged forward, mechanical arms swinging, legs driving into the mat, pistons pumping. The sight took me straight back to the frontlines during the war, when that group of mandroids had surprised us and taken out my entire gunner squad. Good thing I didn't suffer much from post-traumatic stress, or I would have probably started pitching a fit. That's not to say it was easy for me to watch. Truth be told, my stomach seized up and turned over on itself, and my knees wobbled a bit in their sockets. Wanda held me steady.

"You all right?" she said as my hand dropped from her arm.

"Don't worry about me." I nodded toward Enoch, who hadn't left his corner of the ring.

The kid looked terrified. He cowered as Grim Reaper swung a metal fist straight for his skull. Enoch curled into a forward roll, sliding between his opponent's mechanical legs with room to spare. The audience loved that move, and many of them hooted and hollered for the obvious underdog. Others turned to each other and shrugged, confused by Enoch's behavior. They must have been regular attendees, accustomed to seeing him pulverize his opponents—not steer clear of them.

"Either he's never been up against a cyborg like this before," I said into Wanda's ear, "or Yevgeni neglected to dope him tonight."

Her eyes widened as she gazed up at me. "You mean he...wants Enoch to die?"

The pieces fit, as awful as they were. Yevgeni must have found out about Officers Bowman and Sykes investigating his dealings with Hikori Nakano, and he doped Enoch with *tetsu no ken*. Then he somehow coerced Enoch to kill both cops. Now he was going to tie up loose ends by having the kid die in the ring. The two Feds would have no firsthand proof of the 'roid's power tonight, and their hope of obtaining a sample of the drug would die with Enoch. If there was any of the stuff left around, Yevgeni would have buried it so deep even a Federal search warrant would never come close to finding it.

"But he wouldn't have gone into the ring without the stuff, right?" Wanda said. "That would be suicide!"

"Yevgeni could've given him a shot of anything. Painkiller, maybe. Made him think he was all juiced up. Look at him now." We watched as Enoch dodged another lethal blow but didn't fight back. "He knows it. He's not feeling the power that drug gave him."

"Maybe he's just biding his time."

I turned my attention to Yevgeni. His arms were crossed, and he didn't look happy. He too could sense the tide shift in the Arena as Enoch ducked and scampered out of harm's way. The spectators had paid to see a bloodbath, not this poor excuse for foreplay.

"Fight!" Sokolov shouted, the tendons straining in his neck. Tough to be heard over the catcalls and boos that erupted from the audience, but he managed. "Fight back, damn you!"

Enoch crouched against the ropes and glanced down at Yevgeni for just an instant, but that's all it took for Grim Reaper to send a plasteel fist alongside the kid's head, knocking him face-first into the mat. Detective Stankic threw up both his arms, the only spectator in his section appearing to enjoy the show. He probably thought Enoch was doing as he'd been told—throwing the fight. Agents Jane and Nameless conferred in a subtle manner where they stood. Everybody was on their feet, hurling insults and curses at the ring.

"He's gonna kill 'im." Wanda winced as Grim Reaper stomped toward Enoch's sprawled-out body and grabbed the kid by the back of his neck. Hoisting him into the air, the cyborg pivoted and hurled Enoch straight down into the mat again.

The display of violence seemed to appease most of the audience, but Sokolov still looked dissatisfied. He reached into his tuxedo jacket and withdrew a handheld device.

"Fight!" he shouted again, squeezing the device. Some kind of remote control?

Enoch spasmed suddenly, jerking on the mat like he'd been hit with a few hundred volts of electricity. He grabbed his head with both hands and cried out, but nobody heard him. The place was going crazy now. Grim Reaper added to the noise, standing over his opponent with both mandroid-arms raised, roaring like a gorilla prepared to pound his prey into the ground.

"Calls Douglass." I pressed past Wanda, heading for the aisle. "Keep him on the line."

"Where are you going?" She grabbed at my arm.

"Gotta stop this."

I trotted down the steps with Yevgeni in my sights, planning my strategy with every step. I was a couple meters away from him when solid muscle in fancy suits blocked my path. Two security personnel had stepped out of the rows on either side.

"Please return to your seat, sir," rumbled the one on the left with a chest the size of an extra-large beer keg.

"Our prime seating is for..." The other one looked me up and down, smirking at my rumpled attire and battered face. He flipped the lapel of my bedraggled coat. "Our better-dressed guests."

"Tell Yevgeni it's Charlie Madison," I shouted over the noise into their Neanderthalic faces. "He'll remember me."

They shook their heads in unison. "Mr. Sokolov doesn't care about Charlie Madison, whoever you are."

"I'm the guy who got the dirt on his brother. The brother who's dead now, from what I hear. If you don't want to end up the same way, you'll let me speak with Yevgeni." I paused as they glanced at each other. "He's in trouble."

They tried to stare me down. When that didn't work, they parted like the Red Sea, allowing me to pass.

"We will keep our eyes on you," one of them promised.

I was sure they would. Along with Stankic and the two Blackshirts. No doubt I'd caught their attention already as I passed them on the way down.

"What's goin' on, Yev?" I said as I approached, giving his bodyguards a moment to check with the two security goons I'd already met. Some sort of unspoken communication traveled between them, and I was allowed to enter Sokolov's well-maintained personal bubble.

"Madison." Yevgeni forced a tight smile. The bleached teeth were blinding, and his face looked like stretched wax up close, overly tan in a far from natural way. "You are not looking so well. Someone has mistaken your face for a punching bag?"

"Not the first time."

"You should choose better company. I did not realize you were here. I would have invited you to watch the fight from my private box, of course."

Probably not the case, but it sounded nice anyway.

"Not the best fight I've ever seen." I watched as Enoch rolled out from under Grim Reaper's fists in the nick of time. They plowed into the mat, tearing open the thick vinyl cushion, as the kid stumbled to his feet and dashed to the far corner of the ring. "Kid's got no balls."

Yevgeni scowled. "He will fight." He pressed his thumb against the remote in his hand, and Enoch dropped to his knees, his face twisted in agony, hands to his temples again.

"Some kind of remote transmitter?" I nodded toward the device.

Sokolov eyed me coolly. "What do you want, Madison?"

"Can't I visit an old friend?"

"We are not friends. You did a job for me. You were paid. That is all."

I frowned slightly. "Wow. You really know how to hurt a guy's feelings. Here I was thinking we were still chums." I nodded again at his remote. "Let me guess. Some kind of implant in the kid's skull—pain chip? Like what they used to put in dog collars?" Back when there were dogs.

"He is a dog, this one. He must learn to *obey*." He pressed the button again. Same results. This time, Grim Reaper hauled Enoch's agonized body up by one leg and threw him across the ring like a crash test dummy.

"I'd say he's obeyed plenty already, Yev." I waited until his attention returned to me. "Those two cops you had him kill. His previous death duels. Doping him with that new Japanese steroid—what's it called, *tetsu no ken*? He never refused, did he? Doesn't that make him a good pet?"

A cold grin spread across Sokolov's features. "I don't think you want to be here right now, Madison."

"I don't think Enoch does either. You didn't dope him tonight. He doesn't have the strength to take on one of your bouncers, let alone this Grim Reaper monstrosity. You're going to kill him. Right here, in front of God and everybody."

"This is a *death duel*!" Yevgeni laughed, and it was the crow of a madman. "What else do you expect?"

I sighed, nodding sadly. "I figured it was rigged."

Drawing my revolver, I aimed it at the ceiling without ceremony and fired off three rounds. The shots exploded like fireworks in the Arena, sparking off the concrete ceiling, and the audience's cheers and jeers suddenly turned to shrieks of panic. As they abandoned their seats like frightened mice and made for the only exit, trampling each other in the process, I turned the smoking muzzle of my .38 on Yevgeni. His hired muscle had converged on me with eyes bulging and nostrils flaring, but they held their position all around their boss, knowing better than to advance and risk the next three rounds plowing into Sokolov's ugly face.

"You are really trying my patience, Madison," Yevgeni said, oblivious to the pandemonium in the stands behind us. "What is your business here? Surely you do not have an interest in this Enoch Wilson boy. He is no one. You do not work with the police or the Blackshirts. So what business is it of yours?"

I nodded. "Yeah, I should be asking myself the same thing. Only I'm not. Because a friend of mine asked for a favor last night. And that friend just happens to be a cop."

"Ivan owns the cops in this town." He sneered.

"Not this one." Having a hunch Wanda wouldn't have left her seat, I called over my shoulder, "Did the sergeant hear those shots?"

"Loud and clear, Charlie. He's on his way," Wanda replied, tapping the phone over her ear, followed by a terse, "Watch it, buddy. This gun might be small, but it'll put a big ugly hole in you."

Good girl. That double-barreled derringer of hers had come in handy with Yevgeni's hired help.

"You will not leave the Arena alive, Madison," Sokolov said. "Tonight, this will be *your* death duel!"

Grinding gears clanked above me in the ring. I looked up just as Grim Reaper launched himself over the ropes. Both of his bloodshot eyes were fixed on me, his mandroid legs bent, arms curled, ready to crunch my bones to grit. I lunged at Sokolov, pistol-whipping him to the ground. The concrete floor behind us rumbled with the impact of Grim Reaper's landing, chips and dust flying as his plasteel hand grabbed hold of the back of my coat, prying me off Yevgeni and hoisting me into the air.

15

I fired one of my last three shots, hitting Sokolov in the knee before I turned my attention to Grim Reaper. While Yevgeni hit the floor and cursed foully, screaming for his men to kill me, I made my last two rounds count. They hit the cyborg square in the chest, and his mechanical frame shuddered as his torso lurched, spurting blood. His mandroid parts kept him standing upright as he shuddered spastically, and I remained a few meters in the air, dangling from the clenched mechanical fist.

"Shoot him!" Sokolov shrieked, gesturing emphatically at me. But his men weren't moving to obey.

Because Wanda, Agents Jane and Nameless, and even Detective Stankic had their guns drawn, surrounding Sokolov's four bodyguards and security goons.

"Thank you..." Grim Reaper rasped as his flesh became still.

I stared down at his pale face, lined with blue veins. He looked me in the eye.

"...for ending this nightmare." As blood blossomed across his densely muscled chest, his head lolled forward and hung there. Lifeless.

"Who the hell are you?" Stankic scowled at Jane and her partner.

"Concerned citizens, Detective," Agent Jane said, shaking out her platinum blonde locks as she kept her gun aimed at

Yevgeni's men.

"You will not get away with this—any of you! You are *dead*!" Sokolov shouted from the floor. "When Ivan hears of this—!"

"Your boss knows you been killin' cops?" Stinkin' said. With the fire in his eyes, maybe he wasn't thinking about how much he owed Sokolov right now. Maybe he was thinking about Officers Bowman and Sykes instead.

Didn't matter who was on Ivan's payroll and who wasn't, who was dirty and who was clean. When all was said and done, the police of our city were family. Mess with one, you messed with them all.

"That's right, Yev," I said, swaying a bit in midair. I felt like part of a bizarre circus act, but I did my best to maintain some measure of my composure. "I have a feeling Ivan will want to distance himself from you."

"Might even spit on your grave." Stankic stepped forward, ready to shoot Yevgeni between the eyes. One way to take care of those gambling debts. Probably the only thing on his mind, after all.

"Hold it," said Agent Nameless. He kept the gun in his left hand trained on Sokolov's hired muscle while he retrieved a second semiautomatic from the small of his back. He aimed that one at Stinkin'. "We need this man alive."

"Who the hell are you people?" Stankic repeated, incredulous.

"Drop your weapons, all of you, and line up ringside," Agent Jane said to Yevgeni's men. "Detective Stankic, stand down. You won't be killing anyone today."

"Oh yeah?" He didn't retreat. "How the hell do you know my name?"

"They're Blackshirts, you idiot." I holstered my empty revolver.

"I'm the idiot? You're the one up there lookin' like Pinocchio." Stankic tightened his grip on the Glock. "What the hell are Feds doin' in the Arena?"

"We've been in worse places." Jane gestured with her gun for the bodyguards to hurry up. Begrudgingly, they laid down their weapons and raised their brawny arms, standing shoulder to shoulder. "We need to have a conversation with Mr. Sokolov regarding a certain substance he received from Little Tokyo."

"I don't know what you're talking about," Yevgeni said, pouting like a disappointed brat.

"I do." Enoch stood against the ropes, watching the scene play out below him. "I'll tell you whatever you want to know—if you can promise that my parents will be left out of this."

"You will say *nothing*!" Yevgeni barked out insane laughter as he pressed the remote, and Enoch jerked like he'd been hit with an invisible bolt of lightning—eyes rolling, back arched, hands like claws curled inward.

"Enough of that." Jane fired her sidearm, and the remote exploded—along with most of Sokolov's hand holding the thing. He screamed and clutched his bleeding stump to his chest, staring with wild-eyed terror at the blonde Blackshirt. "Now how about that conversation, Mr. Sokolov?" she said, lowering her weapon toward his groin.

Yevgeni nodded quickly.

When Sergeant Douglass arrived with Detective Blinkin'

and half a dozen uniforms, Stinkin' did his best to explain the situation. He lied, of course, saying it was all an undercover operation that he'd been organizing from the start. I could have set the record straight on that score, but I didn't bother. The truth would come out eventually. Or it wouldn't. In this town, you could never be sure about where the truth actually stood.

I lost my favorite coat in the process of being cut down from Grim Reaper's death grip. That was the only way to get free without laser-cutting through the mandroid fingers, and it would have taken a while to get the tech team in there and have them set up their equipment. So I let the cops set up a ladder instead, whip out their trusty switchblades, and slice through my trench coat as well as my suit jacket, not to mention the shirt underneath. Otherwise, I was none the worse for wear.

Stankic hobbled out of the Arena as officers escorted Sokolov's men in cuffs. They'd be released before midnight if Ivan chose to have any say in the matter, but it was a good show nevertheless.

"Don't you try leavin' town," Stinkin' warned me with a scowl.

"Wouldn't dream of it." This city could be real ugly sometimes, but I kind of had a thing for her. And I'd been around the world enough to know the grass wasn't much greener elsewhere. "You might want to stay off that foot for a while."

He gave me the finger, and so did his partner, blinking angrily at me. Had he told her the bad foot was my fault? Most likely. And she knew he'd be trying to get out of all sorts of responsibilities, now that he was injured.

"Thank you, Mr. Madison." Enoch stood before me in cuffs with Douglass at his side. "I know I can't repay you, and I know it's wrong to ask anything more of you—"

"I'll look in on your folks, kid," I promised. Those few moments I'd spent with them at Seven Oaks had been the closest thing to *home* that I'd felt in a long while. Probably something in the air over there, but I didn't mind. "I'll make sure they're doing all right."

Tears welled in his eyes as he nodded and swallowed. "I don't want them ever to find out about...what I did."

Most likely, he'd end up in prison with a stiff sentence. Even if it could be proven that he wasn't acting of his own volition, the facts remained. He'd killed two good cops. Prison time was the only mercy he'd be shown, and for most inmates at the Twin Towers, it was a fate worse than death.

"We'll get everything sorted," Douglass said, gripping Enoch by the shoulder and guiding him up the aisle toward the exit. "Our medics will get that chip outta your head. Flush your system of any drugs Sokolov's given you. You'll start feelin' like yourself again real soon."

Sergeant Archibald Douglass was a good man—one of the last of his kind. I gave him a nod, which he returned. I knew better than to think we'd ever be even. And I also knew the next time he asked me for a favor, I'd step up again without batting an eye.

Wanda sidled up to me as the Arena cleared. I put my arm around her and gave her a squeeze.

"We make a good team," I said with a wink.

"Better believe it." She gave me a light peck on my swollen cheek. "Want to get out of here?"

"Hell yeah."

After spending the past nine or ten hours in the bowels beneath Ivan's Coliseum, I was feeling the early stages of claustrophobia setting in. Not that it would be much better out on the surface with the acid rain to contend with and no overcoat to protect myself, but I'd deal with that when the time came. Assuming Ivan's forces of darkness allowed us to leave. I had started quite a ruckus in the Arena, after all.

There wasn't enough room for us in the lift, so we waited for it to return empty.

"Think we'll ever hear about Sokolov again?" Wanda said, crossing her arms and shuffling her feet in those flashy lavender pumps. They clopped across the concrete floor of the otherwise silent hallway and gleamed in the light of fluorescent bulbs recently replaced. The work crew had acted fast following my scuffle with Stankic. Guess they'd needed to have everything ship-shape prior to the big death duel. "Or will those Feds make him conveniently disappear?"

"It's what they do best."

No loss there. Yevgeni Sokolov was no good for this town. Sure, there would be plenty of others to take his place—lower-level lieutenants in Ivan's organization jockeying for position—but I could be proud of the fact that I'd helped take one of them down. On to the next.

Agent Jane—or whoever she really was—had waited just long enough for me to be released from that cyborg's grip before she and her partner had taken Sokolov away.

"I don't often admit I'm wrong, Madison," she'd said, giving me that coy look she'd graced me with earlier in the day.

"Because you never are?" I raised an eyebrow.

"Something like that." She half-turned away, deliberately

posing in her tight gold-sequined dress that highlighted the perfect curves of her athletic body. "Get in my way again sometime, won't you?"

Not if I had any say in the matter. Feds and me? Oil and water. But I'd given her one of my patented smirks and told her, "Anything's possible."

Wanda and I took the lift up to the main floor of the Coliseum. It emptied us into a lively casino, a regal expanse of opulence peopled by well-dressed men and women with money to burn. Wanda kept her arm across my back to cover the torn portion of my suit jacket, and we did our best to remain inconspicuous. It probably would have been better to leave with the cops. An entourage would have drawn less attention to us, oddly enough.

"Mr. Madison," said a large Russian with the look of *Ivan's Muscle* all over him: a brawny gladiator crammed into a monkey suit. He stood in our way, just a few meters from the gates to freedom.

"That's me," I said, looking him squarely in the eye.

"Mr. Ivan has a message for you."

Wanda tightened her grip on me, but she didn't say a word.

The big thug bared his teeth with either menace or an attempt at looking polite. Either way, it seemed to pain him. "You have earned his interest. He says he will be keeping an eye on you from now on. As you know, his eyes and ears are all over town."

That I did know.

"Message received," I said.

"Good evening." He stepped out of our way with a slight bow.

We got out of there as fast as we could. A blast of cold air and viscous rain greeted us outside, but it felt great to breathe in the fresh fumes of traffic and feel the wind buffet us from head to toe. Lucky enough to hail a cab in just a few minutes, we ducked into the backseat and shook off the oily rainwater as best we could.

I gave the driver directions to my office building and told him to step on it. I wanted to check for any leakage in my repaired wall before heading home to my apartment.

Wanda's place was on the way.

She squeezed my hand as the cab pulled up to the curb in front of her building. "I'll see you tomorrow, Charlie." She waited for me to respond.

"Right." I nodded, squeezing her hand in return.

"Is that all you've got to say?"

I knew what she wanted to hear, and for the most part, I felt ready to say it. But first, I silently ran through my mental checklist.

Came through on my favor for Douglass? Check. Helped Enoch as best I could? Check. Did it all pro bono? Unfortunately, check. Made new enemies in the process? Definitely, check. All in a day's work.

But there were a few things that gave me pause. Hiroki Nakano, a man I'd never met, had met his demise because of the questions I'd asked Katsuo Sanitoro. Yevgeni Sokolov, local scumbag, was now in the custody of our Federal government, and who knew what sort of ringer they were going to put him through. Then there was the drug itself—*tetsu no ken*—something I had no proof existed at all. I'd only seen the results: what Enoch Wilson had been able to do while high on the stuff. Sure, I would follow through on my promise to check in with Enoch's parents. But what would I say to them?

"Hello. My name's Charlie. I know your son. He had to go away for a little while, so I'll be looking in on you from time to time. To make sure they're treating you all right here."

Seven Oaks? Not likely. Without Yevgeni's funding, Enoch's parents would have to be relocated to one of the local institutions. Didn't pay to grow old in this town. Scratch that. This world. You outgrow your use, they put you away to be forgotten.

But the Wilsons would never find out about what their son had been forced to do. I would see to that. And they wouldn't be neglected. I'd see to that, too. Maybe they'd even get to see their son again someday. Stranger things had happened.

What about Paige? She would visit Enoch in prison. She was that kind of girl—loyal to the end.

Kind of like my faithful assistant, Wanda Wood, who'd proven her mettle time and time again. The kid had real spunk and a mind sharper than any supercomputer ever built. I was more than lucky to have her on my team.

So before she stepped out into that awful wet mess dropping from pitch-black skies above our unfair city, I gave her a wink and told her what she wanted to hear:

"You know it, sweetheart. This case is closed."

About the Author

Milo James Fowler is the cross-genre author of more than thirty books: space adventures, post-apocalyptic survival stories, mysteries, and westerns. A native San Diegan, he now makes his home in West Michigan with his wife and all four seasons. Some readers seem to enjoy the unique brand of science fiction, fantasy, horror, and humor found in his ever-growing body of work. *Soli Deo gloria.*

www.milojamesfowler.com

Printed in Great Britain
by Amazon